SEEDS *of* AGGRESSION

FRAN SHELDRICK

SEEDS *of* AGGRESSION

Author Contact: franshel3@gmail.com
Author Website: www.fransheldrick.com
Cover Design: www.bookcoverzone.com

ISBN # 979-8-9932939-2-9

Mac & Shay ❧ Book Seven

FRAN SHELDRICK

SUSTAINABLE GARDENING

An important tenet of sustainable gardening
is using seeds that are native to,
or compatible with the environment.
A plant moved from its natural habitat
could thrive in your garden or develop poorly.
But any new plant will permanently impact
and alter your garden's ecosystem.
It could change the nutritional balance of the soil.
It might attract beneficial insects
or bring unwanted pests.
If you choose to welcome a new species
to your garden,
You'll want to monitor and guide
its adaptation to its new home
so your entire garden can continue to thrive.

- Shay Flaherty

CHAPTER ONE

MAC

Maple Sunrise

New York State Police Lieutenant Roosevelt Cross settled his bulk at the kitchen table and loosened his tie. "How much longer until you return to duty, Llewellyn?" He knew the answer as well as I did.

I set a mug of coffee in front of him and reached for the sugar bowl. "Less than two weeks. I'd like to stretch it to the end of the month, but unless I draw on this year's vacation…"

He narrowed his eyes, creased his brow. "So, you're thinking about retirement?"

I laughed at his default sarcasm. "It's a little early for that."

"Then you need to get back. We're buried. And with everyone in a post-holiday slump, things aren't going to improve." He tilted the sugar bowl over his mug and let granules cascade into his brew.

Rather than comment on insulin levels, I went to the fridge and pulled out material for sandwiches.

"My cousin is due to arrive next week to look after the kids. But if it's urgent, we can probably arrange for day care until she gets here. What have I missed?"

"How well do you know the Cruz family, on the north side of the lake?"

"They sublet part of Shay's booth at the farm market before their winery became profitable, and we've helped each other out a few times. But I don't know them well. They put in long hours with the vineyard and all, and we're busy, here." I shrugged. "I think Shay sees Ami once in a while."

"How about the old man, Rodrigo?"

"Again, I've met him. He seems like a decent guy, knowledgeable when it comes to wine and grapes. He's not in any trouble, I hope?"

"He's dead."

That was a surprise. I split foot-long rolls and arranged them on plates while I considered the news. Drigo was at least seventy but a natural death wouldn't account for Rosie's presence.

"What happened?"

"His grandson found him in the vineyard early this morning."

Instead of assembling the subs, I moved our plates to the table, dumped a collection of containers and packages between them, and ladled out bowls of homemade chicken noodle soup.

While we assembled sandwiches, I nudged the conversation. "Not natural causes then, and since you're asking, I'm guessing not accidental. But if you're looking for leads, I can't help you."

Rosie grunted, shoved his coffee mug aside. "You got any beer?"

"Sure." I pulled a pair of brews from the fridge, popped the caps. "Is that why you want me to cut my leave short? I mean, there's no conflict of interest. I barely knew Drigo and only see Emil and Ami when our paths happened to cross. But I don't have any insight, either."

"That's not it. I assigned it to Braun but I thought your familiarity with the territory and the players might help. Besides, you two have a pretty good success rate when you work together."

I let out a breath. Even if I was enjoying my time off, it didn't mean I wasn't also missing the challenge of the job. "My familiarity could cut both ways, but… let me talk to Shay about child care. Meanwhile, why don't you tell me what you've got."

Cross spooned up soup and swallowed. But before he responded, I spotted movement on the stairs.

"Hold on, Rosie. The twins are up from their nap."

I scooped up a two-year-old in each arm and carried them to the bathroom. "Did you kiddoes have a good rest? Let's do potty and then you can play."

Those tots and their older sister were the reason I was on leave from my job. Shay and I had decided to foster them after their parents were killed, but juggling them and our adopted daughter was a full-time job in itself. I sat the kids on their potty-chairs and handed each one a picture book.

"Call me when you're finished, okay? And no running off until you're dressed."

When I got back to the kitchen, the L.T. stared at me, shaking his head. "This is how you spend your vacation?"

I laughed. "If I don't finish their potty training before Delyth gets here, she's going to give me hell. I assured her she wouldn't have to deal with diapers." At the fridge, I filled a pair of sippy-cups with juice and slathered peanut butter on crackers. "And this isn't all I've been doing. I added a couple of pens in the goat barn and repaired the chicken coop roof, finally fixed a leaky faucet I'd been putting off. Oh, and the kids and I started building a tree house… but that's on hold until spring." I grinned and sank into my chair again.

"Relax, Lieut. It's not contagious. You look shell-shocked." I raised my beer with a flourish. "Go ahead, then. Fill me in."

I set a neutral expression and waited while he pulled out his notes and collected his thoughts.

"Okay. So, dispatch took a call at 0827 from Emil Cruz, age thirty-eight, of… blah, blah, blah. He requested assistance for his grandfather, Rodrigo Cruz, age seventy-four, same address, said the old man went out a little before sunrise to check on the grapevines. That'd be around 0730 or so, almost an hour before Emil found him.

"Temps went down in the low twenties overnight and Rodrigo was worried about the vines freezing. But Emil couldn't find him. He wandered around, calling out, getting panicky—it was still below thirty out there. Finally, he hiked up the hill and spotted his grandfather on the ground, near an outbuilding he calls a lab. Seems Drigo was some kind of scientist, inventing new types of grapes and coming up with different wines. Emil was thinking the old man had an accident, a heart attack or something, but when he got close enough to see, it was obviously more deliberate than that."

"He was the one who called it in?"

"Yeah, he asked for an ambulance, even though the guy was already gone. Dispatch walked him through it until the medics got there. The guy was garroted."

I ran the facts Rosie'd presented: barely dawn, twenty-some degrees, in a snowy vineyard in the middle of nowhere, and an intelligent, genial seventy-four-year-old viticulturist strangled on his own property. "Garroted."

"With a pocket hand saw. Damn near decapitated him." Rosie grunted, returned his attention to shoveling Shay's spicy apple chutney along his sub roll. "I don't know how you stay fit with all the great food your wife makes."

I eyed his waistline. "I'd say Charlene's not coming up short in that department."

He snorted, pointing a fork at me. "Watch yourself, Llewellyn, and keep in mind that you'll be working for me again, soon."

I chuckled and picked up the conversation while he sank his teeth into his culinary creation.

"Whoever did it would have to have some strength to *nearly decapitate* him. It's not going to be Emil or Ami. I'm certain of that. And as far as I know, Drigo didn't have a problem with anyone around the lake. Are there any workers on the place this time of year?"

"Not in the vineyards, no. There are a few employees in the winery but they don't start work until later in the day."

"Have you met them?"

"Braun's probably dealing with that as we speak." He paused and studied me a long moment before raising his brows and shrugging.

I knew what he was doing but I wasn't going to be sucked into it without talking with Shay. "Ty's sharp, he'll handle it. If there's anything he thinks I can help with, he'll call." I got up again. "I'd better see if Bibi and Tolo are finished."

My leave time from the NYSP homicide unit was nearly over. In spite of the many tasks that still needed attention at home, I'd gotten a lot accomplished in a month's time. The most important was that three foster children were now more-or-less comfortably settled into our home.

Six-year-old Gabriella, and two-year-old twins, Bartolo and Bibiana, were still grieving the loss of their parents, but they'd begun bonding with Shay and me, and especially with our daughter Elodie, herself a former foster. Child Protective was trying to locate some family member to take the children but, until then, Shay and I had decided we'd keep them from being separated.

The impact of adding three children to our family was significant, which was why my cousin, Delyth Morgan, would soon become our live-in nanny.

CHAPTER TWO

SHAY

Maple Sunrise

I paced the narrow space at the back of my greenhouse, four steps north, four steps south, rubbing my sweatshirt-clad arms as if to ward off the twenty-eight-degree temperature beyond the glass. I wasn't cold—it was forty-seven humid degrees in the greenhouse—but pre-taping jitters made me shiver. Nerves.

Three technicians crowded in, stomping snow from their feet and wrangling bulky equipment between the potting benches and rows of twine-trellised vegetables. I tried not to cringe when a camera teetered dangerously close to trays of new seedlings.

Lindsey, the TV show's audio engineer and my unofficial video coach, cautioned her coworkers before giving me a wave and shedding her jacket.

"This is going to be great, unlike last night's outdoor interview with a snowplow crew." She made a little shudder. "Mind you don't bump those gorgeous tomato plants, guys. If we're lucky, Shay might share some for lunch." Taking her own advice, she kept the boom microphone carefully vertical until she reached me.

"Don't worry about the mike, Shay. We're only going to use it for the scenes you're doing right here. You can use the lavalier one when you're moving around." She took out the tiny portable mike and pinned it to my shirt. "You look good. That color is perfect on you. What's the topic for the first episode?"

"I'm going to talk about the first steps in planning a garden." I knew Lindsey would have reviewed all the scripts ahead of production, as she always did. Her question was intended to focus my nervous energy and ease me into the taping, something she'd been doing for me every session. "This episode will be mostly basics with a few suggestions to help viewers narrow their choices before they start buying things they'll never grow."

She laughed. "My hubs will be happy to see that. Don't ever ask about the garden-failure bin in our garage."

"That's why Travis wants to kick off the season with that topic. He says we don't need questions about how to grow bananas or what to do with a citrus tree during winter in New York State."

As if on cue, the show's director and my sometime co-host entered and cast a critical eye around the space. "I'd be happy to tell anyone what to do with a citrus tree, today," he barked. "What's with this weather?"

One of the tech's called out, "It's February in New York, Trav. Check your calendar."

Amid chuckles, Travis handed a clipboard to Karla, his assistant director, and took his place beside me. "Okay, folks. Time is money."

Lindsey attached a mike, straightened his collar, and retreated to the sidelines, giving us a thumbs-up.

My anxiety peaked as the A.D. finished checks and raised her voice. "Quiet please. Roll?"

"Sound speed," Lindsey said.

"Camera rolling," Xavier responded.

"Picture up and…" Karla held up three fingers to Travis, counting down, "Three, two, one. Action."

The camera light glowed, Lindsey's recording equipment flashed green, and Travis smiled wide as he began his intro.

"Welcome to a brand-new season of *What to Grow in Western New York*. Whether you're a master gardener with years of experience or just starting to think about planting your first tomato, we hope you'll join us here, every Friday, as we dig into small-scale gardening with

Shay Flaherty from Maple Sunrise Farm. She's going to show us how to turn a bunch of seeds into a bountiful harvest." He angled slightly toward me.

"So, Shay, I know you have some fascinating topics lined up for the coming season. Tell us what we can expect."

And just like that, my nervousness dissolved. I smiled and relaxed as I warmed—both figuratively and physically—to my subject. After a brief preview of the upcoming season, Travis and I discussed the importance of choosing a location, testing the soil, and making decisions about what and how much to grow.

I set my gaze on Xavier, at the edge of the camera, so I'd appear to talk directly to the viewers. "Those of you who watched *What to Grow* last season already know I'm a big supporter of sustainable, organic, permaculture gardening. And one of the basic practices for that is using environmentally compatible plant species."

"Is that the same as companion planting," Travis asked.

"Not exactly, although you could think of them as two related steps in creating a healthy garden. Companion planting is growing mutually-beneficial crops together—like corn serving as a physical structure for the beans to climb, while the beans provide nitrogen for the corn."

"You told us about those last year when you introduced the Three Sister crops—corn, beans and squash."

"That's right. But before we choose plants that are compatible with one another, we want to make certain they're compatible with the environment."

He laughed, drawing on his favorite lament. "Like not trying to grow bananas in western New York?"

"That's an extreme example, but you have the right idea." I raised an eyebrow at the camera in apology. "Without going off on a tangent that would take several hours to explain, I have to tell you it is possible to grow winter-hardy bananas in western New York—not that I'm advocating it."

"Tell us more."

"With sustainable gardening, it's important to plant seeds that are either native to, or compatible with the environment. A plant, moved from its natural habitat, might adapt but it can also result in poor plant development and inferior produce, or simply die.

"Even worse, an invasive, non-native plant might adapt and grow well. But while you're celebrating the new crop, it could also be impacting and altering the garden's ecosystem in destructive ways."

"That sounds like a problem."

"It can be. A new plant might introduce disease, upset the nutritional balance of the soil, or cause damage to other plants, insects, pollinators, and wildlife."

"So, you're suggesting we stay away from new crops?"

"Not necessarily. Only that you rely on careful, professional research to be understand how the new crop will affect the rest of your hard work. In fact, I'd recommend talking with a master gardener or calling your local Cooperative Extension."

"What are some examples?"

Travis had thrown me an unscripted question but fortunately, I was prepared. "I'd suggest any perennial fruits or vegetables should be carefully chosen and managed so they don't take over the garden at the expense of your other crops." I smiled in Xavier's direction. "In fact, your imaginary banana plant is a very good example of that. Did you know a banana plant is a perennial herb? If you've ever planted an herb like spearmint, you know that putting one tiny sprig in the ground can turn your garden into bushels of spearmint that can crowd out every other plant within a few weeks. In time, bananas will do the same. Once you've started it, though, it'll be very difficult contain or remove them."

"That reminds me of a guy my sister dated. She brought him to a family dinner and before we knew it, his entire family started dropping by, siblings, parents, cousins, grandparents…"

I laughed. It was an ongoing routine he used to inject humor into the show.

"Let's stick to garden produce, Travis. They're actually not as complicated as people."

Moving to a white board the crew had set up, I drew a rectangle and divided it into rows. "There are several things to consider when choosing compatible seeds besides growth habits. Things like the nutrients it uses or provides, whether it attracts pollinators or aggressive pests, or if it's prone to a disease or condition that might wipe out neighboring crops. Read the seed packets and ask for recommendations from staff at the nursery or farm where you shop."

Travis raised both hands. "I guess you can't just toss a new plant in the garden without knowing what it can do."

"It's best to choose carefully. Some plants and seeds can adapt and actually improve the balance of your environment. But many are unsuitable associates that cause disharmony and disaster. Those are best avoided. So, if you do choose one, stay vigilant and monitor its effects on your garden."

Travis grinned. "And tell your sister not to add anything you haven't already checked out."

I spent a few minutes going over environmental factors and reminders to avoid chemicals and genetically-modified seed. Travis stepped in again when I finished.

"We've been taping this show for almost a year and I've walked through your gardens dozens of times. But you keep surprising us with things that are going on in there that most of us probably never imagined."

I nodded. "Nature is never stagnant. That's why I take a walk through the gardens first thing every morning, to monitor what's happening. We'll get into more environmental factors and compatibility when it's time to plant. For now, we're only planning our garden. I'd advise starting small the first year…"

When we finished that episode, Travis called a short break before we moved on to taping the next show. I was always amazed at the number of hours it took to create four fifteen-minute segments of air time. And I had no idea how many more hours were spent on editing to polish the shows people actually got to see.

As soon as Travis introduced the second episode, he stepped fully into his director role. I didn't mind because, even though his humor added punch to the show, we wanted to be educational and not just entertaining. I again stood in front of my whiteboard drawings and talked about grouping vegetables by the time and work they'd need and calculating the amounts to plant per person.

"You can find more information and some printable worksheets on the Maple Sunrise website. If you fill those out, using your seed catalogs and garden suppliers, you'll be ready for next week's show when we'll talk about starting seeds indoors."

Travis stepped on-camera with me to wrap up the episode. Then everyone relaxed as lunch break was called, hours late.

As they headed for the exit, one of the techs called out, "What are we having, Shay?"

"Maria Ana made chili con carne and cornbread. There's salad, of course, or sandwiches if you prefer, but you'll have to ask her about dessert. It's probably not bananas." I laughed and reached for my jacket.

As part of our new contract, Travis had requested a meal in the Farm Gourmet meeting room instead of using their usual caterer. Besides adding a little income to our coffers, it provided some variety to the crew's menu and saved them time and travel. I'd handed that portion to Maria Ana for her own one-customer catering company. So far, it had been popular with everyone.

While the production crew went to eat, I slipped into the house for a few minutes with Mac and the twins. I found them racing matchbox cars down a ramp that stretched from the top of the bookcase, across the living room and through the kitchen to the mud room.

I hugged Bibi and Tolo and gave Mac a kiss. "I wonder who built this amazing racetrack? It's pretty advanced for a pair of two-year-olds."

"These are very creative two-year-olds." Mac high-fived the kids as they bounced around, begging him to start their cars from the top of the bookcase again.

"You're a terrible influence… but a great daddy." I poured coffee and found half of a sub sandwich on the counter. "Can I have a piece of this?"

"Sure. Or I can make you a whole one."

I shook my head. "I don't have time. The TV crew is on break and I need to get back there. We still have two more episodes which means we aren't going to finish until four or five o'clock." I looked around the clean but definitely lived-in rooms. "I'll get to the laundry tonight."

"I already threw in a load. Don't worry about it."

"Thank you. But I do worry about my time management. We can't expect Delyth to clean and do laundry on top of watching the kids. And we only have a couple of weeks before you…" I caught his change of expression without realizing I did it. "Oh, Mac."

He held up his hands. "I haven't agreed to anything except a consult. And only because it's someone we know."

"Someone died?" Stunned, I mentally ran a list of friends and neighbors.

"Emil Cruz's grandfather."

"What happened?"

"I'll let you know after I talk to Braun. He's handling it for now." He glanced at the children and reset himself. "Meanwhile, you can focus on your TV show and we are about to build a tunnel for the World's Most Incredible Racetrack." He gave me a quick squeeze. "We can talk about everything tonight."

CHAPTER THREE

MAC

Maple Sunrise

Forty minutes elapsed between the time Shay left and my partner, Tyler Braun, appeared on the doorstep. His arrival coincided with the return of our six-year-old girls, Elodie and Gabriela, which resulted in several minutes of chaos as we all reconnected.

Then Ty, ever the kid at heart, pounced on the twins' race track, giving me a few minutes to look over school papers and discuss first grade events. Since Shay was in the greenhouse with the TV crew, I referred to her checklist for reminders about after-school snacks, homework, and playtime. Somewhere in the midst of that, I managed to make a fresh pot of coffee and get the children settled with biscuits, jam, and glasses of milk. And with the decibel level temporarily below eighty, I finally took a breath.

Ty was in his element. "This is exactly what this house was made for. It reminds me of home when I was a kid. And look at you, bro, you're crushing it."

I laughed. "It's a steep learning curve but I can't say I'm not enjoying life… most of the time."

"At least you've got your priorities straight." He waved a hand at the racetrack snaking through the rooms, under tables, down a cookie-sheet ski slope, and through a long mailing-tube tunnel. "But now I'm worried you won't be coming back to work."

"You're starting to sound like the L.T. Have you noticed the mouths we have to feed?" I turned to Elodie and Gabi, recently dubbed the *Not-Twins* because they wanted to compete with Bibi and Tolo and figured they qualified as same-age sisters.

"Not-Twins, if you've finished your snack, get your barn jackets and take care of the chickens, please. Bibi and Tolo, you can play with the race cars while I clean up and talk with Uncle Ty." I stowed dirty dishes in the dishwasher, returning to Ty's remark.

"I'll be back on the job, all right and it looks like it might be sooner than later."

"Did the L.T. talk to you?"

"Yeah. He stopped by after he left the Cruz place." I signaled my partner to the dining room where I could keep an eye on the toddlers while we talked. "Any news on that?"

"Not much, yet. As usual, according to the family, everybody loved Drigo despite the evidence somebody didn't. His son called him a dedicated winemaker. His employees describe him as driven. It seems he'd been developing a new strain of grape for ages—decades, I guess—and finally got it perfected. Then he used them to make some new wine that's supposed to be so special it's predicted to compete with the finest champagnes in the world. It apparently won top awards at some international wine competition last year." Braun gulped coffee and shrugged. "I didn't understand half the stuff they told me, but the upshot is that this new grape is pure gold to people in the know, literally worth millions."

"Do you think that plays into Drigo's death?"

"The price tag could be a motive. I don't know enough about wine connoisseurs and—get this—oenophiles to know what they consider important."

I laughed. "Ee, no files? Is that a word? It sounds like what you say when your computer crashes."

"Right?" He refilled his coffee mug, grinning. "You have to learn a whole other language to even talk to these people. For the record, all oenophile means is wine-lover but I guess that's too common for people who've never tried ten-dollar, bag-in-a-box wines."

"Fill me in."

Turning serious, Braun glanced to make certain the children were occupied before handing me his phone.

The first picture was a wide-angle shot of Rodrigo Cruz's body on trampled, snow-covered ground. As I scrolled, the pictures became more grizzly and detailed, with close-up views of the area and of Drigo. After a slight shock at the first, I reset myself to investigator-mode and studied each carefully. Drigo appeared to have been strangled with something jagged, sharp, and thin. They'd obviously tried to decapitate him, which was overkill in a literal sense.

"What in hell did they use?"

Ty reached over and tapped the screen forward several shots to a photo of what looked like twisted wires with handles at each end. "It's a pocket saw, in generic terms. The military calls it a survival saw and it's used for various purposes non-military folks are better off not knowing. Veterinarians and brain surgeons cut through bone with a model called a Gigli saw. And there are all kinds of cheaper versions for campers and bushwhackers. Here's a close-up view of the one used on Rodrigo Cruz."

"They left it behind?"

"Yeah. Which I'm sure means there won't be any way to trace it to whoever used it."

I moved ahead to the picture he described, nasty-looking, toothed wires that would account for the horrific mess it'd made."

Before I got any further, the mudroom door burst open to a cacophony of shrieks and giggles.

"Daddy, come see how many eggs we got. I think it's the most ever-ever."

I closed the phone screen and returned it to Braun. Then hurried to take the baskets before any eggs wound up on the floor. By the time I'd sorted that and sent the Not-Twins to wash their hands, I was reset to dad-mode again. Just in time, as Shay bounded in breathless, carrying the jacket she should have put on, and nearly as giddy as the girls.

"We finally finished. I swear, these taping sessions take longer every time. I'm going to have to cancel them altogether if this keeps up. But at least March's shows are ready… or ready for editing, I guess."

I grabbed her coffee mug and filled it while she washed up and hugged the children. "Sit down and catch your breath. Dinner's in the oven and everything's on schedule."

"I'm sorry I wasn't here for after-school snack time. Am I too late to hear the news?"

Elodie and Gabi pulled her to the table where they happily recapped their day while Bibi and Tolo clambered on Shay's lap to add their own two-cents' worth.

The way she put everything else aside to focus one-hundred-percent on whichever child was speaking and still managed to engage the others was amazing. I knew she was taking in every word they said and that later, she'd be able to repeat the conversation nearly verbatim. She even drew in Tyler, suggesting the children show him how well they'd printed their spelling words and asking him about his favorite picture books when he was six.

Shay, who only a few years ago had treated any non-essential conversation like a venomous snake, was as thrilling to me in that moment as she'd been the day I'd fallen in love with her.

ஐ

Our evening spun out at a pace we'd rarely seen when there were only three of us. With the addition of the Marin children, our parenting duties had quadrupled and time became a precious commodity. We were getting better at it though, and Shay insisted on each child taking small responsibilities like selecting their own pajamas and putting their toys away before bath-and-story time. For some reason, they not only complied but took pride in their accomplishments which, according to Shay, helped them integrate into the family without any *fakey, look-at-us-bonding garbage*—her exact words.

There were difficult moments, too. Tolo and Bibi were too young to understand why their parents were gone but that didn't mean they weren't grieving. Whenever they came to us with drooping eyes and trembling chins, we stopped what we were doing and held them close, whispering how much *Mami* and *Papi* loved them. Shay had found someone to make three small blankets with a photo of Luis and Emiliana printed on the fabric and those seemed to give them comfort, as well.

Gabi was better able to articulate her feelings which tended to erupt at unexpected moments, taking everyone—including her—by surprise. Sometimes they took the form of tears and sorrow. But often it was fury or complete withdrawal. At any moment we might find her sobbing uncontrollably for no immediately-discernible reason. Or she might hide in a closet or under a bed, refusing to answer our calls.

The day Gabi's temper exploded in the playroom was a crucial one for her and for Shay, who understood the little girl's need to wreak havoc on every toy in the room. Shay had calmly sent the other children to me and closed the door, allowing Gabi to express the heartbreak she couldn't understand. Like Shay, on the night she'd first learned about her parents, Gabi eventually exorcised her rage and succumbed to tears. Then Shay held her and cried with her. And the following day, Gabi asked Shay if she could call her Mom.

We finally became a family and tucking the children into their beds had become a sweet, peaceful, end-of-day routine for everyone. We knew it might be temporary but that didn't mean it couldn't be real. I only hoped we were honoring Luis' and Emiliana's dreams for their children's lives.

ꟗ

After an hour of clean-up and prep for the next day, Shay and I retreated to the living room couch for some much-needed together time. We agreed it was a non-negotiable ritual when I was at home.

That evening, knowing we'd have to discuss Drigo's death and my probable early return to work, I brought a bottle of merlot, a package of crackers, and some of Shay's semi-hard goat cheese.

Shay stood and stretched before flopping on the couch. "Taping a TV show is harder on my body than working all day in the gardens. So much time is spent standing around while they adjust things or shoot the same scene over and over to get it right."

"They do a good job, though. And it's only one day a month." I handed her a glass of wine and tapped mine to it. "To us, Love. We should do this more often."

She smiled. "And this is where you tell me you're going back to full-time work, starting tomorrow morning."

"Not quite. But I was wondering about calling Delyth. She might be willing to come a couple of weeks early. Would that work for you?"

"It's fine if that's what Del wants to do. But really, I can manage. The majority of our Farm Gourmet products are shipped and we'll only process recipes that run low for the rest of the month. I'll mostly be dealing with last-minute orders and keeping daily deliveries on track. *What to Grow* is done for the month and Elodie and Gabi will be in school, so I should have plenty of time to hang out with Bibi and Tolo."

"Let's see how things go. I'm sure she'll do whatever you think is best for the kids."

She was briefly silent. "Before you go back to work… have you heard anything?"

There was no need for her to elaborate. When Shay learned she had a younger sister she didn't remember—one who'd apparently been adopted out and whose whereabouts were unknown—I'd promised to look for her while I was on leave. Although I'd put out feelers, not a lot of information had come in, but there was one thing I'd been withholding.

"Maybe." I studied my wine to avoid the unwavering trust in her eyes. "It's not certain, Shay. Don't get your hopes up just yet. I asked Warren Kruger, a retired detective in Port Terrence, to do some digging. He found a woman…"

"Who? Is it Annie? Maeve?" Shay scrambled onto her knees, gripping my arm as if the next word or sentence could change everything.

I braced myself to keep a calm tone and deliver only facts. "The woman—her name is Betty—said she had worked with someone named Annie at an insurance company. She told him this Annie-person only worked there a few months but they'd become friendly, occasionally visiting one another or going out for lunch or coffee. She said Annie had some kind of health problems and had to quit her job."

"Was it her? Was it… my mother or Maeve or whoever took me and my sister?"

"We know it wasn't your mother, Shay." I made it a firm statement. Shay knew her mother had died before they wound up in Port Terrence but somehow, she clung to the possibility everyone else had gotten it wrong. "It was not Annie. Whether it was your Aunt Maeve or someone else, we still don't know. The woman couldn't recall her coworker's surname and only referred to her as Annie."

Shay nodded, her eyes demanding more. "The insurance company must have some record of her."

"Of course. But there are privacy laws and we have no proof that their Annie is the person we're looking for." I held up a hand to cut off a tangential argument that would take us nowhere. "Betty did give Warren one useful piece of information. She said Annie had two children. When she got sick and couldn't work, she was having a hard time managing.

"Betty had mostly lost touch by then but she claimed another coworker said that Annie knew a couple who'd been trying unsuccessfully to adopt a baby. She said they'd made arrangements for the couple to take Annie's children."

"Mac…"

I shook my head to forestall her suppositions. "It's possible this Annie placed, or tried to place, both of her children. But not long after that, she passed away. Betty didn't know anything beyond that."

"But that had to be her! That was my… the woman I thought was my mother. Who were they? Who was the couple that took my sister?"

"We don't know, Blodyn. Betty said she never knew their names. And remember, we don't know anything about Betty either. We don't know if her story is even true." I rubbed a hand over my eyes. "I promised you I'd search and that I'd tell you whatever I found, good or bad. I'm doing that, but I don't want you to take any of this on someone's say-so. Betty was reporting something that happened more than twenty years ago. Her recall could easily be distorted or confused. Reconstructed memories are often incomplete or incorrect, even if they're well-intended. And there's always the possibility she made up the whole story. It could be a pack of lies."

"But…"

"People do crazy things, Shay. They'll confess to crimes they didn't commit or make themselves part of a news story that has nothing to do with them. They do it for attention, for excitement, or out of guilt over something completely unrelated. Sometimes they're hoping for a reward—money or a book deal—or simply to be the center of attention for a while. They want to see their names in the paper, their faces on the six o'clock news. We need more before we accept that Betty's story is true or that it's about the person you remember."

As I spoke, Shay slumped, visibly deflated. When I finished, though, she straightened her spine and thrust her chin.

"I don't remember any person," she snapped. "That's the whole point. I don't remember my mother or… or Maeve or my sister or friends or anything else. Don't you get it? That's why I have to know. I need to remember."

I understood her anger wasn't directed at me. It was frustration speaking. I took her hands and returned her gaze, full eye-contact. "We're not finished, Blodyn. We won't stop looking, I promise you. For now, put this information with the rest you've uncovered. Store it in that pending file in your mind and we'll continue to search. Warren is going to keep digging, keep looking for someone else who might support Betty's story, or have other information. There's no legal adoption on the books in Missouri but that doesn't mean it didn't happen in another state or through some private deal. He's an experienced detective and he's tenacious. Let's give him time to uncover something stronger, some proof. You've waited your whole life for answers; try to be patient a little longer."

"All right." Her eyes were moist but she didn't cry or rage. Her willingness to exercise patience was evidence of how far she'd come in a few short years. I only hoped Warren would come through for her, for us. Shay deserved to know.

CHAPTER FOUR

SHAY

Maple Sunrise

Early the next morning Mac went with Tyler to the Cruz vineyard. Minutes later, the school bus arrived for Elodie and Gabi.

I zipped the two-year-olds into their jackets, packed a bag with toys, and crossed our snow-covered yard to the Farm Gourmet building. The delivery vans were out on their routes, the cooks off, and the kitchen silent.

I settled the children in the meeting room adjoining my office and went to my desk. When Elodie was small, I'd worked with her that way, even when we were operating out of my home kitchen. It wouldn't be difficult. Last night's discussion was filed in my mental pending folder, just as Mac suggested. I was going to focus on the children and Mac and my present life. That was all that mattered.

I checked my email for orders, finding a few changes for the next day's delivery, along with two requests for cases of gift baskets. Those had grown in popularity since the previous year and, after the Christmas and New Year's rush, some high-demand items were nearly depleted.

The storeroom shelves had gaps where high-demand products normally stood and, with Valentine's Day approaching, orders for sweet baskets were starting to spike. I took an empty cart and browsed the aisles for substitutions. Bibi and Tolo tagged behind me, apparently unsure if we were playing a game or shopping for groceries.

"Jam." Tolo pointed to the rows of *Maple Sunrise Blackberry Jam* and *Sunlight Strawberry Preserves.*

"Good choice," I told him. "Who wouldn't love a gift of jam?"

"Me love jam," Bibi announced.

"Me love jam, too." Tolo leaned backward to see the top shelves, managing to topple onto his butt. Unfazed, he scrambled to his feet. "Can me have jam?"

I hesitated. I didn't want them to think we could help ourselves to the business inventory whenever we wanted. But then I dismissed the thought. *Our business, our jam*, I recited. With the way Farm Gourmet was growing, one jar of jam wouldn't break the bank. Christmas sales had been beyond anything I'd ever dreamed.

"Blackberry or strawberry?"

As usual, Bibi was decisive. "Strawberry."

Also as usual, Tolo repeated whatever his twin sister said. "Strawberry."

They never seemed to disagree about anything, which I found endearing but strange. I wondered if all twins were that way and couldn't decide whether I should encourage more individuality or let it be. But it did make life easier.

"Strawberry, it is." I pushed my basket aside and took a jar from the shelf. "Let's go see if there's some bread in the kitchen."

I'd just finished making jam sandwiches when my head cook, Maria Ana, came down from her second-floor apartment.

"Oh, we have helpers today."

The children threw themselves at her, squealing *MarNana*—a shortened version of Elodie's MariNana, itself shorthand for her name.

I laughed. "A few more toddlers around here and you're going to be called *MaNa*, or maybe, just *Ma*."

"That is okay." She smiled and cuddled each twin. "Can I help with them?"

"It's your day off and we're fine." I flapped a hand. "I went through today's orders. If we don't restart the recipes soon, we're going to run out of everything."

"That's a good problem."

"It is. But we'll have to schedule more batches, this year. And that means planting more crops."

As she reached for the coffee pot, the back door opened and Terri Gianni breezed in.

"Can anyone explain why people forget how to drive in the snow when it's the exact same thing every winter?" Her words might alarm a non-New Yorker but that was standard conversation for residents.

"Are the roads bad?"

"No. A light coating is all. But is it really possible that people who have lived here their entire lives are surprised when it snows in winter? Or that snow is slippery?"

I waited out her version of what Mac calls the *Annual New York Snow Speech*. We all did it, as predictable as the snow, itself.

After Terri enumerated the number of cars in ditches, the people who drove too fast for conditions, and those who drove so slow they blocked traffic for miles, she handed me a sheaf of papers and turned to chat with the children and Maria Ana.

Terri's husband, Ben, claims that while the average person uses 16,000 words per day, his wife can easily triple that. But I contend it's because her job as a business consultant requires her to actively listen to people all day, so it's really a matter of maintaining balance. And she's always funny and interesting.

I sifted through the purchase requests she'd brought: two more standard case orders, plus several for Valentine's Day baskets.

"More Love Basket orders?"

Terri shed her coat and hat to reveal a bright red, fitted pantsuit and long icicle-shaped earrings to match the season.

"It's less than two weeks away. Easter is early this year, so everyone wants to get a jump on the winter holidays… Lunar New Year, Valentine's Day, St. Paddy's Day." She rubbed her palms together, anticipating the sales. "None of those will be as intense as Christmas but we have to be ready."

"Between increased advertising and orders from another grocery chain, Christmas nearly cleaned out our inventory. We're really low on specialty products."

"Can you switch them up?"

"Yes, but there's only so much that fits a theme. I'm already substituting two items."

She gazed upward, tapping her fingers together. "I wasn't going to say anything yet, but I've been talking to a very large gift shop chain. They're interested in carrying your line as part of their regular inventory… thirty-three stores across twelve states."

"Terri." I stifled a sigh. "We've discussed this before. I refuse to turn Maple Sunrise into a gigantic, corporate farm. It goes against everything I believe in."

"I'm not asking you to expand your farm, Shay. But the Farm Gourmet business is a separate operation and right now, it's pure gold. You're producing unique, delicious foods that people want." She glanced at the children. "If this is a bad time…"

"You go, take care of business," Maria Ana cut in. "I'll take niños upstairs to play." She handed us each a mug of coffee.

"Thanks, Maria Ana. I'm adding this into your week's work hours, though."

She collected the twins and their toys and I led Terri to my office, feeling guilty. Even though the children loved their *MarNana* and I did have work to do, I was supposed to be spending more time with them. How could I be a good foster parent if I depended on everyone else to look after them?

Terri launched into her sales pitch before we were even settled, pulling out her laptop to show me the gift chain's website. "This could be huge, Shay."

I gazed at the yearly garden plans posted above my desk, shaking my head. "Maple Sunrise isn't huge. Farm Gourmet isn't huge. I don't want to be huge."

"You won't need a huge farm if you purchase some of your produce from other growers. And your kitchen facility is fine… for now. But think about what this could mean for your brand."

I loved Terri's enthusiasm and I owed much of my success to her vision but there were limits to what I could do.

"Purchasing from other growers costs money. That cuts into profits. It doesn't make sense. And, depending on how much they buy, thirty-three more outlets could mean…"

A knock at the front door interrupted us. The CSA shop didn't open until noon but I stood and peered out the window.

"It's Thane and Winslow, The Herb Guys."

"Surprise!" Thane Archer's warm smile parted his bushy beard. He ducked his head under the doorframe as he entered.

Winslow Ryan—as polished and professional as his partner was rumpled—followed. "She won't recognize us away from the farmer's market."

"Don't be silly." I waved them into my office. "How many years did we stare across that aisle at each other? I still miss our weekly chats."

"We miss you, too. Although Darius keeps us entertained and updated." They greeted Terri, then Thane produced a long, narrow box.

"We've come bearing tea. How about a cup? We designed some introductory gift packs and I'd like to get your opinion. This one is called the Tea Totaler collection."

Winslow winked. "Get the play on words… Tea Totaler?"

He removed the lid to reveal six compartments of tea sachets. "Each tea is a unique blend of locally grown, organic teas and herbs, selected and created by *The Herb Guys*." He held up one sachet, reciting the tea and herbs it contained along with its recommended uses and benefits, then repeated the spiel for the other varieties.

When he finished his well-rehearsed pitch, Thane applauded. "What do you think?"

"They sound lovely." I bent close to the box and inhaled. "And they smell wonderful."

Terri agreed. "Are you selling them at the farmer's market?"

The men eyed each other, then Winslow pulled up a chair and sat. "We've sold some, but we think they're a little too specialized for that market."

Thane cleared his throat. "I'll prepare some, if you'd like to try… and I can use your kitchen?"

"Sure." I waved him to the doorway. "The tea kettle's above the first stove. Mugs and a teapot are in the meeting room cupboard."

Thane scurried away and his partner leaned forward. I might not have been the brightest bulb, but after seeing Terri's performances, I could recognize an incoming sales pitch when I saw one. The only problem was that I had nothing to offer a tea company beyond purchasing enough for personal use.

"Here's the thing, Shay." Winslow cleared his throat. "You have a lot of subscribers to your CSA program and, while we have a fabulous product, we could never afford home delivery for a few teas and culinary herbs. But I'll bet your subscribers would love a very special add-on to their orders."

The other shoe dropped. I glanced at Terri, expecting her to object but her expression was pure cat with an overturned milk jug.

"That's a wonderful idea, Winslow. It's a product Shay doesn't offer and a step toward something like full-service delivery." She turned to me. "It might be a good addition to gift baskets, too. You'd have to figure out how to manage supply and profits, and draw up a contract. But the benefits could be enormous for both of you."

Winslow practically jumped from his chair. "There's precedent for it. A lot of CSA growers are collaborating, now. Beef and chicken producers are going in with market gardeners like yourself. Small farms are offering milk, eggs, cheese, baked goods, all kinds of products. It benefits customers and the farmers…"

"I can't see it." With Terry on one side and Winslow on the other, I felt like ground zero for two category-five hurricanes. "A collaboration like that requires someone to do a lot of work. I'm already drowning in the million things I have to do every day, and now..."

"Thane and I have been looking into it for months. We were going to start some sort of mail order subscription but then we heard about these collab CSA groups and we thought of you. We already know the three of us will make a great team."

On cue, Thane entered, carrying a teapot and paraphernalia for properly-steeped tea.

"Here we go." He announced. "The proof is in the pudding… or the teapot, I should say."

"Oh, a tea ceremony." Terri clapped her hands. "Can we set up in the tasting room, Shay? Maybe with some crackers or nibblies?"

"We've got that covered." Winslow hoisted a fitted case that contained a set of small tea cups and packages of crackers, Chinese noodles, and shortbread cookies.

I stared, thinking of all the work I'd planned to do that day and the time I wanted to spend with Bibi and Tolo. The morning was half-gone and there was little to show for it. I frowned, looking from the papers on my desk to Terri and the Herb Guys. Then I laughed.

It seemed my day was about to include a tea party. How bad could that be?

ജ

The Herb Guys' teas were a perfect blend of organic herbs and blossoms and the cold-hardy Mao Feng tea they'd been growing for the past few years. Whether or not I agreed to include the teas in my CSA program, I knew I'd be buying them for myself.

Terri was scribbling notes, completely won over. "Personally, I think adding specialty products like these would lure more people to sign up. What if we included one or two sachets with each CSA order at no charge, to test the market? It'd be good P.R. for Winslow and Thane, and would help you decide about collaboration, Shay."

"We'd love to do a promo. How many members do you have?" Winslow pulled out a pocket notebook and a pen. He was in charge of the business side of the partnership, while Thane ran the tea farm and herb gardens… and he'd hit on one of Terri's favorite statistics.

"Shay broke the century mark this year," Terri announced. "She sends out 107 CSA boxes every week."

Thane's eyes widened and he poked Winslow with his elbow. "That's more than twice what we expected."

Winslow's face was classic kid-at-Christmas. "We'll have to discuss logistics but we can definitely meet the demand."

"Tell me how you'll package them for retail sales," Terri urged. "And the price points."

Winslow opened his tablet and brought up a spreadsheet, reading out the numbers and data Terri requested, while Thane narrated their processes. Their energy was high.

My input was only sporadically required but I listened carefully, confident that no decision would be final until Mac, Ben, and Terri and I cast our votes.

When Winslow stood, he shook hands with Terri and me as if he'd just clinched a deal. "I don't see a single downside to it."

"I'm certain you'll all increase sales," Terri agreed, as Thane nodded enthusiastically.

Apparently, I was the only skeptic in the room.

When everyone left, I grabbed my laptop and went upstairs to Maria Ana's apartment. I hadn't accomplished half of what I'd intended but it would have to wait. The children were my first priority and I wanted to spend the rest of the day with Bibi and Tolo, Elodie and Gabi, giving all of them a secure, loving foundation so they'd never spend a single second of their lives feeling unwanted and abandoned.

CHAPTER FIVE

MAC
Cruz Vineyard

The Cruz Vineyard was stark and cold, the wind bitter. The pre-harvest mounds of bright green, heart-shaped leaves and plump clusters of hanging fruit were gone, leaving twisted, woody vines clinging to trellis wires that, from a distance, somehow resembled a mass crucifixion.

Braun and I trudged across the snow-covered hillside to a small brick building draped in yellow crime-scene tape.

He pointed to a marked place in the snow. "That's where Drigo was found, right outside his laboratory."

I turned, taking in a 360-degree view of the area. The lab sat in the middle of the field, some distance west and uphill from a building that held the vineyard's event center and tasting rooms. The winery, barns, and Cruz home were even further away.

"Even if he'd been killed in broad daylight and someone had been around the main buildings, it's unlikely they would've seen anything. The lab's almost completely hidden, given the distance, the angle, and multiple rows of vines."

Braun agreed. "There was probably nobody stirring, since it was still dark and bitter cold out here."

"Which raises questions about the killer." I turned my back to the bitter wind. "They must have known Drigo's routine—that he'd be checking vines in the wee hours despite the cold. But how did they get here? Unless it was a family member or an employee, they had to come in a vehicle and park down near the house. Seems like someone would have noticed."

"Forensics lifted a few footprints but it was snowing almost non-stop and drifting. Also, Emil trampled all over the place looking for his grandfather." Braun pointed toward a buffer zone of trees along the west side of the land. "Yoon found some partials over there. If they belong to our killer, he probably parked somewhere along River Road and walked in through that field."

"Did anyone check the road?"

"Sure. There's not much along there, farms are spread out, no cameras of any kind. The ground was likely too solid to pick up any tire tracks and, by then, of course, any that might've been left were buried. The area under the trees didn't yield anything."

"We can put out a request but the odds are slim anyone took note of an anonymous parked car at that hour." I turned back toward the lab. "Okay. Give me a tour of the scene."

ജ

Walking the Cruz scene was atypical for me. Normally when I arrived at a homicide, the body would be in situ and little disturbed since its discovery. That gave me an opportunity to see everything more or less the way the killer had left it. Not much of importance remained in the vineyard, but Braun took me through it in detail.

After we looked over the exterior of Drigo's laboratory and the immediate area where he'd been killed, Ty unlocked the door onto a combination office and science lab extending to the right.

"Drigo had been in here—possibly interrupted since he left a pen and a journal out on his desk, but there's no way to know for sure."

I took in the entire room before I went to the desk. It was clean and organized with tidy, glass-fronted cabinets and shelves of books and journals. Counters and a table were clear of all but necessary items. The journal on Drigo's desk revealed yesterday's date and a bunch of numbers and abbreviations scrawled on the opened page. His uncapped ballpoint pen sat in the page gutter. There was nothing to indicate a search or a scuffle. The man might have just stepped away for a moment.

Braun turned back. "His grandson said he would've checked on his experimental vines."

He opened a door to the left of the entry and led the way into a warm, earth-scented greenhouse, about half the size of Shay's, with a single crop: grapevines. Each vine had a small handmade sign stuck in the dirt at its base. A few showed the variety but most bore only some kind of alpha-numeric codes.

"Was he grafting vines for new varieties?"

"That's what Emil said. This is where he invented the grape that's causing a sensation in the wine community."

I looked for a gap between vines or some disruption that might indicate one had been removed. There were a few hand-tools and an open bin of soil or compost—signs that someone had been working there—but nothing I could point to as being out of place. "Did Emil look around in here?"

"Absolutely," Braun said. "As soon as the M.E. finished up and we decided Emil didn't appear to be our man, we brought him in. He stated he rarely entered the greenhouse because this was strictly Drigo's domain but, as far as he could tell, nothing seemed damaged or missing."

"What about the office and lab?"

"Same. Except for the journal being left out, he said there was nothing unusual. Forensics went over the whole place anyway because, you never know."

We returned to the entrance where I paused to review. "Drigo walked up from the main house, maybe checked some vines, then came in here. He went to his office." I scanned the room on the right. "Doesn't he have a computer?"

Braun nodded. "He used a laptop. Ami said he left it in his room at the house. Computer Crimes picked it up, along with his cell phone."

"Okay. He probably didn't intend to work out here or he would have brought the laptop. But he would check the greenhouse. Those notes in his journal likely pertain to whatever he observed there. Shay does the same thing." I looked around, then stepped out into the cold wind.

"Maybe while he was making notes, somebody came to the door or he heard them outdoors. He comes out and…" I studied the distance from the door to the spot marked for the body.

"It's roughly twenty-three feet." Braun answered my unasked question. "And the snow was roughed up from about that first flag to where he was found. That's an estimate because of Emil's footprints running through and then all the responders. There were a few larger scuffed areas and blood spatter where it looked like somebody was pushed or fell."

"So they struggled?"

"It looked that way."

"And Drigo was killed with a wire saw." I gazed at the marker, imagining the scenario from the pictures Braun had showed me before. Drigo wasn't a large man but he'd been strong and smart. He would've fought hard... and there would have been a moment when he'd known.

I looked across rows and rows of vines to the west. "Let's follow the trail. Any idea where Yoon spotted the footprints near the trees?"

"Gauging from the partial prints, plus the damaged twigs and scrub Forensics turned up, the guy exited the vineyard near those birch trees. See the white trunks just to the left of that really tall pine?"

"Got it." I nodded, squinting against the wind. "He'd want to get away fast so he'd be running. But if he came in the same way, he's got his route planned... the most direct."

I picked the straightest possible path and we started across.

The wooded area provided less information than the lab and greenhouse. When we reached the other side, there was nothing but empty road and a fallow field across from us.

Braun picked up his recitation. "Nearest building north is a storage barn, up around the curve. There's a house a hundred yards beyond that but the residents are older, didn't see or hear anything." He turned. "South, there's a group of five or six houses just below a rise in the road that prevents any sightline to here. Door-knocks got nothing. A few folks were up but indoors, eating breakfast, getting ready for the day. If anyone noticed a vehicle pass, they would've figured it was a commuter."

Braun would have seen to everything, but I was relying on his recall. "Any cameras between here and the next turn-off?"

"There's a garage a couple of miles north that sells used cars. He's got a couple of cameras on the lot, one of which catches the west lane of the road. That one picked up three vehicles in the time frame. If the guy came in that way, we might have a blurred image, assuming we know what we're looking for. We can probably figure out make, model, and so forth but details or occupants will be sketchy at best."

"It's better than nothing." As we walked back to the vineyard, I gave him a verbal nudge. "What's the next step?"

He twitched, looking surprised. "Huh?"

"You're lead on this, Braun. What do you need me to work on?"

Braun had worked cases on his own before but, when we partnered, my rank meant I was given lead—even though I didn't see it as such. We worked as a team. But if Ty wanted to move up to senior investigator, he'd need to demonstrate the leadership skills he had.

A brief smile lit his face before he refocused on the trail ahead. "You already know the victim's family but, uh, I think we should interview them together to get a better picture of Drigo."

I nodded. It was what I would have done. "You want to do that now?"

"Yes." He paused to consider his plan. "After that, I think we should see what Forensics has for us and start looking into the uh, the interest surrounding the new wine."

"Sounds good. Let's hope Ami's got a pot of hot coffee."

By the time we made our way down the hill, though, cars had begun filling the Cruz's drive and the parking lot near the winery.

"Looks like people are showing up to offer condolences. It might be better if we deal with forensics first and stop back in the morning."

CHAPTER SIX

SHAY

Maple Sunrise

Back at the house, I took out the bin of toy cars and started rolling a few down Mac's racetrack. Tolo joined me, stretching as high as his little arm could reach to set more cars in motion, then squealing and laughing in delight whenever one bounced and rolled off the track.

Bibi carried two cars to a place where the track curved in a wide arc and she'd arranged the dollhouse and figures Mac had made for Elodie a couple of years before. While she quietly rolled her cars and moved dolls around her little settlement, her brother hopped and whooped and cheered, enjoying collisions and wrecks as much as a successful run along the track.

I loved seeing them that way, their paradoxical personalities in full contrast yet so attuned, each would react to the tiniest shift in the other's mood. I wondered if they'd been that way in their mother's womb or had it happened as they'd grown, sharing every minute of each other's lives? Would Elodie and Gabi develop a shared sense if the Marin children stayed with us for a long time?

Of course, considering their relationships led my mind to my own sibling-less childhood and my unknown, missing sister. Of course, when the twins took their nap, I opened my laptop and tugged the tenuous thread Mac had uncovered. Even knowing a professional, experienced detective failed to find her, I had to look. But of course, I found nothing.

I opened a computer file labeled *Family Research – Personal* and selected the document marked *Sinead.* Below the final line on its single page, I typed the date and the information Mac had given me and began a To-Do list:

- *Need Annie's friends' names and the date Shinny was adopted – and where they live*
- *Need name of Betty's friend who told her about Shinny*
- *Why did she keep me?*
- *Need Betty's last name and phone number – maybe she can tell me more*
- *Insurance company – employment records*

After re-reading the list a few times, I realized Mac would have to get information from Warren Kruger before I could begin. I didn't know if Mac would agree to call him, or if Warren was allowed to give us peoples' names and phone numbers. Or even if he did, whether Betty would talk to me.

But there was one person in Port Terrence who would help—the neighbor I'd met when Mac and I went there to search for my mother. Nadia Giordano had known us. She'd babysat me and Shinny. Even better, she was still in Port Terrence, still living next door to the house where we'd lived. It was even possible she already knew Betty.

Very quickly, I added another task. A vital one:

- *Call Nadia*

It wasn't much, but every entry could move my search forward in tiny increments. Baby steps leading into my past. If I kept looking and asking questions, someone would have answers about Shinny's adoption and I could find out where she went. Maybe she knew about me. Maybe she was searching, too. Maybe, finally, we'd meet and get to know each other and be… sisters, again.

ꟹ

That evening, Maria Ana sat with the children while Mac and I went to the advisory board meeting with Ben and Terri. The CSA program took up most of our time because, after The Herb Guys made their pitch, word must have spread. Two more farmers had called, asking to collaborate.

I wasn't comfortable with the idea nor convinced it was the best move for my business but Terri was gung-ho and Ben and Mac seemed in favor of the change. As owner and CEO, though, I got to cast a second, deciding vote if there was a tie.

"It's obviously something your fellow farmers want to do," Ben told me. "And there's no downside to offering a wider variety of products to your customers. There won't be any extra costs involved since you'll charge participating farmers to use your service as well as collecting a small percentage of their sales. The only open question is whether or not this will increase membership. My money's on it happening but we won't have firm data until we run it for at least one year."

I couldn't argue. Terri had gone over the products and costs for each farmer and I already knew them as neighbors and friends. And it wasn't the idea I objected to, it was how I could possibly organize and manage something so large in addition to my own business.

"I guess it could work," I admitted. "I'm pretty sure there's a market for the Herb Guys' teas and fresh and dried herbs. Adding Sullivan's maple syrup products is almost a no-brainer if they can keep their prices down but I don't know how well members will accept Chau Sai's Vietnamese produce. People who aren't familiar with it won't know how to cook or use them. She does grow American vegetables too, but some of those overlap mine so I wouldn't want to add them. We'd have to figure out what to include."

"Those are all things we'll consider when we draw up their contracts." Terri slid a sample form to me. "We can go over the details on Monday."

Ben turned to Mac. "We should look into ordering a new cargo van, too."

They had already discussed my vans and the routes they felt I could cover and decided we needed to expand from three vehicles to four. I didn't want to do it, as much afraid of my business getting too big as of the immediate expense of another vehicle and driver.

Mac looked at me and grinned. "It's only one small van, Shay. The big produce transporters aren't eyeing you, yet."

"It's a lot of money."

"The loan on the first one will be paid off by summer," Ben reminded me. "Your fleet expenses should stay relatively flat."

"There's still additional gas and maintenance," I said. "And the salary for another driver."

"Because you'll have another entire route of customers." He emphasized his words with taps of his pen on the table. "And it's not just CSA members we're talking about. Think of the retail potential."

Terri joined his pitch. "You've hardly tapped into Chautauqua County at all. Everyone who watches *What to Grow in Western New York* wants to buy your products. Think of all the new restaurants, grocers, and gift shops you'll add with just Dunkirk and Fredonia. And picking up Jamestown would be huge. Your CSA membership could double. You could even offer a three- or four-month option for summer cottagers…"

I threw up my hands. "Terri, stop. It's too much."

Mac and Ben glanced up from the map they'd been marking but, wisely, didn't interrupt.

I wasn't going to back down. "The whole point of community supported agriculture is keeping the source local…"

"The Department of Agriculture defines local as under 400 miles. It's not as though you're running big rigs halfway across the country, Shay. Your vans are small and fuel-efficient."

"…and staying sustainable. If I wind up supplying half of New York State, I'll need hundreds of acres of farmland. How would I be any different from those big industrial ag companies?"

"But that's where your collaborating partners come in. You don't need any more land. The Herb Guys and Chau Sai and Austin Sullivan will expand your product inventory and other farmers can supplement what you grow. Your CSA members are going to love it. We'll promote it on your web site and through print ads and with more TV commercials."

"I'd have to make certain the collaborating partners maintain acceptable practices and certifiable organic standards and…"

"The USDA has that covered, Shay. You know how rigorous they are because you have to meet those standards, yourself."

"But…"

"All you need to do is collect annual proof of inspection and certification from each partner and keep them on file with your own inspection records."

Terri and I batted every point like tennis balls until the men called time-out.

"You two have analyzed it to death." Ben used his coffee mug for a gavel. "Let's vote."

I tried one last angle. "Can we vote on a trial period—a temporary program?"

Mac shook his head. "That's asking a lot from your partners, Shay. They'd have to withhold products from their direct inventories to fulfill the CSA needs. If it turned out to be short-term, they could lose out on other opportunities."

He was right.

"Okay. I guess we can vote."

By the end of the evening, I'd reluctantly agreed to add three collaborating partners to the Maple Sunrise Farm CSA program and, potentially, the consideration of others. We'd also approved changes to the budget to cover another refrigerated cargo van, an additional driver, and the split-time garden worker/kitchen porter I'd promised my cooks. I was excited and nervous, optimistic and scared, all at the same time.

With the official meeting adjourned, Mac reached for bottles of whiskey and wine, pouring the latter for Terri and me. While he and Ben returned to the table for an in-depth discussion of engines and refrigeration units, Terri and I took our glasses to my office.

She pulled a chair alongside mine at the desk. “Let’s put an ad on the job board for a route driver. You’re going to need one soon.”

I turned on the computer and opened the site. “I can use the one from last time. All the information is the same.”

“Maybe mention it’ll be in Chautauqua County in case someone prefers that area or already knows the territory?”

“Good idea.” I opened the app and started typing.

“How about the kitchen porter position?”

“I thought I’d offer it to the garden workers, first. One of them might like the variety. And those positions are easier to fill with college kids coming home for the summer.”

After I posted the driver opening, Terri tapped my arm. “Don’t close out, yet. I think you should put out an ad for another cook.”

I turned in surprise. “A cook? I can’t afford that… and we didn’t vote for it. I don’t need another cook. We’re managing fine with three of us.”

“That’s the point, Shay. You’re barely managing during mid-harvests, even with you in the kitchen and pulling overtime. This year, you’ll have additional administrative duties and a lot more customers than before. You’re going to need another cook at some point.”

“But we…”

She held up a hand. “Not right away. Maybe not even full-time. But you can’t possibly work twelve- and fourteen-hour days the way you did last year. You’d barely have time for your children.”

I opened my mouth but my protest died with the realization I couldn’t compromise my time with the kids.

“If you place the ad now, you can have someone lined up when you need them. You don’t want to wait until the last minute and find no one’s available, do you?”

I glanced back at Mac and Ben, bent over a laptop. “We’re supposed to vote on major expenditures.”

"Running an ad isn't a major expenditure. And trust me, Shay. You're going to need another cook and, when you do, we are going to approve it with no argument."

Deep inside my resistant self, I knew Terri was right. I just couldn't get my head around another cook in the kitchen and another employee on the payroll. Most of all, if I were completely honest, I didn't want to imagine myself further removed from the work I loved and did well. I was a cook and a gardener, not some hot-shot business executive.

As if she read my mind, Terri signaled me to fill out another app. "You won't have to give up cooking entirely. It's in your DNA."

ဆ

Mac and I walked through fresh snow to the house where Maria Ana was knitting, the TV playing low.

"You're doing the right thing, Blodyn," Mac assured me. "Everything will work out for the best."

"You voted?" Maria Ana looked expectant.

"Yes. For CSA partners, a new van and driver… and a part-time porter for the kitchen."

She smiled at the last item. "Everybody's happy, then."

Mac grinned and squeezed my shoulders. "Almost everybody. One of us might take a little longer to convince."

CHAPTER SEVEN

MAC

Cruz Vineyard

Braun and I returned to the vineyard lab, the next morning to see if any of Drigo's journals mentioned a name or an investment offer related to his discoveries. It was a cold hike and a waste of time since most of his notes referenced experimental grafts and his observations of their development.

After snapping a few pictures of the plants in the greenhouse for my own reference, we relocked the building and angled downhill toward the cluster of buildings that made up the winery's public face. As we dropped below the crest of the hill, the wind seemed to lessen a little, although it was just as probable I'd grown too numb to feel anything. I'd be glad to get indoors.

Braun's uncharacteristic silence lasted until we passed the event center and he cleared his throat.

"I'm wondering if you could give me your impressions of the Cruz couple before we interview them. A quick run-down of their personalities and relationships with Drigo and with each other? They were upset and in shock the day it happened, so I'm not certain I have an accurate gauge."

I slowed my pace and pretended to check out the buildings, giving him a moment to consider his strategy. I guessed our reversed roles was causing his indecision since he had no reason to second guess himself. But his request was exactly what I would have asked.

"That makes sense." I signaled him into the center's recessed entryway to get out of the wind. "I'm not sure I'll be a lot of help but I know them a little."

"Neither struck me as suspicious."

"They're not. I'd stake a year's salary on them being completely innocent of any involvement. In fact, I'm a little worried their close relationships and general tolerance might blind them to any insight at all. Drigo was training his great-grandson, Ruy, to take over the business, but I'm not certain Emil inherited their enthusiasm for grape breeding. He seemed to enjoy farming and winemaking more than the experimental stuff."

"Was Drigo unhappy about that?"

I shrugged. "As I said, I wasn't close to them. Off-hand, my guess is he accepted it. Drigo's family has been making wines for generations in Spain and his education was in plant genetics or whatever it's called. Emil got his degree at Cornell and spent a year or two in Spain. He loved the vineyards but he never showed much interest in Drigo's laboratory. If I had to guess, I'd say Drigo was hoping his great-grandson, Ruy, would follow in his footsteps."

"That's Emil and Ami's son? He wasn't here the day of the murder."

"He's in his first year at Cornell. He's probably here now."

"How about Ami? Any problems with her grandfather-in-law or in her marriage?"

"God, no. Emil and Ami are really solid and, from what Shay's told me, Ami adored Drigo. I think her own grandparents passed before she was born, so he was her only grand generation. And the feeling was apparently mutual since Drigo never had a daughter."

"Any other family?"

"Not local, as far as I know. Ami grew up on the west coast, maybe Oregon. Her parents are out there, I think. Emil's parents died in a plane crash when he was in his teens. That's when Drigo stepped up."

"Anyone else? Anything I'm missing?"

I gave it some thought. "Nothing that comes to mind."

"Okay. Let's go talk to them… indoors."

ꟈ

There was no mistaking the grief in the Cruz home. It was visible in Emil's slumped posture, Ami's reddened eyes, and Ruy's listless mood, in addition to their shell-shocked expressions.

Tyler and I expressed our condolences and I told Ami that Shay would be stopping by with dinner later. We answered their immediate questions as much as possible while Ami poured coffee and handed it around, making the requisite attempt at small talk. But, once we'd covered the weather and Ruy's new life at college, it was time to get down to business.

Ty asked Ruy to wait in the TV room while he and Emil went into a smaller parlor, and Ami and I stayed in the kitchen.

At first, Ami had little to offer. I asked about her relationship with Drigo and his recent mood and behavior, all of which she reported to be normal.

"I haven't been actively involved in the vineyard operation in a few years. When Emil and I married, I helped with harvests or pruning, especially if we were short-handed. Later on, Drigo turned most of the vineyard management over to Emil, and started training me to run the winery. That allowed him more time to do what he really loved, working in his lab and greenhouse."

"How did you all get along together? You must have run into conflicts from time to time."

"Nothing serious." She smiled for the first time. "Drigo was always open to discussion if there was a problem or one of us wanted to try something different. He'd listen to everything we had to say, ask questions, and take it all quite seriously. Then he'd tell us whether we could go ahead with our idea or not. If he did agree, he'd always finish by saying, *We'll try. But I'm the boss and decision is mine. If it don't work, we scrap it.* Emil and I have quoted that line to each other a million times and it still makes us laugh. If we're going somewhere and whoever's driving wants to take a different route or we're in the grocery store and one of us picks up a different food or brand, the other will always say, *We'll try. If it don't work, we scrap it.*" She laughed, hiccupped, and covered her face, sobbing.

I laid a hand on her arm. "I'm sorry to put you through this, Ami. I know it's not easy but what you tell us could help catch the person who did this."

She nodded, scrubbing at her tear-drenched cheeks. "It's not fair. Drigo never hurt anyone."

I brought her a glass of water, let her eulogize the old man for a few minutes before getting back to my questions. "You have staff working here in winter, don't you? Who else is on the property?"

Ami sipped water and swiped at her eyes with a tissue. "We scale way down in winter, but there are some." She ticked her fingers as she spoke. "On the production side we have an assistant winemaker, the cellar master, and a lab tech. Emil and Drigo keep an eye on the vineyard, and Nico comes by to help with any routine jobs, but they have a few men on-call if there's pruning or maintenance needed.

"Then there's my staff, the sales and hospitality side. My assistant, Paige and I split most of those duties and we bring in trained regulars for tours and tastings. We don't have many drop-in customers at this time of year, but I have a part-timer in the wineshop and to answer the phones. That's about it."

I jotted the list in my notebook, counting at least a half-dozen more individuals to interview. "Is there anyone in that group who had a problem with Drigo or with any of you?"

"No. Most of us have been together quite a while and we work too closely to allow any conflict or dissension."

"I'll need names and contact information on all of them. Someone might've seen or heard something."

She hesitated, then sent a text. "Paige will email you our complete employee roster, both current and from the harvest season just past."

"Thanks. I'd like to talk to your son, now. Drigo may have mentioned something to him that will help."

The idea was to get Ruy's perspective without his parent's influence but, because he was under age, we also didn't want any problems if he revealed something we'd need when the case went to court.

Ruy couldn't decide whether he was sad or angry, whether to rage or weep, so he did neither. Normally an animated, outgoing young man, he seemed to have withdrawn overnight. He shuffled to a kitchen chair where he slumped, silent and avoiding eye contact.

"I know the last thing you want to do right now is answer questions, Ruy. And I wish I didn't have to ask them. But you had a special relationship with your great-grandfather and he might have told you something that will help us." I rambled on for a few minutes, watching his physical reactions. When he showed he was at least listening to me, I tried some low-key inquiries about the things he and Drigo enjoyed together.

Ruy raised his chin but kept his eyes downcast. "Bisabuelo said I have the character to become a world-class biogeneticist… like him. That means a plant breeder." He hesitated, as if expecting me to contradict him.

"That's high praise from someone who was respected and consulted internationally, himself. You must have inherited his patience and dedication."

He didn't smile but a light flush touched his cheeks. "He was teaching me everything he knew. But he said I also had to get my formal degree and then spend a few years doing hands-on study with other viticulturists. After that, he said I'd be ready to come home and take over his job."

"And you want to do that?"

"It's all I've ever wanted since I was a little kid. Bisabuelo started taking me to his lab before I even went to school. By second or third grade, he gave me a section of the greenhouse and my own vines to experiment with."

"That's impressive. Did he talk to you about the new grapes he was developing?"

"Of course. You've probably heard about his chardling blanc grapes. He worked to perfect them for many years before he submitted it for approval and registration. But it wasn't until he produced his EnElCee Vintage Brut that the world took notice."

"EnElCee..."

Ruy finally made eye contact. "It's spelled e-n-e-l-c-e-e, but it's actually the acronym NLC, which stands for Neoka Lake Cruz. One of Bisabuelo's little inside jokes." He gave a half-smile. "It's a sparkling wine, brut means dry—in this case, low sugar—and vintage is a designation that means it's produced from a single, select harvest—the best of the best, in other words."

"Sounds pretty special... and expensive."

"It is. Bisabuelo restricted it to vintage only. He also insisted on a minimum six-year aging that makes it even more special. And pricier."

"So, a privately-developed grape variety and a select, six-year-aged, limited-production wine? Have I got that right?"

Ruy nodded. There was a small light in his eyes and he'd corrected his slumped posture. "The vines will be commercially available in another year or two, but it will be difficult for anyone to replicate our blend and processes, even if they could match our soil, conditions, and so forth. And, of course, we have a very good head start."

"Your great-grandfather taught you well, Ruy. I can't get my head around making a new grape, let alone all the rest of that stuff."

"Would you like to see what I'm working on? It's a different variety of grape. In the early stages you never know how things will turn out but if you'd like to go up to the lab..." He stopped as if he'd been gut-punched.

"I'd like to see it, if you're comfortable going up there." I put a hand on his shoulder. "There are a few markers and some tape left, but the scene is cleared, Ruy and the lab building is intact. Nothing inside was disturbed that we could see."

He turned to Ami. "Mom?"

"It's up to you, Son. If Mac says it's clear, then it is. And we have to check the greenhouse vines soon, in any case. Take the Ranger, though. The snow's piling up out there."

The boy grabbed his winter gear. "I'll get the ute from the barn and pick you up by the back door. Shouldn't take more than a couple of minutes."

I gave Braun a heads-up and reached for my jacket and boots.

Ami stayed at the table. "If you don't need me, I'll let you two go together. It's good for him to take charge, to do something he's good at."

଼

Minutes later, Ruy parked a Polaris Ranger utility terrain vehicle by the back steps. It was a rugged looking beast, set high over twenty-nine-inch tires and outfitted with a snowplow and room in the back for cargo or passengers.

I took the shotgun-seat and strapped in. "Looks like a solid ride. Can it handle the bluff or do you stick to the trails?"

Ruy didn't respond and when I turned to look, he was hunched forward over the steering wheel, squinting up the hill.

I leaned in too, craning my neck to see what he was fixated on. All I caught was a quick flash of something beyond Drigo's lab building. Between blowing snow and the distance, I couldn't have sworn if it was human or animal.

"Somebody's up there." Ruy sounded confused. "It's not Nico. He has the day off."

Before I could speak, he slammed the gearshift, loaded the clutch, and took off, full-throttle.

CHAPTER EIGHT

MAC

Cruz Vineyard

The Ranger bucked. I snagged the rollbar grab-handle and braced my feet. The ute shot ahead, bouncing and fishtailing, but Ruy worked it like a pro.

"Shouldn't be anybody… up there." He growled through gritted teeth, focused on the steep, snow-covered farm track.

I pulled out my phone, called Braun. "Grab the vehicle and get up to the river road, code 3. We got a runner from the lab." I was shouting from adrenaline rush and engine noise when the ute slewed sideways and thumped a fencepost. My phone slid from my grip, landing by my feet.

Ruy shifted into reverse, swung the wheel, and kept going.

As we crested the hill, visibility worsened. Vineyards sloped away on all sides and, with nothing to block the wind-propelled snow, we were caught in a whiteout.

Ruy was forced to a crawl, beating his fist on the wheel.

ဢ

We met Braun on the verge, digging in his vehicle trunk when we broke through the trees. "I wasn't fast enough. He was gone when I got here. I might've caught his tail lights as he rounded the curve up there but it was too far to ID anything—if it was even him." He held up a spray-can. "Good news is we've got some clear tracks. Bad news is they'll be obliterated in no time, and forensics can't get a tech here for at least an hour."

I grunted, calculating the cold hours ahead. "You might as well go back to the house, Ruy. We'll be out here for some time."

I took the can of gray primer from Braun and stuffed my pocket with evidence markers. "Show me where you want to start."

He led me to a stretch of trampled snow along the road's shoulder. At a glance, I noted a set of tire impressions and several boot prints. I crouched down for a closer look. "We've got a vehicle—probably a truck from the looks of it. And a fair-sized footprint with good tread."

"See if you can pick a clear section of tire prints. There's a half-bucket of snow-print plaster in the trunk. I'll grab that and my camera while you set up."

We operated at a fast and steady pace, marking, spraying, and photographing; then mixing and pouring plaster to get a cast. It was finicky work and our hands and faces were numb with cold.

We'd lifted several impressions from the road and the trail to Drigo's lab, when a minivan pulled up.

"Coffee and soup," Emil shouted. "Both hot."

"Throw in a hot shower and we'll nominate you for sainthood." Braun had just lifted a cast so the timing was right.

I finished pouring another one then followed him into the van, the sudden heat on my skin so extreme it stung. I resisted an urge to down the entire contents of the thermos in a single gulp.

"Ami was worried about you." Emil raised his own travel mug in a toast. "You guys are really earning your pay, today."

"Yeah, the job's not all donuts." Ty scrubbed at his frozen face, his mouth so stiff he sounded drunk.

"Any reason you'd expect someone to be at Drigo's lab today?"

Emil scowled. "No. What did you find?"

"Nothing certain," I told him. "We hadn't even left the yard when Ruy spotted someone leaving the lab. He drove up as fast as he could, and Braun came around by the road, but the guy got away. We never got a good look at him or his vehicle.

ꝏ

The short break did us good. Once we were warmed up and caffeinated, the rest of the collection went quickly. But we weren't finished. A call from Ruy brought another issue.

"I came to Bisabuelo's lab to check, to see if that guy stole anything. He did."

"I told you to go back to the house. You're contaminating a crime scene." I paused to reset my tone. "Ruy, can you step back outside, please? You can return here or go back to the house and call me again, but we need to go over everything… away from the scene."

"Sorry. I only meant to look."

"Don't worry about it, it's done now. Just don't touch anything else. Are you outside?"

"Yeah. I'm locking the door. I'll head up to you."

Braun and I loaded up and got into our vehicle, ramping the heat. Ruy appeared a minute later.

"I'm really sorry," he repeated. "I didn't touch anything in the lab or the office, only looked around. When I got to the greenhouse, though, I could see some of the vines had been moved."

"You said something was stolen. What was it?"

"Vines. He tried to cover up the empty spots with pots and stuff moved around but I spotted it right away. He ripped out a whole flat of new grafts. I'll have to check the journal but I'm pretty sure they were all chardling blancs."

Braun looked up from his notes. "That's the new one that's causing excitement throughout the wine business?"

"Yeah."

He made another note. "What do you suppose they're worth?"

"Thousands?" Ruy blew out an exasperated breath. "Millions? Definitely a lot. Maybe my dad will know."

"Okay." My partner tucked his phone in a pocket and frowned. "We'll have to go over the greenhouse again, take some photos and maybe borrow those journals your great-grandfather kept."

He glanced at me, to see if he'd missed anything.

I gave him a nod. "We're going to have to get Emil or someone else who understands this stuff to explain the implications."

ꟾ

The lab and greenhouse didn't yield much information. The cheap pine door had been smashed with a foot or hammer making access simple. As Ruy had reported, the only disruption inside was a large gap between vines in the greenhouse. I wouldn't expect anything as obvious as fingerprints, but plant pots and gardening tools had been tossed in the empty space and some soil dropped on the floor indicating the guy was in a hurry. Forensics might find fibers, hair, or other trace evidence we couldn't see.

"I'll call Yoon to get somebody out here, see if they can find something useful."

CHAPTER NINE

SHAY

Maple Sunrise

After Mac left for work that morning, I got to work cleaning house and restructuring my plans for the coming season. School was closed for some kind of faculty meeting so all four children were home but I sent them to straighten their toys and games in the playroom before they played.

I wasn't at my best, working in short bursts on my laptop while sweeping, mopping, folding laundry, and tending to four chattering children. Mac had done a better job of keeping up with everything so the housework wasn't overwhelming and the children played happily together, but he wasn't also juggling paperwork.

I paused to watch the kids huddled together over some game and thought, for the thousandth time, how difficult it would be when the Marin family came to claim their babies. I braced for it every day, knowing they would leave another empty place… no, three empty places… in a heart already riddled with them.

Unexpectedly, I thought of Leah, a long-ago foster sister, shouting *Swiss Cheese* and a laugh escaped me. It was a silly reference we fosters had created to signal when one of us was caught bending a rule in a home filled with taboos.

I didn't steal the children, I told Leah in my mind. *We got them the way families got you and me… and we really love them.* Leah had never minced words. *Maybe so,* her memory-image agreed. *But you'd steal them if you could.* In a way, she was right. I would steal them and a hundred other children if I could save them from the heartache she and I had endured.

I put Leah's memory away, along with my mop and bucket, and returned to the laptop. If I wanted to solicit new CSA subscriptions, it was past time to get it done.

Terri was working on a direct marketing campaign to announce our presence in Chautauqua County but it was up to me to find customers. I began with a few stores near the county line that already purchased gift baskets, then expanded my search west and south.

By noon, I'd made some progress but I needed to fix lunch and help Elodie and Gabi set up their paint supplies while the toddlers napped. Somehow, in the midst of everything, they'd also convinced me to take them sledding that afternoon.

ଌ

With everyone bundled in snowsuits, hats, and mittens, I trudged uphill through at least a foot of snow, towing Bibi and Tolo on Mac's old toboggan. Elodie and Gabi ran ahead with their snow tubes, laughing maniacally whenever they stumbled and fell.

Our hill flowed in an easy slope from Little Wolf Mountain before it widened and leveled out around the lake and river basin. At its lower end, it was steep enough to thrill the six-year-olds but not too scary for the twins. When we reached the first level area—a sort of natural terrace—I stopped to catch my breath and make sure no one had lost a mitten or boot.

The older girls immediately took their first slide, screaming all the way down. Then the toddlers and I followed on the toboggan, managing not to overturn along the way. I marveled at the kids' stamina as we climbed and slid, again and again.

After an hour of play, I was ready to lure everyone back to the house with promises of hot chocolate. But before I could say the words, Mac appeared, running across the field below, waving and calling out. In no time, hill-rolls and sled races and snowball fights were underway, small bodies running and tumbling with renewed energy as Mac whooped and cheered them on and I snapped pictures with my phone.

When we were all half-frozen and exhausted, Mac put Elodie, Bibi, and Tolo on the toboggan and I hauled Gabi on one of the tubes, following our well-trodden trail home. Mac supervised baths and pajamas while I prepared soup and biscuits for a warm supper in front of the fire, knowing the children would fall into bed early that night.

"That was a work-out." Mac flopped on the couch and pulled me down beside him. "How long were you out there before I got home?"

"We went out right after nap, but we were only sledding." I poked his ribs. "None of that crazy stuff until you showed up."

"Lucky for you that I did. I'll bet that's the first time you ever rolled down a snowy hill. And, by the way, your snowball pitch could use a little work."

"My pitch would have been fine if you'd given me time to make proper snowballs…"

My phone rang—an unusual interruption at that time of night—and I frowned as I checked the screen. "It's Maria Ana."

"Shay." Her voice was a soft moan. "I need help. I fall down…"

I leaped to my feet. "What happened? Where are you?"

"Stairs."

Mac was already pulling his boots on, telling me to stay with the children while he ran to her apartment.

Everything happened fast after that. An ambulance and a troop car showed up, sweeping the snow with red and blue lights while people scurried back and forth between them and the Farm Gourmet building. The lights were on in Maria Ana's upstairs apartment but I couldn't tell if she was up there or in the stairway.

It wasn't until a gurney was wheeled to the ambulance that Mac came running to get his coat and give me an update.

"They're taking her to the E.R. She fell down the stairs, might've broken her hip. Are you okay staying with the kids or would you rather I stay and you go with her?"

I wanted to be there for her but Mac could offer both reassurance and practical help while I'd be little more than a comforting presence. He was used to dealing with crises and the E.R. staff already knew him.

"We'll be fine. You go… but call me as soon as you know anything."

Before he left though, I raced out—coatless and bootless—to peer into the ambulance and tell Maria Ana I loved her and would come to the hospital in the morning if she wasn't home by then.

She looked so small and alone on the gurney, for a moment I nearly changed my mind about going.

ꙮ

As tired as I was, I couldn't sleep for worrying about Maria Ana. Mac called to tell me her hip was broken, as he'd thought. And when he finally came home, he looked grim.

"She's going to be okay, but she needs a hip replacement. They're trying to schedule her surgery for late tomorrow… uh, tonight, or Monday morning."

"Is it too late to call her?"

"Pain meds, Love. But if you like, I'll take you over to see her in the morning."

I pulled at my hands, always feeling useless in situations like that. "What can I take for her? Is there anything we can do?"

"She'll have to stay a few days, maybe a week, but we need to figure out something for when she comes home. She won't be able to use the stairs for at least a month."

"She can stay here, with us." My mind flew over the possibilities which weren't promising. "She won't want to be in the living room with all of us running through. Could we turn the playroom into a bedroom for her?"

Mac had converted my tiny office and food pantry into a playroom when Farm Gourmet had moved to the Hawley house. It wasn't very spacious but I thought we could at least fit a bed in there.

He nodded. "Sure. I'll get Braun to help me move the couch and toys out and we can set up a bed before she comes home. You can let me know what else you think she'll need."

"Is the doctor sure she'll be okay when she heals? We can have a granny flat built on the back of the house. Or even a little house of her own, with no stairs?"

He chuckled and wrapped an arm around me. "You're getting ahead of yourself again, Blodyn. Let's slow down and see how she does. From what the nurse was telling me, people get new hips all the time and once they recover, they use stairs, run, bike, even play sports."

"I hope so. Maria Ana would hate being inactive and unable to do the things she enjoys."

It wasn't until four in the morning that I jolted awake to the realization Maria Ana wasn't only going to have to leave her apartment while she recovered, she wouldn't be in the Farm Gourmet kitchen either. Jennie and I would never be able to manage without her. I was going to have to find a temporary cook.

CHAPTER TEN

MAC

Iroquois County

Weekends are theoretical for homicide investigators. Braun and I planned to spend Saturday tracking down and interviewing workers from the Cruz vineyard. We weren't expecting any brilliant revelations, but it was work that had to be done… and you never know.

Before that, though, I had snow to clear, livestock to feed, and actual shit—of an animal nature—to shovel. And most important, four kids to be bundled into coats and boots to assist me.

I assigned egg collecting to Gabi, while Elodie instructed the toddlers on the finer points of feeding chickens and ducks, and I tended the goats. Barney, as usual, tore madly from one of us to the next, trying to manage all of his self-imposed responsibilities.

"I can see why you chose Barney for your dog," I told Shay, over breakfast. "You're both obsessed with multi-tasking."

She laughed, doling out pancakes and sausages, as she reminded the six-year-olds to make their beds, helped Bibi mop up spilled juice, and explained to Tolo why we don't brush our teeth with maple syrup. "Barney's better at it than I am. But he can't be expected to herd goats and mind the children at the same time. He's going to need an assistant."

"Funny you should say that. I've had my eye on one of the vet's Great Pyrenees. She's due to whelp sometime in March."

"One of those giant bear-dogs?" Shay looked doubtful. "Why not another border collie? And why not an older one?"

"Border collies are herders and Barney's got that covered. But the herd is growing. He'd have a hard time with a panicked herd if a pair of determined coyotes show up. We need a dog that'll get along with him, bond with us, and do guard duty for the goats. Pyrs are proven livestock protectors that become part of their herds, but an older dog might be problematic due to previous attachments." I turned away to pour orange juice as I added, "Two would be best."

She squeaked more than screamed, but her intent was clear. "Two? Two dogs besides Barney? Two puppies?"

At the word *puppies*, the kids all started whooping and begging.

I gave Shay my most appealing smile. "The herd's getting too big for one dog. The Pyrs will protect the whole farm while Barney will still do the herding."

"But three?"

"They won't be house dogs. Guardian Pyrs live with their herd. And they're great around children. Gentle giants."

Shay looked from our four giggling children to me and flung a dishtowel at my head. "Honestly, Mac. Sometimes you're the biggest kid in the house."

But I caught her smile before she tucked it away.

"Come on gang, let's help Mom clear the table. Then, I've got to go to work… and tell Doc Hutchins we want pick of the litter."

ꕤ

As foreman and vineyard crew supervisor, Nico Carbone probably knew the Cruz workers as well as anyone. Middle-aged and stocky, he had the look of a former middleweight boxer whose nose had taken a few too many hits, but his disposition was relaxed and easy. His home reflected the man: sprawling, lived-in rooms marked by pieces of sports equipment, books, and video games. One glance at the array told me he had at least two or three active teenagers.

He didn't withhold his disgust with the way his employer had died. "I don't know what their problem was, but there wasn't any reason to kill Drigo. He would've given them the shirt off his back if they asked for it."

Braun sat in one of the big club chairs and took out his phone. "Were there any workers who didn't get along with him? Somebody with a gripe or a long-standing feud?"

Nico shrugged his meaty shoulders. "You always get a few agitators and complainers. Some might've resented the Cruz family in general, just because they're successful, well-respected, got some money and land. But there's never been anything extreme or that serious that I recall. If someone wanted to complain, I think it'd be at Emil rather than Drigo."

"Emil didn't get along with the workers?"

"Oh, sure he did. Emil's a very likable guy. But he's the one out there, working alongside the rest of us, so he's the one to correct or poke at the slackers if they need it. He's not a loud-mouth bully. He stays polite, keeps it private, but it's his business on the line and he expects fair value for his money."

Ty studied the names on his phone and glanced at me for direction. I gave a slight nod but no advice. He knew what to ask.

"We've got a fairly long list of names. If I read them off, could you point out anyone who might've had a problem with Drigo? Not only as potential suspects, but also to give us a different point of view… somebody who might have noticed or overheard something."

"Sure, I guess I can do that." Nico stood. "It's Saturday. Are you guys allowed a beer?"

I recognized his need to busy himself while we talked. "We're on duty but water or coffee's fine."

While he rummaged around the coffee maker and fridge, Braun read out each employee's name and Nico responded without hesitation, usually with a forthright *he's no problem* or *she seems level-headed* and only a few questionable ones. By the time they finished, Braun had checked off eight or nine names for follow-up. Some were people who'd expressed dissatisfaction with their jobs or with the

Cruz family, others were workers Nico described as *talkers*, people who liked to chat and gossip and might have useful information.

Braun finished his coffee and pocketed his phone. "You've been a big help, Nico. You've saved us a lot of legwork. We'll start with these and maybe one of them can point us in the right direction."

"Just so you catch whoever did this." The man closed his eyes briefly. "It's going to be hard without Drigo. His enthusiasm always kind of lit up the place."

While Braun drove to our next stop, I checked in with forensics. Ji Ho Yoon took my call and rummaged through the reports he'd received. "Rodrigo Cruz. That the one?"

I said it was. "Braun and I took casts of some footprints and tires. They're probably not the quality your team would've pulled but it was one of those days. We did what we could."

He didn't respond immediately but emitted a few grunts and hums that suggested he was reading.

"You're right about the footprints. We didn't get much from them. Possible size twelve boot but the tread's iffy… could be any of three or four brands and, well, that's about it. But you got lucky with your tire casts. You're looking for a pickup—something like an F-150 I'd guess—with three Michelin Defenders, on the front and the left rear, but a BF Goodrich A/T on the right rear." He clicked a few times before continuing. "That one, the Goodrich, has a pretty good tread… I can't swear one way or the other, but I don't think it's brand-new. Still pretty good condition, though. The other three are fairly well-worn. I'll send you Eddie's report with his specs and measurements but that's the gist of it. If you find the truck, we'll match it for you."

"Anything from the greenhouse?"

He shuffled papers again. "They're not all complete, yet. From what we've got so far, I wouldn't get too excited… uh, hold on a minute." There were sounds of movement and muffled conversation before he returned to my call. "We've got one point of interest, Mac. Those boot prints from around the truck? They don't match the ones from the Cruz murder scene."

"Meaning we're looking for two suspects?"

"I'd bet on it. The prints from both scenes were too messed up to get a brand. The ones from the first scene were trampled and partially blurred by snow and the ones from the second weren't full prints due to the road surface and they were also snow-blurred. But they aren't the same size. Your vine thief looks to be a size, size-and-a-half bigger than your killer."

"Seriously? I didn't see that coming." I glanced at Braun who only scowled. "Okay, Yoon. Looks like we're back to the drawing board. You'll send the reports?"

"On the way. Good luck, guys."

I thanked him and disconnected.

"It feels like a step back," I told Braun. "We need to look at potentials who connect. But the vehicle info is good. And it's more than we had."

ꙮ

The next few workers we called on led nowhere. One was a thin, scowling man with a broad-ranging list of complaints from his brother's drinking to government oppression. The Cruz family fell somewhere in his generalized disdain for all *rich people.*

Another, a young female who said she worked some days as a picker in the vineyard and other days as a quality sorter, insisted everyone liked Drigo. Nico had tagged her as a *talker*, an outgoing, chatty type—which she certainly was—but she didn't exhibit any dislike toward the Cruz family or her job, and her attitude toward her co-workers was mostly positive.

A few people weren't at home, but the last name on the list, Keith Sands, raised a different problem.

The stout, worn-looking woman who opened the door, eyed us with suspicion. "How do I know you're who you say you are? Where's your uniforms?"

Braun explained our rank and the purpose of our call, and we showed her our IDs.

"If you're really cops, then how come you don't already know Keith's missing?"

"What do you mean, missing?"

"I mean he's gone. MIA. Not here." Her weary voice couldn't pull off the intended sarcasm. "He got a phone call, said he was gonna help out a guy at work and he'd be back in a coupla hours. I ain't seen him since."

"Maybe we should come in."

After shooing off three young children to *go watch TV*, Hope Sands sank onto a kitchen chair as if she'd never get up. Her house was also well lived-in but, unlike Nico's, it hadn't seen a cleaning in a while. Dirty dishes sat in the sink and on the table, cupboard doors stood open, and the kitchen counter was buried beneath food containers, papers, and what appeared to be a pile of unmatched socks.

"Am I gonna have to go over the whole thing again?"

"You reported your husband's absence to the police?"

"Yeah. When he didn't come home and nobody'd seen him, I got worried he had an accident. A deputy took a report but it seemed like he figured Keith was gone on a drunk or cheating with some woman." She raised her eyes toward the ceiling. "As if he could be bothered going anyplace else to drink. And, trust me, he don't have enough interest to chase a woman."

"When did you last speak to him?"

"When he went out the door. That was… Thursday? Yeah, Thursday afternoon."

"The day before yesterday?"

Two days after Drigo was killed. I eye-checked Braun to see if he'd caught it. The set of his jaw said he did.

"It was so cold I couldn't see why they'd need him. They done the ice wine picking already. But Keith said there's always stuff that needs doin' and a buck's a buck." She rubbed at her temple. "Can't argue that."

"Do you recall what time he left?"

"It was after lunch. Maybe two o'clock, two-thirty? He got a call and said he had to go to work."

"And he said *a couple of hours.*"

"I expected him home for dinner. I wouldn't of bothered cooking if I'd known it was just the kids. They're happy with frozen pizza."

"Was it usual for him to get called in like that?"

She half-shrugged. "Not too much. But he'll go if there's a few bucks to be made."

Braun scrolled his phone. "Was it Emil Cruz who called or someone else from the winery?"

"I dunno. He just said *work*. Tell you the truth, it coulda been Cruz or maybe one of the other places. Keith does jobs for a coupla vineyards if Cruz doesn't need him." She chewed a thumbnail. "I forgot to tell the deputy that. But it probably don't matter."

"If Keith was headed in a different direction when he went missing, it does matter." Braun cleared his throat and adjusted his growing irritation.

I stepped in to give him a break. "Where else does Keith work, Mrs. Sands?"

"Black Crow sometimes and the foreign-sounding one on Silverdust Lake. He used to work over to Keuka Lake but it's too far of a drive so he don't go there no more."

"Where's Black Crow?"

"North, on Lake Ontario."

"And the other one?"

"That one's east of here, right before you get to Silver Rapids."

I jotted down the information. "The sheriff's probably on it. What was he driving?"

"His pickup truck."

"Do you know the make or model? The year?"

"I think it's a Ford. It's black but it ain't new. I don't know what else. He bought it off some guy he knows."

Braun stepped in again.

"Another thing, Mrs. Sands. Where was Keith on Tuesday?"

She looked blank. "Tuesday?"

"This past Tuesday, four days ago. Two days before he went missing. Was he home that day?"

"I dunno. Let me think." She studied her hands for a moment, her lips moving as she ticked her fingers. "Tuesday was the day I went to the dollar store. The kids needed cereal and they had canned pork and beans on sale."

"What time?"

"Around noon. Me and my friend, Lois, had a BOGO coupon for the burger place so we went there after."

"Had Keith gone anywhere that morning?"

She scratched her head and shrugged. "I don't think so?"

In spite of her detailed recitation of the coupons she'd used for shopping and her bargain lunch, she seemed unable to recall if her husband was home or not.

Braun persisted. "What time did you get up that morning?"

"Seven. My alarm's set for it. I have to get my coffee before I get the kids up for school or I'd be good-fer-nothin' all day."

"Okay. And where was Keith? Did he have coffee, too?"

"Keith don't get up if he don't have to work…" She hesitated, frowning. "He mighta been gone to work that day."

"Are you saying he wasn't here that morning? Tuesday?"

"It hadda been Tuesday. Lois come by early to bum a cuppa coffee because she run out. We had a cup here, after the kids left for school, and I give her a ten-percent-off coupon for some at the dollar store."

"And Keith wasn't home?"

"Not when Lois was here." Hope rubbed her forehead. "I don't remember him sayin' he had work, but he must of. He might of got called late, after I went to bed."

Braun prodded her about the night before and again, about her morning but she insisted she couldn't remember anything else. When we were certain she had nothing further to offer, we thanked her and prepared to leave.

"Are you gonna look for Keith now?"

Braun shot an eye-roll in my direction but gave her a smile. "We'll talk to the sheriff, Mrs. Sands, and see what they've got."

"Well, if you find him, would you tell him the kids need milk for their cereal? He can pick it up on his way home.

CHAPTER ELEVEN

SHAY

Maple Sunrise

Jennie came by on Monday to help work out a kitchen schedule. She hop-danced across the snowy driveway, carrying a box of breakfast pastries. She always claimed she couldn't function without a little sugar in the morning.

My mood was low with worry and a sense of being mired in a time-and-money quicksand, so the temporary distraction was more than welcome. I poured coffee and filled her in on Maria Ana's condition while she doled out sweets to Bibi and Tolo.

"Her doctor says she'll be as good as new once she recovers but that could take anywhere from a few weeks to a few months." I paced from the kitchen to my office, feeling the acidic burn of too much stress and caffeine. "I posted an ad for a cook on the job boards but finding the right person will take time. Then we'll need at least a week to train whoever we hire, even if they have cooking experience. On top of that, I have to hire and train a driver and the kitchen porter and get the Chautauqua County CSA membership drive going." I spun and dropped into my chair. "The only good news is that Delyth arrives tonight. Fingers crossed she can handle the kids and our chaotic lives."

Jennie pointed to my still-untouched pastry. "Eat. You can't think straight on an empty stomach."

"I told the route drivers to ask around while they're making deliveries. One of our customers might know a cook who's looking for work… or someone who'd take a two-month job."

"Maybe I could work more hours. If my mom can watch Poppy in the evenings, I wouldn't mind."

Even as I thanked her, my mind was calculating the impact of overtime on the shoestring budget. I took a deep breath and a bite of pastry, resetting my mood while I chewed. Mac would say I was over-reacting, that the problem would be resolved in a few months. But those months, going into a new season, were a critical time in market gardening.

"It's going to be rough. But I guess I should be thankful it's not June or July when things get really crazy around here."

"Can't you just picture that?" Jennie snickered. "Maria Ana would demand we put her hospital bed in the kitchen so she could keep us in line, and you and I would be bouncing around like pinballs—totally unfit for anything. We'd have all the kids lined up, chopping vegetables and tending kettles. Can we get little aprons and chef hats for the twins?" As she expanded her description of a kid-staffed Farm Gourmet, her snicker rose to a howl and I began laughing with her. It didn't solve any of our problems, but she lightened the mood in an instant.

"Maybe we could invite Travis to tape a few TV episodes," I suggested, setting us off again. "Viewers might not learn anything but it would make a terrific sit-com."

Once our hilarity—or hysteria—passed, my stomach roiled again. "Seriously, Jennie, I'm not sure we can make it. Those early weeks, when the gardens are opening and we're racing the clock to turn out dozens of batches of veggie pickles before the spring demand starts? There's no way I can do that and train the garden crew and a driver."

I turned to my email and, almost immediately, spotted a message on one of the job boards where I'd placed the ads. I mentally crossed my fingers and opened it. A generic notice informed me that someone had responded to my listing and the attached link would take me to their resume. Excited, I clicked and announced, "Someone answered the ad."

But when I scanned the resume, my hope dissolved. The applicant listed three previous jobs, two of them as a hair stylist for which she'd been trained.

"Never mind. She's a hairdresser, not a cook. Her only food-related experience was at a restaurant where she lists her position as waitress and kitchen assistant."

Jennie frowned. "Maybe an assistant cook?"

"It just says kitchen assistant. And she has almost six years in salons, so she must be a decent hair stylist. Maybe this came to me by mistake."

"It'd be nice to have a hair stylist who also cooked. She could give us cuts during lunch breaks." Jennie laughed and hip-hopped her way to the kitchen.

I scanned the rest of the email list but that was the only job response. Hopefully someone qualified would apply soon because, once spring planting began, I'd have to work more hours in the gardens. That would leave Jennie on her own in the kitchen.

ৼ

That afternoon, we processed batches of jam with fruit we'd frozen at harvest.

"We're managing," Jennie assured me for the dozenth time.

My laugh, as I poured sweet blackberry jam into sparkling pint jars, sounded weak. "Do you really believe that or are you hoping to make it real by repeating it?"

"Both. We've refilled several shelves in the last couple of weeks. But I don't want to get complacent and jinx it."

"In a few weeks, I'll have to be in the gardens more, getting the first gardeners trained and prepping new beds. And after that…"

Jen held up both hands as if warding off demons. "Don't say it! By then, you'll have hired another cook and a full garden crew and Maria Ana might be back to work. Everything will be back to normal."

"The garden crew, okay. Maria Ana, maybe. But I haven't had any qualified applicants for the cook position."

"What about the hair stylist? Maybe you should talk to her." Jennie slid another tray of sterilized jars into place.

"She doesn't have any experience, Jen."

"I didn't have any experience when I started, either."

"You'd been a restaurant line cook and you were familiar with home canning procedures. I don't think this woman has even that much."

"She might have done something similar when she was a kitchen assistant. Maybe she's a fast learner. That's more important than experience, isn't it?"

I swallowed my objection. "Equally important, I guess."

"So why not talk to her? If she's not a good fit, you don't have to hire her. It's possible someone else will apply."

"You do realize you're a relentless optimist, don't you?"

"Yeah." She grinned and crossed her eyes. "And I'm cute."

I laughed and bumped her shoulder with mine, thinking she was also a very good friend and the perfect complement to Maria Ana's measured caution and my own over-analysis of every detail.

Despite my pessimism, when we finished the last batch, I went to my office and checked the job boards again. There were no new applicants so I brought up Harley Forsythe's resume and dashed off a message, asking her to call for an interview.

Jennie was correct. The worst that could happen was that she'd be completely unfit for the job and I wouldn't hire her.

I straightened my desk, stuffing my notes into a folder. "Now it's time for the school bus to drop off the girls. And tonight, we pick up their new nanny at the airport. That'll be one problem resolved."

Buffalo-Niagara Falls International

Delyth Morgan's cornflower blue eyes and dark, wavy hair marked her as Mac's relative, as did the mischievous grin she flashed when she crossed the airport terminal and spotted her cousin. We'd met through video calls, so introductions weren't necessary and, after a brief hesitation, the children threw themselves at her as if they'd known her all their lives.

Once she'd greeted each of her future charges and they'd begun the argument of who got to sit next to her in the car, Mac wrapped her in a hug.

"You've grown up, Del." He tugged a strand of her dark, shoulder-length hair. "Am I going to have to put locks on the doors to keep the lads away?"

She punched his arm. "You better not dare. I am grown up, a legal adult." Squirming out of Mac's arms, she reached to hug me. "I don't know how you put up with him, Shay. He's such a tosser."

I laughed, enjoying her accent as much as their banter. "Welcome to New York, Delyth. We're excited you're finally here."

CHAPTER TWELVE

MAC

Maple Valley

Braun came by early Monday morning, gung-ho to track down Keith Sands and close the Cruz case. We needed a break—that was certain—and the vineyard worker's disappearance two days after Drigo's murder didn't feel like a coincidence. So, while I didn't quite share my partner's assurance, I agreed Sands could be the key to our case.

I was beginning to enjoy riding shotgun, letting my partner lay the groundwork and do the driving and directing. He might lack confidence but he'd always been a solid investigator and taking lead forced him to exercise his decision-making skills. If I had any reservations about him getting promoted, they were personal ones. I'd be losing the best partner I'd ever had. On the flip side, it would give us equal standing in the same region, maybe the same unit. That would almost guarantee some crossover on complex crimes where teamwork can make or break you.

I filled him in on Maria Ana's progress while we grabbed take-out coffee.

"Shay was at the hospital most of the day, yesterday. The doc said Maria Ana's surgery went well but they want to keep her for a few days. We're going to put her up in the playroom until she can manage stairs again."

"Tell me when you want to set up her room. The band's performing next weekend, but I can give you a hand any evening this week." His unsolicited offer of help was a perfect example of how he could parse a conversation to its essence and decide what was needed before I'd even made a request.

"I appreciate that, Ty. I'll let you know."

Back on the road, I turned the conversation to work. "What's our plan for today? Any ideas how we can chase down Sands?"

He nodded. "I called Deputy Gaines. He says it's still a toss-up whether the guy's missing or off on a bender. Contrary to what Sands' wife told us, it seems Keith's been known to disappear before, although his previous absences never extended more than forty-eight hours."

"So he might have nothing to do with the Cruz case?" I wondered if we were wasting time. "Emil Cruz listed Sands as one of their employees, but he didn't report seeing him. How about the other wineries Hope mentioned?"

"I called them both. The Black Crow people said he hasn't worked for them since last winter's ice wine harvest. The one on Silverdust Lake claims they use him off-season for day work because he doesn't mind if the job takes a couple of hours or several days. The woman I spoke with described him as reliable and versatile, meaning he can handle pretty much any kind of vineyard work or maintenance job. She said she hasn't seen him in several weeks but she said she'd ask around." He paused and shrugged, clearly second-guessing himself. "I thought we might as well talk to them, first. Eliminate it completely, if we can."

"Good plan. Let's do it."

Vignes d'Argent Winery

Vignes d'Argent was an upscale winery with a country club vibe. The sprawling, glass-walled Coteau Hall was easily twice the size of the Cruz events building. Beyond it, a cluster of small B&B cottages—no doubt denoted as *chalets*—sat among the trees.

"What's with all the French?" Braun studied the signage. "Do I even need to know?"

I laughed. "Their name, Vignes d'Argent is just a play on words, silver vines. Technically, it ought to be called Silverdust vines for the lake. Coteau is what you call a hillside or a vineyard on a hill."

"They couldn't say that in English?"

"It adds a touch of *Je ne sais quoi* don't you think?"

He snorted. "As long as I'm not expected to use my high school French to communicate, we ought to be okay."

Charlotte Harmon was attractive, fit, and nearly my height. She not only didn't expect us to speak French, but appeared to be as all-American as Braun, welcoming us to the hall and introducing herself as the winery's hospitality and events manager, as well as part-owner of the operation.

When Tyler explained the reason for our call, she led us to an executive mezzanine-level office that presented a birds-eye view of the entrance and main floor on one side and a panorama of vineyards and lake on the other. Sleek white oak and deep raspberry furnishings managed to convey success, wealth, and strength with a nod to its vineyard origins, and a corner cabinet held several volleyball trophies and medals—including an FIVB world medal—and a couple of martial arts awards. Harmon's wall-hung credentials attested to degrees in viticulture and oenology, plus a very exclusive Master Sommelier diploma and a Master of Wine certificate. The entire space oozed power.

"As I mentioned on the phone, we're looking for information about one of your occasional workers, Keith Sands." Braun didn't waste time getting down to business.

"I did check with our staff." The woman took a chair, crossing shapely, well-toned legs. "Apparently, Keith was here on Thursday although I didn't see him, myself. That's not surprising if he was working in the vineyard. I had a number of appointments during the afternoon and two wine tastings scheduled that evening, so I was focused on preparations."

"Who would have seen him?"

"Philippe Beaumont, my business partner. He's in charge of the vineyards and must have requested Keith for some reason. But it was two of my servers, Jack and Lily, who told me they'd seen him in the winery."

Braun tapped the names into his notes. "We'll want to talk with them and with Beaumont. Are they here, now?"

"The servers aren't scheduled until Thursday evening's tasting. But Philippe is on the property, I believe. Shall I have someone check?"

"We'd appreciate that. If he can clear up a few questions, we'll be able to move on."

She used her phone briefly. "He's in the wine cellar. I can take you to him, if you'll follow me?"

ꟸ

I'd visited a few western New York vineyards over the years. They'd become popular corporate and tourist destinations, and wine-tasting tours were often booked months in advance. The ones I'd attended were casual affairs, genial and laid-back, in bright rooms with a single, long table or clustered bistro seating that was designed to encourage conversation, with an emphasis on fun. Vignes d'Argent took the experience to a whole other level with a luxurious, continental ambiance that suggested their price tags were well above my budget.

Charlotte took us to the rear of the main level where a thick, arched door opened onto a softly-lit passage completely encased in stone. A barrel-vaulted ceiling curved above us, while the floor canted downward in long, winding turns. The only relief to the mottled tan stone was in the old grape-rakes, earthenware jugs, and other antique vintner implements set in randomly-spaced niches. The air was cool and the silence palpable.

"We are now underground," Charlotte announced as we passed an 18th-century wine press. "This passage, and the rooms below, are naturally maintained at fifty degrees Fahrenheit throughout the year. That's an ideal temperature for aging wines but, as you'll see, we also have separately controlled zones for particular vintages."

As she recited facts and figures, we rounded a final turn and passed through two more sets of doors into an elegant room designed for private tastings.

The vaulted stone walls rose higher and wider, punctuated with arched alcoves containing spot-lighted, stamped wine barrels. A long, dark walnut table, lined with two dozen tufted leather chairs, took up the center of the room. Suspended above it was an astonishing chandelier that resembled giant silver grapevines twining and stretching in long, sinuous curves that dripped glittering clusters of pale-purple LED grapes. The effect was stunning.

Braun's expression mimicked a kid's first glimpse of the queen in full jewel-encrusted regalia. I probably had a similar look, although I tried hard not to gape at something that must've been tagged near the national debt.

"Impressive, isn't it?"

I turned to see a bespoke-suited man in his late fifties, with vigilant eyes, a classic box-beard, and confident military bearing.

"I commissioned it from a French designer whose name you might recognize."

Charlotte intervened. "Philippe, this is Investigator Tyler Braun and Investigator MacAlistair Llewellyn from the state police." She smiled at us. "And this is my business partner, Philippe Beaumont, who will talk your ears off if you let him."

"That's good news," I told her, wondering how their partnership survived amidst all the power display. "A lot of the people we meet are reluctant to tell us anything."

That got a discreet laugh from Beaumont. "I hope this isn't about that unfortunate incident, last summer. I promise I've had the speedometer repaired."

I couldn't place his accent. It was a blend of upper-class British and standard Parisian but with a blurred undertone that reminded me of the American South. There could be a million reasons for it, inherent or acquired, but it made me curious.

"I'll be in my office if you need anything further." Charlotte excused herself and returned the way we'd entered.

Braun took out his phone. "We'd like to talk to you about one of your employees, Mr. Beaumont… a casual worker, name of Keith Sands."

"Keith? He's not in any trouble, I hope? I know he enjoys a drink now and again, but…" The man waved an arm at the barrels and bottles surrounding us, grinning. "I can hardly fault him for that."

"We're trying to determine Mr. Sands' whereabouts since last Thursday. He's been reported missing."

Beaumont's smile faded, replaced by questioning, raised eyebrows. "I'm sorry to hear that. How long has he been… unreachable?"

Before Braun or I could respond, he held up a hand. "Please sit down. I can offer a very nice Riesling or… I'm sorry, are you allowed a glass of wine?"

Braun sat but shook his head. "We're on duty. This will only take a few minutes. If you wouldn't mind?" He established control, gesturing the vintner to a chair across from him. "We were told Keith Sands was called in to work here, last Thursday. Were you aware of that?"

"Of course. I was the one who called him. I was concerned the extreme cold snap would damage our young vines, so I asked him to evaluate their condition."

"Is that the kind of work he does for you?"

"Keith has been working in vineyards since he was seven years old. Despite an unfortunate lack of formal education, he's one of the most talented phytopathologists I've ever encountered."

"What's that?"

Beaumont raised one finger like a lecturer about to make a point. "Phytopathology is a fancy word for botanical diagnostics. Keith is a plant doctor, his ability in that area is pure, unparalleled genius. He could earn a fortune three times over if it weren't for a regrettable lack of ambition. Instead, he's a laborer."

Braun narrowed his eyes. "So, you get genius-level work for minimum wage?"

"It's a bit more than minimum. Our staff members are well compensated." His tone was imperious but he couldn't resist a smirk and a Gallic shrug. "We are, after all, artisans engaged in commerce."

So far, I'd pegged him for a fake accent, phony charm, massive ego, and blatant greed. None of that was indictable but he'd get no humanitarian awards from me. I cut him off.

"Let's get back to Thursday, Mr. Beaumont. What time did you call Sands and what time did he show up?"

The man's eyes widened slightly as he switched his attention from Braun to me. "I don't recall the exact time I spoke with him. It was afternoon and he drove here immediately. Within the hour."

"What hour? When did he get here?"

"Mid-afternoon. Around two-thirty or two-forty-five, I'd say."

"So then, what? Did he report to you? Punch a clock? Go out into the fields?"

"I believe he examined the vines when he arrived, before he came in to report his findings."

Braun's phone-taps were turning to jabs. He paused to hard-eye Beaumont. "We can play twenty questions with you all day, if you like, Philippe. Or you could just give us your statement, tell us how everything played out on Thursday afternoon. Who, what, where, when, why, and how. You know how that goes?"

The man feigned a long-suffering sigh. "*Certainement.*" He pulled his cell from an inner jacket pocket, swiped, and read the screen.

"On Thursday last, I phoned Mr. Sands at two-oh-six PM." He pursed his lips to add, "Eastern Standard Time," with a pointed glance in my direction. "I requested Mr. Sands' assistance in evaluating the condition of some of our more vulnerable vines. He arrived here within the half-hour. He did not punch a clock since we do not use such devices, however, he did report his findings to me after completing his inspection. We discussed the need for precaution and decided to call a few workers to heel-in that parcel. I directed Mr. Sands to immediately contact three of our experienced vineyard assistants to complete the work. He did as directed. The men arrived and Mr. Sands left shortly after."

"He didn't stay for the actual work?"

"He did not. These are experienced workers so his continued presence wasn't required. I believe he had another appointment, something else he needed to do."

"What time did he leave?"

"I can't say precisely. I was in my office, dealing with other concerns. I didn't see him again. Perhaps someone else can answer that question."

Philippe wasn't going to get off that easily. Braun aimed at steady, measuring look at him. "About how long would you say you spent with Keith Sands on Thursday?"

"In total? No more than thirty or forty minutes. Possibly less."

"So you should be able to walk me through your conversation, what he said, what you said. Let's start with your phone conversation at…" Braun stressed his enunciation as he read from his notes. "Two-oh-six PM."

I set my face to neutral, swallowing a laugh. This was Braun at his finest. Beaumont had rubbed him wrong and it was going to cost him in time and energy, if not more.

Philippe either realized his mis-step or decided cooperation would make his life easier. "Two-oh-six, yes. Keith answered my call and we exchanged greetings and small talk…"

"What sort of *small talk*? Did he mention what he'd been doing, any plans or concerns he had?"

"I think it was simply how-are-you and general remarks about the weather, its likely effect on the coming season. Nothing terribly important."

"How was his mood?"

"He seemed normal. Flat. He wasn't angry or depressed, he wasn't hung over. Keith is never inclined to be especially jovial, so I would say there was nothing unusual about his mood at all."

"Okay. How are you, the weather's cold, blah-blah-blah. Then what?"

Beaumont glanced at me as if he were hoping for a reprieve. I returned an impassive stare and he shifted back to Braun.

"I suppose I then told him my concerns about the first-year canes and asked if he would take a look at them. He agreed and that was it."

"You didn't set a time?"

"I'd already expressed an urgency. I believe Keith, himself, suggested doing it as soon as he could arrive here."

"When was your next contact with him?"

"When he came to my office with his report."

"And how was he then? Did he seem agitated? Worried? Unhappy? Did he express any concerns?"

It was obvious my partner was setting the bar high for any future interviews or discussions with the vintner. Gauging his stamina for at least a twenty-minute session, I settled back in my chair to enjoy the show.

Beaumont's words were becoming clipped with impatience. "He appeared exactly the way he normally appears: low-key, serious, and focused on the task at hand. As I've already stated, Mr. Sands is not a particularly emotive person."

"Did he give any indication about other plans for his day?"

"He did not." Philippe paused and his jaw jutted slightly as he leaned toward Braun. "Let me amend that. When I expressed my regret about calling him in at the last minute, I believe he did make an off-hand remark about another appointment."

I went on alert, at the same time noting my partner's tapping fingers had paused. "What about another appointment?"

"It was only a passing comment, nothing specific." He hesitated, as if searching his memory, then raised his eyes. "I have it. Keith shrugged off my apology for interrupting his day and said it was fine because he had a similar engagement nearby, anyway. He said it was no trouble to stop here on his way to that one."

"Did he say where his other appointment was?"

"Not then. But when he came back to give his report, he mentioned the Cruz vineyard had also expressed concerns with the weather."

"So, his other appointment was at the Cruz place?"

Beaumont leaned back again and crossed his legs. "I have no specific information as to that, one way or the other. I'm simply telling you what he said."

ꝏ

"Back to Emil Cruz," Braun grumbled when we were back on the road. "Although Philippe Beaumont's got my full attention."

I chuckled. "He didn't like being on the receiving end of your questions."

"He's also arrogant, too full of himself. And from what I could tell he'd have no trouble taking down a guy Drigo's age."

I couldn't disagree. "It'd be easy to incorporate a few stolen vines in a vineyard this size."

No one was at the Cruz home when Braun and I stopped by. A young man at the winery informed us they were meeting with their pastor and then with Drigo's attorney.

Since we had no idea how long that would take, we opted to return to H.Q. to take care of loose ends and paperwork.

CHAPTER THIRTEEN

SHAY

Maple Sunrise

Delyth was relaxed and natural and she shared Mac's upbeat approach to life. Her interactions with the children were a lot like his, playful and fun yet appropriate and responsive. I could see they were excited to have her attention and fascinated by her energetic personality, trendy clothing, and her Welsh accent. Elodie and Gabi hung onto every word and competed to help, while the twins followed her around like a pair of puppies.

For the first time in my life, I felt a twinge about my age. We were only seven or eight years apart, but Del was youthful and carefree, almost a child herself. I couldn't recall ever being that way but perhaps I'd forgotten.

I smiled at Gabi struggling to put one of Del's dresses on a hanger, while Elodie carefully arranged shoes in the closet.

"I know you've put a spell on them," I teased.

Del grinned. "Sadly, it's a one-time spell that wears off pretty quickly. My little brothers are totally immune to it."

"How many brothers do you have?"

"Three." She made a face as if it were three too many, but her eyes were laughing. "I told my mam if she had to burden me with that many siblings, she might've done a kindness with at least one of them being a girl. But now, look at you with a houseful of them."

"They're a bit young," I said. "But I'm sure they'd love to be your pretend sisters."

"Or you could. I always wished for an older sister, somebody to share the burdens and show me how to get on."

Before I could speak, a flash of singing echoed in my mind—*Shinny-Shanny, Shanneeee-Shinneeeee.* It was so sudden, so brief, it barely registered before it was gone. Something must have shown on my face, though, because Del froze, then turned quickly to gather a pile of tee-shirts.

"I'd love to be a big sister to this bunch, but nanny is good."

I lingered for a few minutes more, watching the way she charmed the children and imagining her as my sister, as Shinny. What would it have been like to grow up sharing every day of my life with a sister? I wondered, when I found Shinny, if she and I would be able to make up for all the years we'd lost? If I could love Elodie and Gabi and the twins like my own, I was sure I'd feel the same about a real sister. But how would she feel about me?

ꙮ

When I got to my office, I found a message from Harley Forsythe agreeing to the interview I'd suggested. Since there were still no other applicants, I decided that, barring any serious problems, we'd make do with whatever skills she had. An extra pair of hands—even with the minimal ability—would be better than none.

I took care of my immediate tasks, then unpacked the new CSA flyers and divided them up for the drivers to distribute on their routes. But when I turned to the database of potential customers in Chautauqua County, I felt my stress level rise again.

Terri had collected an extensive list of residents—most of whom I was certain wouldn't sign up for the program—and several dozen businesses that could become regular retail customers. If even a third of those wanted fresh produce, I was going to be stretched down to my last radish and bean.

"This is a bad idea. We have to stay local and small." I'd recited that mantra a million times over the past month and it was still true.

Even when I included the collaborative partners' contributions, I wasn't convinced we'd succeed, no matter what Terri claimed.

All you have to do is test the waters, Terri had insisted. *It's still local. You're under twenty minutes from the county line and Jamestown is less than an hour. You already go further than that for some of your current customers.*

Terri knew her numbers and she wasn't wrong about the distances. But predicting the quantities of produce I'd need to grow and the additional hours required to do so was a different matter. Farming is a gamble in the best of times.

I started to reach for my phone to call her, then stopped my hand. It wasn't just Terri's opinion. Mac and Ben also believed the move was right. And now, I also had to consider the collaborative partners' investment and opinions. Winslow, Thane, Chau, and Austin had already signed contracts. They had each agreed to supply specific products for my CSA customers and, in exchange, I'd include them on my website, take care of delivery, and collect a small percentage of their sales.

As news of our collaboration spread, other farms and producers inquired about partnerships. I had no interest in turning Farm Gourmet into a grocery wholesaler, but I made one more exception when Brooke Warner, a neighbor and professional baker, asked to join. Her fresh loaves of traditional and specialty breads were the perfect addition to our CSA baskets.

Adding a partner required a lot of time and work. I'd need a half-day to visit Brooke to ensure her processes and ingredients met our all-natural, sustainable, organic standards. It also meant another contract, coordinating her production schedule with our deliveries, and a million small details. I was learning that every partner also brought another set of opinions to consider.

I could manage the delivery of loaves of bread, packets of tea, and jugs of maple syrup as easily as my fruits and vegetables. The products never argued or tried to change the way I run my business. Human partners, on the other hand—even the ones I otherwise liked and respected—were much harder. Those humans were depending on me to honor our agreements, though, and that meant providing the customers I'd promised.

I took a deep breath, opened the new Chautauqua flyer on my computer, and set up a merge with the database. The worst that could happen was that I'd fail miserably and have to go back to what I'd been doing. How could I argue with the common sense of at least giving it a try?

ꝏ

Delyth did so well on her first day that, when Maria Ana called to say she was being discharged, I had no concerns leaving the children in the care of their new nanny.

Maria Ana was eager to go home. I loaded her bags and new folding walker-frame into the back of the van and drove slowly to avoid jarring her hip.

At home, Del had helped the children make signs and drawings to welcome Maria Ana and they'd assembled the makings for a tea-and-cookies party. Elodie tucked herself possessively at her substitute-grandmother's side while the other children settled around them.

In spite of her discomfort and the effects of the pain medicine she'd been given, Maria Ana was in good spirits. She enjoyed the children's hugs, tolerated their repetitive questions, and even allowed the older girls a trial use of her walker. When I handed her a cup of her favorite herbal tea, she smiled gratefully.

"I'm sorry being so much trouble for you. Is the kitchen a problem?"

"You're no trouble at all. The kitchen is in mid-winter lull and Jennie's doing a great job. I posted an employment listing for a temporary cook to fill in until you're well, but Terri's pushing hard to expand our territory. If we find a temp who's a good fit, we can offer a permanent position, later. And if they like working with us, they might stay on."

I continued to chatter, telling her about the unlikely applicant I was going to interview and giving her any news I could think of until she seemed to tire and set her teacup aside. Shooing the children from the room, I rearranged her pillows.

"We'll let you rest, now. The TV remote and your knitting basket are right there. If you need anything else, I'll be in the kitchen."

CHAPTER FOURTEEN

MAC

Iroquois County

Gabi, Elodie and I completed morning barn chores and I helped get them off to school before leaving Shay and Del with the twins to work out the rest of their day.

Shay and I had decided to make Tuesday as ordinary as possible to introduce Delyth to our family routine. Even though the farm and food processing were in slow season, Shay had a lot going on, gearing up for spring planting and the CSA expansion. I knew Maria Ana's absence also increased her workload and would add to the household confusion when she came home, but what I didn't know was that she was being discharged that very day.

Braun swung by on schedule and we went to talk to the Cruz family. He took the long way around the lake, stopping at the diner to pick up coffee he didn't need. It seemed he was stalling, that something about the case was eating at him. When we reached the turn-off where the road curved around Spicebush Mountain and the state conservation area, he finally brought it up.

"You've known these people for a while, Llewellyn. They seem okay, but they've got a lot of money tied up in their grapes and wine business. Anybody can snap under pressure. What are the odds Emil and his grandpa fell out over the stress and expense of creating this new wine? Maybe it impacted the rest of the business?"

I felt I knew the answer to that, but I gave him the courtesy of considering it. "First off, I can't say I know them really well. But, from what I saw, Rodrigo was a reasonable man, the epitome of patience and respect toward everyone. I can't imagine any problem he couldn't resolve with some common-sense discussion. And he doted on his family."

"How about Emil?"

"Emil's young but it seems like he inherited his grandfather's judicious nature. Ruy, too, for that matter. The Cruzes tend to think things through before they speak. No shooting from the hip in that clan."

"Okay." Braun would accept my take. "Yet, we have one killed on their property and one possible MP within a three-day period."

"We aren't certain our missing person ever went to their place. Or if he did, that he didn't leave voluntarily and intentionally. He's got DUI charges and an assault on record, this isn't the first time he's gone missing and, so far, nobody's spotted his vehicle. It's possible he's halfway to Mexico or he could be holed up with a bottle somewhere nearby. Or, he could be dead. If we can pick up his trail, maybe we'll get some answers."

ꝏ

Emil Cruz assured us he hadn't seen Sands since the Christmas party he'd hosted for employees.

"It's a casual lunch deal here, in our events center," Emil told us. "We do it as a thank you, but it's also a way to keep in touch with the workers so we don't lose them next season."

He was insistent that Keith's mood had been normal as far as he could recall, and that nothing out of the ordinary had occurred. When Braun asked about his relationship with Drigo, he didn't hesitate. "Anything to do with grapes and wine, they practically read each other's mind. You couldn't imagine two more different people to mesh the way they did. I know my grandfather had a lot of respect for Keith's opinions and ideas."

"How about Keith? Did he feel the same about Drigo?"

"I'm sure he did. He was always considerate and helpful when they worked together."

"We were told he was called to Vignes d'Argent during that cold snap. Something about the vines freezing. You didn't need him to look at your vines?"

"The storm when Abuelo was killed?" Emil shook his head. "He and I tracked that ourselves, like we always did. We take precautions as part of our post-harvest routine and Nico, our field supervisor, also keeps a close eye on any young or vulnerable plants if there's a concern."

"If there was a problem, would Nico have called Keith?"

"No. Nico would report it to me. If we needed a crew, we'd figure out who to call for how many hours, first. A call-in like that can put a big dent in our operating budget."

Braun started to pocket his phone, a signal he was finished, so I spoke up.

"There's one thing I've been wondering about, Emil. I know you covered this at the beginning, but I wasn't involved then. Can I ask about the pocket saw… the weapon used?"

Emil stiffened, taken by surprise. "Sure. There wasn't anything unusual about it, though. Most of us carry one when we're working in the field."

"For cutting vines?"

"Right. They tend to grow fast and we keep them pruned to manage the crop, limit the buds to get higher quality, mature grapes."

"That's an ongoing process? I mean, do workers carry pocket saws throughout the season?"

"Generally, yes. After the harvest, we cut back any greenwood that'd be killed by frost. And in winter, we remove dead and diseased growth, plus any canes that aren't going to produce well. Then, when the new growth starts, we cut back lateral shoots on the trunks to force development of the ones we want… the season's crop. So regular workers are apt to carry a knife and a pocket saw pretty much all the time."

I gave that some thought, comparing it to Shay's system of thinning her veggie shoots when they came up, allotting space for the best and strongest shoots. "Okay, I can see why they'd need the saws. Do they buy their own or do you provide them?"

"We keep a case of them in the barn with the other tools and equipment. The workers can grab a new one whenever theirs breaks or gets dull."

"Is the barn ever locked?"

"Off hours, sure. But during the workday, it's open."

I glanced at Braun who gave me a nod, acknowledging that our list of potential suspects had widened to just about anyone familiar with the tools in the barn.

"Thanks, Emil. I don't know if that tells us anything but it helps to know what we're dealing with."

We questioned Ami and the two employees who were in the winery but only the family had been on the property during the early morning hours when Drigo was killed. And no one reported seeing Keith on the property the afternoon he disappeared.

"Emil, Ruy and I were out to take care of the arrangements that afternoon," Ami recalled. "Then we stopped for dinner, so if he were here later, we might have missed him. But it isn't like him to just drop in."

As we drove away, Braun spent several minutes rehashing the information we had. "We don't have any proof Sands killed Drigo, or that these two cases are even connected. For all we know, Sands is lying on a beach somewhere, soaking up the sun and tossing back margaritas. Should we keep chasing this or dig deeper on Drigo Cruz's activities?"

I grinned, seeing he'd momentarily forgotten he was lead. "It's your call. We don't have much on either one."

"How about we work the employee lists and at least get it pared down to a workable number?"

"Makes sense."

By noon, we knew we were spinning our wheels. As far as I could tell, the general reaction was shock and sadness for Drigo and either mild concern or resignation toward Keith. But no one offered anything useful. In fact, we hadn't even picked up a hint of deception or withheld information. Just bewilderment and more dead ends.

℘

Since we were near Maple Valley and out of ideas, we decided to confront Hope Sands with the information we'd collected on her husband. She hadn't been entirely truthful with us.

The Sands' sidewalk hadn't been shoveled and the kitchen looked as if it hadn't seen a broom or a dishwashing since our last visit. The only notable changes were an untidy stack of magazines and papers that replaced the pile of socks, and the addition of a pair of overflowing laundry baskets in the middle of the floor.

Braun glanced around before opting to stand. "We won't take up too much of your time, Mrs. Sands. Have you heard from your husband since we last spoke with you?"

Hope was nearly as disheveled as her home. "No."

"Have you spoken to any of his friends or checked at the places he usually goes?"

"I called some. Nobody's seen him. They don't know any more than I do. And the sheriff's not lookin' for him." She rubbed the side of her face. "You gotta find him. I know somethin' bad must of happened."

"We've asked around and got the same answers you did. No one has seen him and no one has any idea where he might be. The sheriff put out a BOLO—a *be on the lookout*—for his truck. If he's on the road, maybe someone will spot him."

"I'm telling you he wouldn't go nowhere without sayin'. Something bad happened. He's in trouble. Or hurt."

"We do have a few questions about the statement you gave us." Braun hard-eyed her for a moment but her blank expression never wavered. "When we spoke to you on Saturday, you told us your husband hadn't done this before, that he'd never disappeared without telling you. According to the records, not only has he done it before, but it appears he's done so on multiple occasions."

Hope's gaze dropped to the unswept floor. She remained silent.

"Would you like to explain that, Mrs. Sands?"

"He wasn't never gone more than a day or two." Her voice began as a low mumble before becoming defensive. "It was because of his drinking. He knew if he tried to drive, you'd stop him. He wasn't gonna chance that so he stayed where… wherever he was."

Braun stifled his reactive sarcasm. "But you lied to us. Do you want to correct that now? Tell us where he might go if he chose not to drink and drive?"

It took some prodding before she gave up the names of a few bars Keith went to on his more serious benders and some of the people he'd mentioned seeing. "But he don't hang out with them anymore. He does his drinking at home, now."

Braun slapped his card on the cluttered laminate table. "Let us know if you hear from him. We'll be in touch."

It was possible Keith Sands had decided to walk away from his wife and kids. He might also return soon, hungover and repentant. Or not. In the meanwhile, if he didn't figure into Drigo's killing, we were wasting valuable time looking for him.

"You want to make the rounds of Keith's bars and drinking buddies, now?"

"Might as well get it over with." Braun echoed my thoughts. "But this is the last shot. If we don't connect him to the Cruz case today, we drop him. Let the sheriff deal with it."

CHAPTER FIFTEEN

SHAY
Maple Sunrise

Over the next week, my life resembled a hamster's world, if the subject hamster happened to live in a small cage with seven others. I seemed to be running on an unstoppable wheel—somehow never moving as fast as required—while everyone around me kept coming and going, asking, needing, wanting, talking. Especially talking. There seemed to be no end to the conversations and questions that arose and overlapped until I wanted to plug my ears.

Before Mac entered my life, I'd managed to live in a kind of muted bubble where no one intruded. Then he'd burst in with all his enthusiasm and energy… and the rest of the world had followed. My quiet, empty house was now overflowing with people I hadn't even met five years ago. I was never alone. The privacy and stillness I'd worn like armor no longer worked. I was so tired, so consumed by everything that needed doing, my fatigue only registered when I collapsed into bed at night. But even dead-asleep, the exhausting list of responsibilities invaded my dreams and never stopped growing.

As always, the mornings began in the cold room, helping my drivers sort and load orders into their vans. Then I moved to the greenhouse, to manage the crops there, and to sow seeds and set seedlings for early season transplanting. At noon, I moved to the

Farm Gourmet kitchen where Jennie had prepped and started the day's recipes and we worked together to finish and process them. In between, I stole minutes to field phone calls, take new orders, and set up deliveries for the steadily-increasing list of CSA customers. Deep within some part of my brain, I knew I should feel excitement over the burgeoning success, but there was no time to pause and actually experience it.

At Mac's insistence, I hired two garden workers a bit earlier than usual and brought them in to prep and tarp new beds for spring planting. Between the recently-recruited grocers and gift shops I'd picked up in Chautauqua County and the growing number of CSA subscribers, I was worried I wouldn't have enough produce to meet the demand. I'd checked and changed my garden plans so many times the numbers lost all relevance and I often woke in the middle of the night, fretting over the many ways Maple Sunrise and Farm Gourmet might collapse and fail completely.

ஐ

When I joined Jennie in the Farm Gourmet kitchen that afternoon, I'd made several plans and a couple of decisions.

"First of all," I announced. "Harley Forsythe's interview is tomorrow. I'd like you and Maria Ana—if she's feeling well enough—to spend some time with her, too. You can show her around, give her a feel for how we operate, and see if your styles and personalities mesh. If she seems interested, you could have her try a few simple tasks. I'm hoping she has basic food prep skills, but she might need training with knife-handling or how to operate some of our equipment."

Jennie was immediately on board. "That'll be fantastic. And it's a great way to get acquainted without all the *who's your family* and *where'd you go to school* stuff."

Back at the house, Maria Ana's response was more cautious but still agreeable. "It will be good if you can slow down a little. I worry when I see you running like headless chickens."

I chuckled at her garbled idiom.

"I'd really like to get your opinion and input," I told her. "And we'll put a chair in the kitchen so all you have to do is observe. You won't have to do any work."

ഇ

The next morning, Maria Ana, Jennie, and I were gathered around the prep table with our coffee, when Harley Forsythe walked into the kitchen.

She looked like a hair stylist. Or, she looked the way I imagined an expensive, couture hair designer would look. She had style and flair, and when she flashed her brilliant smile, it gave a friendly, open personality to her sophisticated, high-maintenance finish. No one could avoid smiling back.

The bubblegum pink highlights in her blonde, spiked-pixie hair reflected soft color on her high cheekbones and accentuated her long-lashed, kohl-lined, brown eyes. I could picture her posturing, center-stage on a Hollywood movie set much more easily than chopping onions in my kitchen.

I introduced everyone, gave her a sixty-second business bio, and led her to my office. Her sharp interest and enthusiasm took me by surprise, making me wonder if she'd created the chic façade to impress us. According to her resume, though, she'd worked in a restaurant kitchen so she would have known there'd be no reason to get fancy here.

Once we were seated, I chatted generally to give her a snapshot view of my business and the foods we cooked. Harley listened attentively and responded with bubbly assurance.

"After I applied for the job, I found some of your products in a shop in Maple Valley. Your *Honey-Spice Apple Chutney* is so good I nearly ate the whole jar of it at once." She laughed easily at herself. "I'm going to try one of the jams next. Which would you recommend, your *Lake Neoka Spiced Pear Butter,* the *Sunlight Strawberry Preserves,* or the *Maple Sunrise Blackberry Jam*?"

Pleased, I took note of her careful selection and recall. "You researched us, well. Those are all very popular products."

"That's what Kara, the shop owner, told me. She said the pear butter is her favorite."

For a split-second, I wondered if there was something rehearsed about her words but I shrugged it off. She was probably a little nervous and job-hunters were often advised to research prospective employers for that very purpose. I was pleased she'd taken the trouble to try my products and, if an opportunity arose, I thought I might ask Kara for her input.

I picked up the application I'd printed and scanned it. "We were hoping to find someone with cooking experience but, because this is such a small operation, I think it's equally important that the person I hire is someone compatible with the rest of the staff. We can always teach cooking skills to someone who's willing to learn."

Harley flashed her smile and pressed her hands together. "I was hoping you'd say that. I mean… I'm no slouch in my own kitchen and I did help out in the diner where I worked, but there's a lot I still need to learn." She hesitated, then leaned forward slightly. "I want you to know I'm very willing to learn and I usually catch on fast to new things."

"That's good to hear…"

"You should also know I'll be a very responsible employee because I'm a single mom and it's important to me to show my daughter that a woman can achieve anything if she's willing to work hard for it."

Her remark was such a common, overused one I couldn't tell if she was sincere or blowing smoke, so I returned to her resume. "You mentioned you trained to become a professional hair stylist and it looks like you were doing very well at it. Why did you decide to change careers?"

Harley described her previous jobs with enthusiasm and no complaints. She claimed the owner of the salon where she'd last worked had developed health problems and had to retire.

"I would've stayed. I even offered to manage the salon for her when she wasn't feeling well, but she said she was tired and her doctor thought she had too much stress in her life." Harley thrust her lip in sympathy. "I could have taken another hair stylist job but salon hours aren't great when you have a kid to consider. And I know the last one hired always gets stuck with what nobody else wants. I figured it was a good opportunity to make a move and try something that fits better into my life."

"You moved here from Ohio?"

"Right. That's where I grew up. I have a friend from high school who moved to Maple Valley. When they heard what was happening, they suggested I come here and give New York a try. So, I did." She shrugged and smiled. "The area is beautiful and everyone I've met has been friendly and helpful. It seems like a nice place for my daughter to grow up. She's already made friends in the neighborhood where we're staying."

I reminded her the cook position was intended to get us through Maria Ana's recuperation period, but that I'd consider making it permanent if we both agreed.

"That's perfect for me. I'll be able to try out something new and I promise I'll work hard. But if I'm a total failure at cooking, neither of us will be too upset when Maria Ana returns." Her confident expression told me she had no intention of being a total failure at anything.

When I'd finished my questions, I asked Jennie and Maria Ana to show Harley some of the daily routine. While Maria Ana calmly explained our working style and probed Harley's familiarity with cooking, Jennie launched into a series of amusing anecdotes and began prepping the recipe we'd agreed on. Harley perched on a stool, taking in everything they told her and asking good questions.

After a few minutes, I excused myself to take a phone call. When I returned, the former hair stylist had donned an apron and was gamely following Jennie's instructions. It probably wasn't proper interview procedure but I thought their interaction was better than any job test we could have devised. I was certain Maria Ana was taking a serious measure of Harley's personality, character, and skills. And Jennie, being Jennie, would probably have her entire life story before they finished the recipe.

Again, I only took a brief glance at what they were doing but it was obvious Harley's knife skills were good, if not chef caliber, and

I'd never reject her for that. Neither Jennie nor I had begun with professional-level skills.

I refilled my coffee mug, eye-checked Maria Ana who didn't appear concerned, and returned to my office. I'd give them another ten or fifteen minutes, then wrap it up.

ઞ

Later, after we'd thanked Harley for coming in and waved her off, I turned from the doorway to see Maria Ana smiling and Jennie bouncing on her toes.

"I take it everything went well?"

Jen seemed ready to burst. "She's really good, Shay. Her skills are at least as good as mine were when I started and she follows directions to a tee."

I looked to Maria Ana, raising my brow in question.

"Jennie is right. Harley listened and understood what we need, very quick. If she not know, she asks. She can learn."

"And how did everyone get along together, personality-wise?"

"Very good."

Jennie was even more enthusiastic. "I can't believe how well we clicked. I feel like I've known her forever and we have so much in common. Harley's only a year older than me. She's also a single mom, and our daughters are the exact same age. Can you believe it?"

I raised my eyes heavenward, laughing. "I'm guessing your vote is a yes?"

"A big yes. And you know what else? Harley said she thinks I'd look great with dip-dye tips and she offered to do them for me. I'm trying to decide between blue and blonde."

"I guess we're talking hair and not sirloin tips," I told Maria Ana in my most ironic tone.

Maria Ana doubled over, laughing. "How I'm supposed to put up with two of those?"

"It'll be hard." I grinned to make sure Jennie wasn't bothered by our teasing. "Okay, then. Let's take a vote. Shall we hire Harley as our assistant cook or should I keep looking?"

Three thumbs-up and the motion passed.

"I'll call her this afternoon and let her know. She can start work on Monday."

CHAPTER SIXTEEN

MAC
Vignes d'Argent

A charter bus was parked outside Coteau Hall, the building bustling with activity. I could see a large group beyond the front window-wall, stowing coats and bags before beginning their tour.

Tyler asked the receptionist if Jack or Lily were there and, if so, whether they'd be available to speak with us.

She made a call and directed us to a courtesy office reserved for guests for computer services or private meetings. "They'll be with you as soon as they finish setting up. It shouldn't be more than a few minutes."

Jack arrived first. He was young, eager, and earnest, but couldn't tell us a thing except that during off-season Sands worked a semi-regular schedule, generally reporting directly to Philippe, and that he seemed quiet, a bit of a loner.

"I don't know what kind of work he does. He's mostly out in the vineyard but Philippe calls him to help with jobs in the winery sometimes, too."

Braun tried to probe deeper with little result. "Is he friends with anyone in particular?"

"Not that I know of. He mostly keeps to himself. He'll answer if you talk to him but he never has much to say." Jack laughed.

"That's probably why he and Philippe get along so well. They're complete opposites."

"When did you last see him?"

He tilted his head, pursed his lips. "It had to be last Thursday. I remember because we had double wine tastings and that doesn't often happen at this time of year. We were really busy."

"But you saw Keith Sands. Do you recall what time?"

"Had to be between set-up and serving. Both groups were right on schedule. Lily and I had to help out in reception because we're on half-staff in winter. So, we were directing guests to the correct tasting rooms and Keith was on his way out. I think he stopped to talk with Lily, but he just gave me a wave. That was it."

"Time?"

"Oh, right. The tasting was scheduled for five o'clock, so guests would've started arriving around four-fifteen or four-thirty. It takes a while to get everyone in and seated, explain how the flight presentation is conducted."

"Great. That's very helpful."

Blonde, shy Lily was less inclined to talk with us but, with Tyler's careful questioning, she gave us a better picture of the man.

"Keith only stopped to say hi. I think he made some remark about the size of the crowd coming in and said he hoped we didn't get them all drunk, that he'd better go straight home so he wouldn't be on the road when they left."

"He said he was going straight home?"

"It was a joke. I don't know if that's what he did or not." She blinked. "No. I know he didn't because then he said something like he had one more job to do before he could call it a day. I don't know if he went back to the vineyard or what, but I guess he didn't go home right away."

"Did he seem annoyed or upset that he had more work to do?"

"Not at all. I think he's glad for any overtime he can get, like most of us. Some people think he's grumpy and unfriendly, but I get along with him okay."

Braun gave her an approving smile. "How well do you know him?"

"Not real well. I worked reception a few times when we were short-staffed. It's really boring during off-hours or if there aren't any tours coming in. Once, when I was sitting there, doing nothing, and Keith was waiting to talk to Philippe, I asked him about his work. Just passing time, you know? After that, he'd stop and talk when he saw me. Not a lot, but he told me a little about his family and how he grew up working on farms and in vineyards. I got the impression he hardly ever went to school so he didn't have much education. But I've heard he knows a lot about how to grow grapes. He's always polite and he seems nice."

"Did he chat with other staff, too?"

"Not often. I think he was uncomfortable with some of the winery staff, like he felt he didn't belong in here. When he's with the other vineyard workers, though, he looks more relaxed."

"You see him in the vineyards?"

"No. We aren't allowed in the areas we don't work, like the lab or the fields. Sometimes a few of the workers come in around quitting time if they need to see admin about insurance or something. Or I'll see them in the parking lot. I don't even know most of their names except Keith and Gus, one of the foremen." She ducked her head. "I'm hoping to make movies… produce and direct them, I mean. So, I like to watch how people act and talk in real life."

"You're observant," Braun said. "I guess film directors and investigators have something in common."

She smiled, flushing lightly.

"What was Keith wearing Thursday night when he came in to talk to Philippe?"

"Wearing? I don't..." Lily closed her eyes briefly. "Wait. I do remember. He had on one of those tan jackets the field guys all wear in winter, the heavy ones with zippered pockets? And he had a pair of work boots with knitted cuffs. The cuffs were red and gray."

"You're good." Ty grinned. "How about Philippe? Do you recall how he was dressed?"

Again, Lily thought a moment before rattling off a fairly detailed description similar to the way he looked when we interviewed him. We had no way of knowing how accurate she was, but she'd given

Braun an opening he could use. He asked her a couple more playful questions about other staff, then narrowed his focus to Sands' facial expressions, body language, and what she overheard. Lily was amused and charmed.

When we heard the tour group returning and moving into the large presentation and tasting room, it was time to end our chat. But Braun wasn't finished.

"One more. This is a tricky one that requires both observation and drawing some conclusions. Ready?"

She peeked at the crowd still navigating the corridor. "Ready."

"Thinking about the times you've observed Philippe and Keith together, how would you describe their overall relationship?"

"Friendly?"

He squinted and drew his brows inward, as if disappointed. "That's it?"

"No, but… Okay, I'd say they act friendly but not equal. I think Keith likes Philippe but he's a little… not afraid of him but not relaxed like you'd be with a friend. And Philippe acts over-friendly. Don't tell him I said this, okay? He talks too much and laughs too loud when he's trying to pretend you and he are besties. He does that a lot with Keith. I think Keith gets it though. Philippe is one of those people you can tell what he thinks of you by the size of his smile. Like, you guys would get a much bigger smile than I would because I barely register on his people rating. He'd give you his best laugh probably."

"But if Keith's kind of low on the hierarchy, then why do you think Philippe gives him a higher, uh, *people rating*?"

"That's easy. It's because Keith works extra jobs for Philippe whenever Philippe calls him. And he calls him a lot. I like my job here and Charlotte's easy to work for. But Philippe is a user and he's fakey." She slid from her chair and adjusted her hair clip. "I'm sorry, I need to get in there before the tastings start."

"Sure, that's fine. Thanks for your help, Lily. You're very insightful, by the way. If the movie director thing doesn't work out, you might want to try for a job with us."

She hurried away, giggling, and Ty pumped his fist. "Not a lot, but it's something."

I chuckled. "Nicely played."

"Maybe we should talk to Philippe again."

When we returned to the reception desk, the woman was unable to reach Philippe. Charlotte Harmon was in the presentation room but Braun sent her a text and a few minutes later, she replied. He read the screen with a frown.

"Philippe left. He's going out of town and won't be back until mid-March."

CHAPTER SEVENTEEN

SHAY

Maple Sunrise

Harley surprised us all. From the first day, she fit into our kitchen like she'd been born to it. Jennie was thrilled to acquire another cook, a new friend, and a fellow single mom who fully understood the subtext to her child-rearing tales. Even Maria Ana approved because Harley was a conscientious rule follower. That would allow Maria Ana to relinquish the more physical parts of her job without worry, knowing both of her cooks were dependable.

To cap it off, Jennie quite naturally stepped into a mentor role for her new friend and, after only a few weeks, the two women were talking about combining households to share expenses and childcare duties. It seemed premature to me since they knew very little about one another. But Harley said she needed to vacate her friend's small apartment and enroll her daughter in school, while Jennie had a spare bedroom and could use the rental income.

I kept my opinions to myself; happy my employees were getting along so well. Having Maria Ana back in the kitchen—sometimes part-time and only doing light-duty—lifted some of the burden from my shoulders and lessened the need for me to monitor every detail. Adding that to Harley's contributions and my own continued efforts to work alongside the kitchen team seemed to restore a little of our previous balance. That didn't mean slowing down was an option, though. Like spilled molasses, other demands, and things I'd let slide quickly oozed into every tiny gap in my schedule.

Mac had once recited an old saying about nature not wanting a vacuum, or something like that. But I told him the only vacuum in my life was the Shark Upright I ran through our house in spare moments… which he found hilarious.

By mid-March the gardens were taking on that pre-spring urgency I loved. I hired two more garden workers, one full-time and one to split between field work and kitchen cleanup. And, to my great surprise, the increased payroll I was certain would destroy the budget was nearly offset by the boost in CSA membership from both the Chautauqua County enrollments and additional sign-ups in our original territory. It was so unexpected that, every time I recorded employee hours, I kept rechecking the numbers, convinced I'd made a mistake.

My slightly-lighter hamster-wheel existence continued as I ran from the gardens and greenhouse to the kitchen and office, to home and back around again, with side trips for school runs, groceries, and supplies, plus an occasional training update and ride-along with one of my delivery drivers. Most of my evenings still included an hour or so of updating journals and sorting accounts. I was tired, but a growing sense of excitement made it less exhausting than before. I wasn't sure, but I thought it might be a hint of what real success could feel like.

ℵ

One morning I rolled out of bed at 5:30 to find Mac already gone. It was the first time I could remember not waking, or at least half-waking, when he was called out in the night and I thought it spoke volumes about my depleted energy. I had to manage my schedule better.

Fifteen minutes later, I dragged myself to the cold room to find two of my drivers, Tucker and Chi-Chi, checking orders… along with Mac. Thinking a crisis had come up and he'd caught the message while I slept, I looked around for some sign of trouble. Everything appeared normal.

"I thought you'd been called to work, Mac. What are you doing here?"

He grinned at my confusion. "I wanted to give you a break, today. Why don't you sit down while we finish loading the orders?"

I hesitated, then shook my head. "That's okay. I can jump-start Naldo's orders. He'll be along shortly."

By the time Naldo and Jeremy arrived, most of the orders were loaded and ready to go. I gave the drivers last minute reminders to check each customer's product inventory and to drop off more CSA flyers. Then, as the vans rolled out, I turned to go to the greenhouse, but Mac caught my arm.

"Hold up. Let's go for a walk."

"What? I can't. I've got four cases of seedlings to prep for the garden crew this morning."

"Shay, it's not even 0630. Your crew won't get here for at least another hour and a short walk won't hurt. We never get time alone anymore." As a teaser, he handed me an insulated travel mug and picked up a backpack.

"What's that?"

"Come with me and find out." He grabbed a matching mug to mine and leaned in for a lingering kiss.

"There. I didn't know if it was poor form to kiss the boss in front of her employees but we can't start the day back-footed, can we?"

In response, I grinned and stretched up for another. Then he grabbed my hand and led me past the dark Farm Gourmet building to a path that wound away toward Beaver Inlet.

The channel that rarely froze over completely was now ice-free and only a few patches of snow remained beneath shrubs and pine trees. When we reached the spot where the stream widened into a pond, and stick-and-mud lodges dotted the surface, we side-stepped down the embankment to a long flat rock surrounded by cattails.

Mac spread an old blanket to sit on and used his pocketknife to clear away some growth that blocked our view of the water. Then he sat beside me and pulled breakfast sandwiches and containers of fruit from his backpack. It was a perfect re-creation of the breakfast hike I'd done to surprise him during our first spring together.

"You remembered everything," I whispered. "How did you find the time?"

"Sometimes the rigors of being a 24/7 investigator come in handy." He smiled at my gratitude. "Look."

I tracked his pointing finger in time to catch sight of a pair of sleek brown heads pushing branches upstream. We leaned in to watch until they dove underwater near their lodge, then reappeared to nudge and rearrange their construction. Later, there were more beavers, dining on water lily and cattail roots and gnawing tender aspen branches.

Despite a chill in the air, the soft lap of water, birdsong, and spring peepers combined with the rising sun to spread contentment throughout my being. Mac wrapped an arm around my shoulders and I curled close to his side.

"Thank you for doing this. I needed to… to stop for a minute."

"You did. And we're going to rework your schedule, Blodyn. You can't keep up the pace you've been going. But let's talk about that later. For now, just enjoy this moment."

ᘓᘐ

The gardeners were in the greenhouse and Mac had to get ready for work, so we kissed goodbye in the barnyard and went our separate ways.

I enjoyed the physical work of my mornings whether I was planting seedlings, amending soil, harvesting greenhouse crops, or laying out new garden beds. My body moved to the pace of familiar tasks while my mind registered the presence of organisms in the soil, its structure and health, and its placement in relation to the sun's path and adjacent crops. Without taking notes, I made subconscious decisions about what and when to plant. If Craig or one of the other gardeners were working alongside me, I'd try to remember to speak my thoughts aloud—although I was happy in my head—because all four were learning the methods that contributed to Maple Sunrise's good health and abundance.

Ethan and Justin had each done some type of farming while growing up, but were limited in their knowledge of market gardening. Craig had more experience and was evolving by consensus into a crew leader. I was hopeful he'd be ready to take over the training of new workers as the season progressed.

I wrapped up my morning by picking a couple of bushels of greenhouse tomatoes. Brett would wash and pack those for the next day's CSA baskets when he finished his morning porter chores. Then I ran to the house to shower and change for my afternoon kitchen and office jobs.

There were some daffodils left from St. David's Day so, when I left the house, I took one blossom for my office. I'd saved all the little bud vases Mac had given me when I was hospitalized, and the one I kept by my desk—a swirly, heart-shaped, blown glass design—was currently empty.

ꟸ

The Farm Gourmet kitchen smelled sweet and spicy as Jennie and Harley tended kettles of apple butter, using up last season's apples. Maria Ana was seated at the finishing table, applying labels to rows of filled jars. I was pleased by how many they'd done.

"Give me a few minutes to pull tomorrow's change-orders and I'll start shelving the apple butter in the storeroom. They all look perfect."

When I went into my office, my bud vase wasn't on the shelf where I'd left it. Even though it had always stood in the same spot, I looked around the room. It wasn't there. I went back to the kitchen.

"Has anyone seen the little green-and-white vase I keep on the shelf by my desk?"

Three blank faces turned in my direction. "It's not there?"

"No. Maybe Brett moved it when he was cleaning." I put some water in an empty jar and set the flower in it. "I'll look for it later."

Several inquiries about the CSA program had been posted on our web site. I answered those, took care of the order changes for the next morning, and paid a few bills. By the time I finished, my *few minutes* had run into an hour.

I grabbed a shopping cart from the storeroom and pushed it to the kitchen to load jars of apple butter, then spent several minutes organizing shelves to accommodate them. We tried to keep orderly rows of products but, in our rush to do so much, things tended to get moved around and forgotten.

I took a towel and cleaning spray and wiped each shelf before shifting jars into place. When I cleared a lower shelf and swiped it with the towel, my hand struck something and I leaned down to peer to the back.

Reaching in, I grasped my favorite bud vase, wondering how in the world it had wound up there. Then I remembered Del and the twins stopping by a few days before. Perhaps Bibi or Tolo had spotted it and carried it from my office. It was colorful and sparkly and I could imagine a child finding it irresistible—although how they'd reached it on the top of my bookcase was a mystery. Laughing at the children's resourcefulness, I carried it back to my office.

"I found my vase," I told the cooks. "One of the twins must have climbed up and swiped it."

I replaced my vase, added the daffodil, and went back to work.

CHAPTER EIGHTEEN

MAC
Batavia

Monday morning dawned wet but mild. Braun and I met up at headquarters to coordinate schedules and talk through our nearly non-existent strategy for the Cruz homicide. We'd been stalled for too long and, faced with the specter of a case going cold, Lieutenant Cross prodded and questioned us on a daily basis. We were as frustrated as he was.

I returned a couple of phone calls and checked with forensics for updates on Drigo, but they had nothing new.

"Drigo's been on my mind all weekend." I hitched a hip on my desk and slugged coffee, trying to organize a collection of unrelated thoughts.

"Too much time on your hands?"

I chuckled, considering my family's activity-packed days. "Not likely. Shay was talking about some new chutney Terri thinks is competing for her market and it got me wondering about Drigo's chardling blanc grapes. If this new wine is the big deal Emil and Ruy seem to think it is, would another vintner want it bad enough to kill? Is it even possible to duplicate both the grape and the wine? Or what if someone came up with another, similar product and figured Cruz was trying to cut them out?"

"Are you thinking Philippe?"

"Philippe, Keith Sands, or some other vintner who hasn't pinged our radar yet." I stood and circled our desks. "I was thinking how the challenges of running a family-owned vineyard are a lot like the ones Shay faces with her crops and products. They have issues with weather, pests, what-have-you, plus competition from other family-run wineries and the large corporate operations. Big ag already has a foothold in California's wine industry, buying out small farmers and snapping up massive acres for vineyards. And now that New York wines have become popular, it's inevitable they'll try to take over here, too."

"Huh. I didn't realize that. Are there any now?"

"Not yet. But it's probably only a matter of time."

"Then how does this connect to Drigo?"

"There's got to be over 200 wineries in this end of the state. That's a lot of competition for a niche market, even considering the tourism dollars."

"I follow. But it presents us with a pretty large number of people to cull."

"Maybe I'm off-track but it's an angle to look at. We know someone stole Drigo's vines. It might've been his killer or an opportunist, but the link is there. I thought we could get Emil to give us some names of individual vintners around the area… anyone who might be in financial trouble or who had a grudge against Drigo, someone who seems overly ambitious. If we talk them through, one by one, maybe we can jar something loose."

Elliott Baker was fiddling with my coffee machine. He dropped in a pod and punched buttons, then gave me an exaggerated fish-eye.

"That's your plan for the Cruz case? Why not just ask the troopers to run checkpoints on… oh, I don't know… every road in the state?"

Ty grunted. "You need a little sarcasm with your coffee this morning, Baker?"

"Sounds like you could use an expert opinion, that's all." Baker's grin was equal parts collegial and challenging. As half of our unit's other homicide team, Elliott and Chuck Ryder's cases frequently overlapped ours, but that didn't stop us from engaging in friendly competition whenever the opportunity arose.

"With ideas like that, the open/unsolved unit must be buried in your cold files."

Baker retrieved his mug, dropped a buck in the cash jar, and moved to join us. "Seriously, are there any loose threads Ryder and I can pull for you?"

I glanced at my partner but he shrugged. "We're in a pickle, El… somewhere between second and third base. And we can't even get a positive ID on the runner."

"In that case, your best strategy is to run hard and force him back to second."

I dropped back into my chair and propped one foot on an opened drawer. "If you're going to compare the case to baseball, a more realistic analogy is the bases are loaded and the batter just hit a Canseco."

Braun barked a laugh. "On that note, let's get to work. I need to head out. Do you have time to talk to Emil, today?"

"Sure," I said. "I'll make time."

ꝏ

The rest of the day offered mostly mundane, cleanup work. Braun was scheduled in court, presenting testimony on a previous case, while I interviewed a witness in another and went out on a call for a pair of neighbors whose property-line dispute had escalated into a gunfight.

Nobody was dead—not for lack of trying—but since the case fell under violent felonies, I had the questionable privilege of arresting the hot-heads, taking their statements and those of a witness, and writing up the reports… hours of work over a moment of stupidity that would likely wind up with nothing more than fines and some anger management classes. I recommended installation of a high, solid fence and some productive hobby for each of them.

By the time I finished with that, I was looking forward to a drive.

Cruz Vineyard

It was late afternoon before I made it to Emil and Ami Cruz's home. Unlike Beaumont's place, their vineyard bore only the hallmarks of a working farm during the weekdays. Wine tastings and social events were limited to evenings, weekends, and occasional special bookings.

I could see crews working among the uphill vines and a forklift shifting barrels into the cellar, so it was no surprise when I reached the door and Ami informed me Emil was supervising the pruning.

"Come on in and I'll call him."

I sat in the same kitchen chair where I'd first talked to her and Ruy about Drigo's death. Ami handed me a big mug of coffee and a blueberry muffin while she made her calls.

"Emil's on his way."

I asked after Ruy and the family in general and Ami mouthed the expected replies but I saw the hesitancy in her eyes, the assumption of security that had been taken from her.

Emil carried new responsibilities on his shoulders, as well. It was evident in his abrupt stride and firm stance that looked almost challenging. But he smiled and shook my hand.

"Great to see you, Mac. We ran into Shay and the kids on the lake trail the other day. Did she tell you? That's quite a family you've got."

"She did mention it. Yeah, the kids are a handful but they're going to keep us young… or age us fast. Not sure which, yet."

"I hope I get to see you when they all hit their teens together. I bet you weren't thinking about that when you decided to take them. We only had one and those years were… an experience." He settled into the chair on my right and took Ami's proffered mug. "But you didn't come here to talk about kids, I'm guessing."

"No, and I wish I had something positive to report. As Braun told you, we need a break in your granddad's case so we're trying a different tack. What can you tell me about your competition in the grape and wine industry? Has anyone offered to buy you out or tried to cut into your market?"

"Not in a long while. We're small potatoes as wineries go. Average size for a vineyard around here is fifty, sixty acres. We're only thirty-five. I'm hoping to plant another five or six this season."

"You bought more land?"

"Nah. This is the north section, behind the pond. It was mostly trees and scrub up until a couple years ago when we started clearing it. If we convert it all, we'll add another twenty, thirty acres. But that'll take time."

"Sounds like good potential, though."

"It is. But my point is, nobody's looking to cannibalize us. Not yet, anyway."

"How about Drigo's new grapes, the chardling blanc?"

Emil's eyes hardened briefly. "Plenty of outfits would like to get their hands on that. They're likely waiting for the public release though, to see how well it's accepted."

"No one's approached you about it?"

"Not directly. There have been a lot of questions but it's mostly curiosity about how we'll move forward now that Abuelo Drigo is gone. Even if someone was considering an offer, they'd probably hold off for the moment."

"Okay. There's something I'd like you to do for me, Emil. Could you and Ami compile a list of local or regional vintners and viticulturists around the area that Drigo interacted with over the last… let's say, six months? And, if it's possible, give me an idea of their relationship, how well they got along, if they disagreed about anything, maybe something Drigo mentioned that gave you a clue he mistrusted them or felt someone was being dishonest?"

"You're thinking he was murdered by another vintner? That doesn't make any sense."

"Bear with me, Emil. I'm not really thinking anything, except that, when it comes to competition and money's involved, a lot of things can go haywire."

He stretched out his legs and ran a hand over his face. "If you're thinking it was about chardling blanc and EnElCee, I can tell you a lot of people are interested—nearly everyone in the business—domestic and foreign. But interest doesn't necessarily mean they want to own it or have the capability to develop it. And, if you restrict it to this area and the last six months, I can narrow it to three."

"Only three? I was expecting more."

"Like I said, everyone's interested because it is a big deal for the industry. And if EnElCee is the success the experts are predicting, even a small investment could have a major impact. They'll all want chardling blanc grapes eventually and for a variety of reasons beyond EnElCee. It's a volatile market but nothing is going to happen for a little while, and nothing is guaranteed."

"Okay. Then what makes these three different?"

"Part of the difference is location and part is knowledge. Since all three are in the same geographic area, they can almost count on producing a very similar, possibly exact grape if they buy stock directly from us, which they most certainly will want to do. And, of course, anyone local has been following Abuelo's progress from the beginning. It's no different for us. We keep tabs on what other vintners are growing, what works and what doesn't. That's just basic research."

"I get that. So… who are they?"

"Well… it's not that I believe any of them killed my grandfather. These are just vintners who have shown serious interest and have the means to do something about it." Emil looked to Ami, who gave him a nod. "Bull Duncannon at Black Crow Vineyard is the biggest producer. He and Abuelo were good friends, saw each other every few weeks."

I jotted the name and added a tick-mark, remembering Hope Sands had mentioned Keith working at Black Crow.

"Then there's a newer one in the Finger Lakes, Patrick Hogan. He's only been operating ten or twelve years but he's a go-getter. I can't think what his place is called."

"Ten Trees," Ami said. "It's the Ten Trees Winery. He's on one of the smaller lakes, Conesus or Canadice? Maybe Keuka."

"We can check. How about the third one?"

"That would be Vignes d'Argent on Silverdust Lake. Philippe Beaumont and Charlotte Harmon are co-owners."

CHAPTER NINETEEN

SHAY
Maple Sunrise

My days were more regimented than ever, yet they also ran with a precision I'd never managed when I worked alone. The Farm Gourmet kitchen was producing at an all-time high. For the first time, I had three full-time cooks who no longer had to pause their work to transfer compost, clean equipment or mop the floor. And I managed a regular schedule of half-day sessions in the kitchen as well as my morning farmwork. Adding Brett to the crew had provided a more focused atmosphere and, within days, I asked him to move to full-time Farm Gourmet duties.

Besides maintenance and porter tasks, Brett had begun pulling the daily orders of Farm Gourmet products in the storage room and taking them to the customer bins in the barn. It was a time-consuming chore Jennie and I shared in the past that—like most duties—continued growing as our customer base expanded. Brett's presence in the kitchen also lessened the cooks' need to stop to mop spills or fiddle with temperamental equipment, and cries of *clean up in Aisle Jennie* were becoming a regular source of amusement for everyone.

As a surprise bonus, Jennie and Harley's shared-housing arrangement brought a new ease to their lives. One morning, Jennie walked in with stunning blond highlights in her newly-styled ginger hair. Smoky shadows and darkened lashes enhanced her gray eyes.

"You look sensational," I told her.

She sauntered with a hip-slung, catwalk stride, grinning at Maria Ana and me.

Maria Ana nodded her approval. "Has Brett seen?"

"Not yet, but don't say anything. Let's see if he notices."

Jen giggled, her cheeks turning pink. "Everyone should have a live-in hair stylist. And it's so great to have help with school runs and looking after the kids."

Harley, coming into the kitchen, caught her last remark. "I agree with that, one-hundred percent. Our girls are getting along, too and they're in the same class at school."

Maria Ana indulged their chat and laughter while they prepped and cooked but kept a close eye on schedules and production. She also continued to work alongside the younger women even though she no longer lifted heavy kettles or stood for long periods of time. With Brett and Harley taking on more of the physical duties, I was able to gradually shift some of my desk duties to Maria Ana—alleviating my own workload and giving her time to be off her feet. But as soon as her hip healed, she'd moved back to her little apartment—often climbing stairs instead of using the motorized stairlift Mac had installed.

Mac teased that she and I made a great pair because we were both stubborn, but Maria Ana remained adamant about her agility.

"Good hip needs using," she insisted, but I could see she was pleased by the change of pace.

Once I saw how well she settled into her new routine, I made another decision. "How would you feel about becoming the official Farm Gourmet Kitchen Manager? We'd work together to coordinate the recipes with what's ripening in the gardens, but you'd set up the kitchen schedule, assign responsibilities, and oversee production."

Her forehead creased with concern. "No more cooking?"

In my enthusiasm to promote her, I hadn't considered that Maria Ana actually loved cooking as much as I did; she might not want her job to change. "You don't have to give that up. I meant for you to switch to lighter work, at least some of the time, and let Harley and Brett take over the heavier stuff. It would be up to you, how much cooking you'd do."

She gave that some thought. "I could do that, I think. Are you going to stop cooking, too?"

"Never," I laughed, relieved. "I'm like you, Maria Ana, I always have to be meddling around in the kitchen one way or another. For now, I want to spend mornings on Maple Sunrise chores and afternoons in the kitchen. And when I'm in here, we'll follow your schedule. You'll be in charge."

ꟸ

The changes and improvements weren't limited to the kitchen.

The Maple Sunrise three-man garden crew—plus me—was working all out, planting, transplanting, and direct-sowing for the season ahead. Like the kitchen team, they seemed to work well together. Craig had taken the lead by consensus so, once a chain of command was established, I made it official with a small pay increase and the title of field supervisor. Having him oversee the rest of the workers would be one more step toward making the operation more efficient, especially when the summer crew joined us.

Even though my farm and business had undergone a rapid growth spurt, it hadn't happened without a few bumps. It was hard for me to be hands-off in the gardens and kitchen. Practical or not, a part of me wanted to personally handle every step of every process to make certain nothing went awry. But when I interfered, it became obvious I was causing more problems than I solved.

Craig diplomatically assured me he had *everything under control* while Maria Ana was more direct in asking, with a grin, *do you want to manage today or do you want me to do it?*

Comments like those quickly became a signal I should retreat to my office and take care of administrative duties. Given the need to set up accounts for all the new customers, and to coordinate deliveries for our collab partners, there was no shortage of those to keep me busy.

ஐ

I was in my office, updating garden journals, when my phone signaled a call from Nadia Giordano. It had been a few weeks since I'd left a voicemail asking if I could talk with her again, about my past. There'd been no response and I assumed she'd either forgotten who I was or had nothing more to say.

I got up and closed the office door for privacy, my voice shaking a little as I answered.

"Your voicemail took me by surprise, Shanny." Her precise way of speaking and use of my baby-name removed any further need to identify herself as my former neighbor in Port Terrence. She did so, anyway. "This is Nadia Giordano."

After a few minutes renewing our brief acquaintance, I told her about Detective Kruger and the mysterious Betty who claimed she'd known my mother.

"I spoke with Warren Kruger back in January," Nadia said. "He was just starting his investigation, beginning here, with your first known residence in Port Terrence. He was quite thorough in his questioning, but I could only tell him the same things I told you and your husband when you were here. He didn't mention anyone named Betty."

"If he was just starting out, he probably hadn't found her yet. Warren only told Mac about her recently. I was wondering if you might know who she was, a woman named Betty who was friends with or worked with my… my mother?"

Nadia didn't respond immediately but I waited, in case she was searching her memory for the name. It had been over twenty years since everything happened.

"Your mother had a few visitors after she stopped working, not many. There was one woman who dropped by once a week. It's been so long, it's hard to remember, but I think that was it. She always came by a little past five o'clock, maybe on the way home from her job, and she always brought a picnic cooler. I assumed it was your evening meal, but it was only once a week and always on Thursdays."

She gave a dry laugh. "Funny, I'd forgotten all about her. Now, I can see her as if it were yesterday.

"Once a week, on the dot of whatever time she came—I remember thinking I could set my watch by her—she parked her car, opened the back-hatch for the cooler, and marched up to your house. She'd stay a while, maybe an hour? Then she'd take her cooler back to the car and drive away. I don't remember seeing her any other time, but it's possible she came and I didn't notice. But every Thursday, right after five, every week, she was there."

I'd been holding my breath, hoping for more information, but it seemed that was the end of her story. "You don't know if that was Betty… or who she was?"

"I don't recall ever meeting her or hearing her name but maybe Jenna, my daughter, will know. I'll ask her. If she knows, I'll call you."

My focus was scattered after that conversation. I sat for a few minutes, replaying it in my mind, then I typed the information into my file. There was nothing else to do. Except wait.

ꝏ

When I went to the kitchen, I found Terri perched on a stool while the cooks updated her on our progress. To no one's surprise, she was delighted with how well the new systems were working.

"Look at you, Shay," she greeted me. "I hear you're delegating and directing like a born executive. Smucker's will be trying to hire you away."

I laughed. "I don't know about my directing but I'll admit both Maria Ana and Craig are perfect in their new positions. They're the ones the big corporations will want to hire."

"The changeover couldn't have gone better. And now you'll be able to do your website updates and paperwork without working twenty hours a day." She pointed to my office. "Let's take a look at your production stats and see what's next."

Terri had suggestions for linking products on the web page to increase sales. Offering a recipe for a broccoli-carrot-cauliflower casserole and then grouping the three veggies for the week's sale promotion would almost guarantee requests for add-ons. And ideas for using veggies in a fruit smoothie could help customers improve their diet and feature our more plentiful produce.

"A recipe page is also the perfect place to tempt members to try different produce. If you feature Chau's yardlong beans with her sesame-ginger recipe or a simple stir-fry and then offer the beans at discount that week, customers might decide to try them."

It was one more item on my task list, but she wasn't wrong. "I'll ask Chau for some recipes. Maybe she and the Herb Guys could do something together."

"Wouldn't it be fun to have a pot-luck dinner meeting with all your collabs? Everyone could bring a dish that featured their products and talk about ways to combine…"

"No." I held up a hand to stop her. "We all have farms to run. There's no time and no need to get into that in the midst of planting season. I'll do the recipe page but that's it."

Terri's grin told me she'd postpone, but not eliminate her plan. "Maybe next winter when things quiet down."

She dug in her bag for the list of retail prospects she'd compiled, pulling it out along with a small gift-wrapped package. "I almost forgot. I found this in my travels one day and thought of you."

When I peeled back the tissue-paper, I found a framed sign that read:

Delegate.
One Person can do Anything.
But it takes a Team to do Everything.

I flashed an amused eye-roll. "You must have ordered this custom-made for me."

"Nope." Terri laughed. "It was a lucky find. But whoever designed it must know you."

I laughed and propped it on the bookcase over my desk where it would serve as a daily reminder. "It's good advice. Just hard to do."

Later, she followed me to the barn to talk with the delivery drivers as they returned from their runs. She also caught up with Austin and Brooke, two of my collaborating farmers who were dropping off products for the next CSA delivery. She was excited by their enthusiasm and success stories and I felt both grateful and proud. It seemed we were making customers' diets more interesting and healthier, and improving our own lives at the same time.

ℬ

It was late when I returned to the Farm Gourmet kitchen. The staff were gone. I needed to make dinner and spend time with the kids so I went to my office to lock up, but when I reached for my keys, something didn't look right.

I'd left my computer open to our website, papers and flyers were strewn across the desk, and the table behind my chair was a jumble of sample jars, labels, and flyers. Given the state of the room, it was surprising anything caught my attention. But something felt off.

I scanned my desk two or three times, then walked back to the doorway and studied the room from there. Almost immediately I spotted an opened drawer in the normally-locked filing cabinet.

Crossing the room again, I pulled the drawer and checked the tabbed sections, all of which seemed to be in order. I rarely opened that cabinet. Two drawers contained nothing but paper, pens, and other office supplies. Only the opened drawer held any real files. Those included important correspondence and reports I needed for the health inspections, tax information, and a few business filings. But I was fairly sure I hadn't accessed any of those recently, and the cabinet was always locked.

I ran my fingers along the tabs again: business plans, customer agreements, health inspections, certification reports, personnel records, supplier contracts, tax returns… Everything was where it belonged.

Maria Ana had probably taken a call and needed the tax ID or something. If so, it was unusual that she hadn't re-locked the cabinet or left me a message, but I knew how busy the kitchen could get. She'd probably been called away and forgotten.

As I turned away, I glanced at the bookcase where I'd set the little delegation plaque. It was gone. I searched the shelves and floor in case it had fallen, finding nothing. Had someone been in my office, nosing nosed around in my files and taking my little sign? I had no idea who would do such a thing or why.

Then I remembered my missing bud-vase and wondered if the children had visited when I was in the barn. That would at least explain the missing sign. I was certain that whatever happened would turn out to have a simple explanation.

I shut down my computer and locked the file cabinet and my desk. When I grabbed my bag, though, a glint from the trash-bin at the side of my desk caught my attention, and there, among the discarded papers and refuse of the day, lay the little sign. I picked it out with a mixture of relief and confusion. I was going to have to have a serious talk with the children that evening.

CHAPTER TWENTY

MAC

Iroquois County

Rodrigo Cruz's homicide case took us to yet another vineyard, The Black Crow, on Lake Ontario's southern shore. The vineyards must have covered twice the acreage of Vignes d'Argent, but the winery was housed in a rustic old barn, apparently catering to large, country-style events rather than the smaller, formal tastings favored by Beaumont and Harmon. The owner, a tall, broad Bunyanesque character named Bull Duncannon, had a personality to match his venue.

When we identified ourselves as state police, he pulled a comic double-take.

"Had you come around when I was a youngster, you might've had good cause," he boomed. "These days, much to my dismay, I've turned into a fairly dull old codger."

Ty cracked back. "I'll bet you're still sharp enough to know what's going on though. We're looking for information."

"Prob'ly don't have much of that that's useful, either." He doffed the predictable ten-gallon hat and scratched his thinning scalp. "It'll depend on how far back we're talking. You boys want to come inside? I don't suppose you're up for wine but there's spring water and pop in the cooler. We can sit down while you tell me what-all this is about."

Despite his willingness to speak with us—and he seemed happy to spend the rest of the day talking—Mr. Duncannon had no suggestions about the identity of Drigo Cruz's killer. He and Drigo had been friends and friendly competitors for years but, like many older men, friends were not necessarily confidantes.

"If Drigo had any trouble, he'd've kept it to himself. He was never one to air problems. We mostly talked about crops, conditions, predictions, weather… work-related stuff. Maybe the odd discussion about our grandkids and families, politics, or something from the old days. Last time we talked must've been a month or so before he went." Duncannon paused and bowed his head. "Drigo was a good man. He didn't deserve to go that way. Not that anybody should, but especially not him. Things won't be the same without him to keep me on my toes."

ꟼ

On the way to Ten Trees, I notified Region E we'd be invading their territory, getting some good-humored slap-back and an invite for coffee.

Patrick Hogan was as intense as Bull Duncannon was laid-back. A thin, tense man, he made no secret of his dislike for Drigo when we explained the purpose of our call.

"Cruz stole his so-called chardling blanc species from me. I'd been working on a complex hybrid grape for years. I bought this vineyard specifically to grow and develop it."

Braun went on alert. "Rodrigo Cruz stole grapevines from you?"

Hogan shook his head but continued to glare. "He couldn't have gotten my grapevines, but he somehow got his hands on my notes. He used my work—more than twenty years of experimentation and research—and took credit for it. Claimed it was his."

"How did he get your notes, Mr. Hogan?"

"I don't know how. He stole them. Probably paid one of the vineyard workers to copy them when I wasn't looking."

"You give your vineyard workers access to your notes? Do you have any idea who might have copied them?"

Hogan was beginning to deflate. Whether he really believed Drigo had stolen his notes or not, it was obvious he had no proof.

"He had to have gotten them at least five years ago to give him enough time to replicate mine. I don't know how he did it, who he used. But I know that he did."

"Did you ever confront him about it?"

"No. I was working on it. The minute I heard the rumors about his new grapes, I looked into it—curious about what he'd come up with—but when I saw them, when I tasted them, I knew immediately they were mine. The profile is very distinct."

"When was that? When did you realize Drigo's grapes were the same as yours?"

"Last summer, early fall."

"Okay." I could see Braun calculating time and opportunity. Five years of planning seemed implausible but it wasn't impossible. "Walk me through your discovery and your conversations with Cruz if you had any. How did it come about? What did you do?"

"I suspected he was up to something for a long time, going back years. But the first time I saw evidence was at one of our regional vintner meetings. Cruz brought some chardling blancs, planning to have a private discussion with his friends. But someone overheard the conversation and word got around. I'd had my suspicions about his *experiments* for a while—his questions and interest in the work I was doing while acting all secretive and sneaky about his own."

"You suspected he was trying to copy you."

"That's right. He'd be talking to someone—his close pal, Bull Duncannon, for instance—but when I'd come near, they'd clam up. Like I said, sneaky."

"So, at the meeting last fall, what happened?"

"Cruz and Duncannon had their heads together as usual. But somebody picked up on their conversation, that they were talking about some new grapes. I'm not sure how it got around, but pretty soon, everyone was talking about Drigo's EnElCee wine and the chardling blanc grapes he'd used to develop it. The discussion got kind of tense with everybody wanting to know details and Drigo being cagey. He had some grapes with him, though, just a handful he was apparently going to show Bull. But with all the clamoring he was kind of backed into a corner. The upshot was, only a few people got to taste them. There wasn't anywhere near enough to go around. But I made sure I got one… and that's when I knew he'd stolen mine."

"From one grape?"

"I told you, it's distinctive."

"Did you confront Cruz?"

"Not then. I kept it to myself until I talked to my lawyer. He said he couldn't take any action until we had proof my notes were stolen. I was working on that—questioning some of my workers, ones I can trust—and keeping an eye out for any signs of deception."

"What did you learn?"

"There was one guy. A free agent sort who worked for me, time-to-time with special issues in the vineyard. He used my office on at least one job, which would have given him access to the books where I keep all my research notes. I asked him about it but he played dumb, denied knowing anything about my research. It was too late—the damage was done and my private records were out there—but I fired him anyway."

"Who was the guy?"

"Same one who worked on-and-off for Cruz and a few others, like he did here. I should have known better than to hire somebody with no loyalty to anyone but himself." Hogan's shoulders slumped in defeat. "And now, my lawyer says proving the case will be next to impossible with Cruz gone."

Braun prodded. "We'd be interested in talking to that guy if you'd tell us who he is."

"Really?" For the first time, something resembling optimism lit Hogan's eyes. "I haven't seen him in a few years but the other vintners in the area will know how to reach him. His name is Keith Sands."

ജ

We already knew Sands was MIA, but two days later, on St. Patrick's Day, Philippe Beaumont surfaced again. While we were waiting for his return, I'd run a deep dive into his past. What I found was exactly what I'd expected: a carefully assembled history.

Beaumont had been born and raised, not in France, but in Louisiana where his father purportedly ran a very productive and profitable moonshine business. When Philippe graduated high school, he'd used his skills to start a legitimate beer distillery and later, he partnered in a short-lived vineyard operation. Around 2002, he sold the distillery and his share of the vineyard and moved to England where he worked for a small winemaking operation and spent time traveling to vineyards around Europe.

We didn't pick up a lot on him until he reappeared in the States a decade later and purchased a small vineyard in New York's Finger Lakes region. Presumably, he'd developed the continental persona and distinctive accent he now sported during his expat years.

"Literally a self-made man." Braun chuckled over the compiled history. "Aside from his father's moonshine still, there's nothing illegal on record, but it seems like he was always hanging around the fringes. I want to talk to him about his last meeting with Keith Sands."

So, when Philippe called in response to our weeks-previous message, Tyler immediately arranged for us to speak with him that afternoon.

Vignes d'Argent

Temperatures were in the sixties, people were emerging from winter hibernation, and *Vignes d'Argent* was bustling. A pair of fifty-six-passenger motor coaches and a half-dozen cars sat in the front parking lot when we pulled in. Inside, Philippe—sporting a healthy, sun-tanned complexion and conspicuous vitality—stood beaming and glad-handing the guests that filed into his tasting rooms.

Braun studied the milling, exuberant crowd. "We're in the wrong business, Llewellyn. What do you suppose the take is on a group like this?"

I snorted. "More than we make in a month combined, I'd guess. But don't forget there's overhead."

It was no more than a ten-minute wait until Beaumont bounded across the lobby, hand extended. "Greetings, investigators. We couldn't ask for a finer Saint Paddy's Day, could we?"

We agreed, shaking hands and following him to a mezzanine office as luxurious as Charlotte Harmon's. His space, outfitted with a dark-walnut desk and bookshelves, smoke-gray leather couches, and garnet-and-silver wallpaper, offered similar views of the lake and vineyards but gave off an old-world, masculine vibe.

"You look tanned and rested, Philippe," Braun told the vintner. "I'm guessing your vacation went well?"

"Semi-vacation, yes." He waved us to the couches, offering wine or sparkling water. "It was a combined personal and professional trip. That's something people outside the industry rarely realize, our work is never-ending."

"I get it," I told him, aiming for common ground. "My wife runs a market garden operation and it's the same for her."

"Of course. Agriculture and its attendant businesses take a special dedication. I think that's why the country is suffering a loss of small farms, vineyards, and the like. It's much easier to turn it over to big ag producers. But the environmental impact and decreasing quality? Those are unforgivable."

I smiled. "You're preaching to the choir."

Braun gave us a moment to exhaust that topic, then turned the conversation to the reason for our visit. "We're following up because Keith Sands is still missing. Have you or any of your employees heard from him?"

"I certainly haven't." He waved a hand toward some distant figures pruning vines above the lake. "As far as I know, neither has anyone on the field crews. But they're not all back yet."

"It's been a while since we last spoke. In February, you told us Sands was going to the Cruz vineyard the night he disappeared."

Philippe blinked. "I did? I don't recall but if I told you that, it must be so."

Braun swiped his phone. "This was on February seventh. You told us Keith mentioned having another appointment the last evening you saw him. I'll replay your response.

"I'll start where I'd just asked you for details about that conversation." He switched the phone to speaker.

Beaumont:	**I have it. Keith shrugged off my apology for interrupting his day and said it was fine because he had another engagement nearby, anyway. He said it was no trouble to stop here on his way to that one.**
Braun:	**Did he say where his other appointment was?**
Beaumont:	**Not then. But when he came back to give his report, he mentioned the Cruz vineyard had expressed similar concerns with the weather.**

Beaumont frowned. "Now that I hear it, it does seem familiar. And it's believable the Cruzes would have wanted their vineyard checked and protected that night. The wind was brutal. Honestly, though? I don't remember that conversation."

"According to the Cruzes, there was never an appointment with Sands that night. In fact, they were away from home all evening." Braun aimed a hard glance at Philippe but it was obvious he'd hit a brick wall.

"I did say *the Cruz Vineyard*. Did I mis-speak or might I have misunderstood Keith? I can't swear to either." Beaumont shrugged. "I do wish I could help you, Investigator Braun. Even more, I wish Keith would return. It's going to be very difficult—make that impossible—to replace him."

Maple Sunrise

When I arrived home, I found the front porch festooned with glittering tinsel shamrocks. Indoors, Delyth and the children had swapped the St. David's Day dragons and daffodils for St. Patrick's shamrocks and leprechauns. Shay, for her part, had a nice corned beef brisket and cabbage in the pot and a loaf of soda bread, fresh from the oven.

I slipped up behind her to kiss the nape of her neck and she spun, wrapping her arms around me.

"You've made everyone in the house as holiday-crazy as you are," she murmured, chuckling.

"Everyone? Does that mean I've finally won you over?"

"Maybe."

"Aw, come on. You're as Irish as they come, Shannon Kathleen. Surely you must love a Saint Paddy's Day celebration."

She slid from my arms and turned to her cooking. "I have to say, I don't mind the food part. Dinner smells so good I can't wait to eat."

"It does," I agreed. "And I'll bet it'll taste as wonderful as the *cawl* you made for Saint David's Day."

She grinned. "That was pretty yummy, wasn't it? And the daffodils you bought were lovely."

"And your *bara brith?* It tasted like home to me." I rubbed my belly remembering the Welsh speckled bread she'd baked. "You have to admit we *Cymry* have it all over you *Gwyddelod* when it comes to food."

Swatting my arm with a tea towel, she burst into real laughter. "Go say hello to the children before you start a war in my kitchen and you won't get any dinner tonight."

"I'm gone. I'm gone." I snatched a piece of the soda bread she'd sliced and ran from the room.

The children were all in the playroom hanging more shamrocks in every possible space. They dropped their cutouts and came running for hugs when I entered.

"Happy Saint Patrick's Day, Elodie-Gabi-Bibi-Tolo. And to you, Maria Ana. Do we have enough shamrocks, yet?"

She smiled from her chair. "Happy Saint Patrick to you, Mac. I think the children have missed only one or two places."

I chuckled. "How's your hip?"

"Much better, thank you. I walked around outdoors after work today."

"Are you managing all right? I could install a sidewalk to make it easier…"

"No. I'm doing okay. It's nice to get outdoors in the warmer weather."

"She'll be ready to run a marathon, soon." Del popped in and started scooping up dropped shamrocks and bits of glitter. "Bibi and Tolo and I walked with her today and you'd hardly guess she'd ever been injured."

While we chatted and the children scurried around, I found myself sinking into the pure contentment of a house filled with family. It was something Shay had agonized over her entire life. What took me by surprise was how much it changed me, as well. Maria Ana, our volunteer grandmother, had lived with us before Shay opened the Farm Gourmet building. But Elodie, then the Marin children, and now Del, were filling our rooms with their energy and chatter and companionship. It seemed we'd become the family Shay always longed for, and it felt absolutely right.

Over dinner, I watched Shay split her attention among the children while keeping up with the adult conversation and making certain everyone had plenty to eat. But when she went to the kitchen to load the dishwasher, I sent her to relax and spend time with the others.

"I've got the kitchen, Blodyn Tatwes. Go enjoy our family."

The look of gratitude in her weary eyes shamed me. I'd been holding up my end with the children and barn chores, but Shay still carried the bulk of the household tasks in addition to working long days in both of her businesses and keeping everyone else happy and comfortable. I needed to do more.

CHAPTER TWENTY-ONE

SHAY

Maple Sunrise

As March was winding down, two of Mac's original goats, Ingrid and Heidi, kidded, adding four more does to the herd. Fortunately for me, they each managed to deliver at night when Mac was home.

The previous spring I'd helped Heidi deliver two kids—Pebbles and Patches—in a raging sleet storm when Mac was at work. I was hoping I wouldn't have to repeat that drama but we had four more pregnant does this year, including Pebbles. Mac laughed and told me the odds were against me.

Of course, all the children were excited and overwrought for days, wearing a permanent trail through the orchard and over the bridge between our house and the goat barn. But then, only three days before April Fool's Day, what had been forecast as a heavy rain event turned into a late-morning freak storm that buried the land in slush and wet snow before turning to frozen sleet. Schools closed and classes were dismissed, creating havoc on the roads as people rushed to collect their children.

Rather than leave Maria Ana alone in her apartment, I suggested she wait out the storm with us. As I helped her cross the sodden, slippery yard to our house, I tossed my keys to Jennie. Neither her old sedan nor Harley's compact were safe or large enough to transport all our children. While they drove a mile-and-a-half to Neoka Crossing, I raced to the gardens to move acclimating seedlings back to the greenhouse and put frost covers on the early crops we'd already transplanted.

A bed of seedlings had been lost to a cold snap the previous spring, so Mac and I had installed bamboo hoops over the garden beds that held vulnerable plants and those I'd use for early transplants. All that was necessary when the storm hit was the addition of burlap covers. It was a frantic scramble as the crew and I fought stinging sleet and blasts of icy wind to get them positioned and fastened before the plants were destroyed. But my gardeners understood the crisis and, despite conditions, we finished the job. The minute the last plant was protected, they ran to their vehicles to head home. But I had more to do before I could take shelter.

Sleet pelted my shoulders and hood and stung my face while the ground turned to ice under my feet. I grabbed a set of ice-cleats from the mud room, strapped them over my boots, and stomp-stepped my way to the poultry shed to make sure all the chickens and ducks were secured. Then I crossed the bridge to the goat barn.

I checked that the newly-freshened does and their respective offspring were in separate pens with sufficient water, feed, and hay, and that the rest of the herd were in maternity or group pens. To be safe, I examined the expectant mamas' bags and tail ligaments for signs of impending delivery, but their udders were loose and bands still thick. There'd be no kids arriving that night.

I set out dry food and fresh water for Muffin and Bruin, our Great Pyrenees dogs. They had free rein and would stay in the warm, protected barn with their charges. I called Barney and closed the sliding door. As we clomped back over the swollen, racing creek, I saw my SUV creeping slowly up the drive—and finally exhaled the breath I hadn't realized I'd been holding. The storm was worsening but everyone was safe.

Jen, Harley, and I hustled the girls indoors where Del welcomed Storm and Poppy along with Elodie and Gabi, offering everyone cozy wraps and cups of hot chocolate.

"The roads are a mess," Jennie whispered. "I think I might be able to get home if I'm careful, but visibility is awful, the pavement is black ice, and the wind and sleet are ferocious."

"Why risk it? The storm won't last long. I think everyone should stay here." I took a head count and did some quick calculations.

Jennie opened her mouth to protest but I held up a hand. "We're warm and dry and there's plenty of food. If the power goes out, we have a backup generator so we won't freeze." I eyed Jennie and Harley, getting relieved nods from each. "Good, then."

I raised my voice for the children. "Who wants to have a sleepover party?"

Six young voices chorused and cheered, including Bibi and Tolo who—I was pretty sure—had no idea what a sleepover even meant.

ꟹ

The rest of the day really felt like a party. We played cards and board games, grazed on sandwiches, snacks, and bowls of soup, and consumed pots of coffee and tea. Harley got a kit from her car and gave everyone manicures, delighting the kids with more than a dozen polish colors to choose from. And Del taught us the hilarious Welsh goat-counting song that Mac and Elodie used to sing.

It was nearly five o'clock when Mac finally called. "I wanted to check in on you earlier, but it's weather-insanity out here. We're all hands on deck. How are you doing?"

I told him about covering the gardens and Jennie and Harley collecting the children from school. "I took care of securing the livestock. Now, we're planning a big sleepover with Maria Ana, Del, Jennie, Harley, our four munchkins, and Poppy and Storm. Oh, and me." I giggled at the picture he must have imagined. "At the moment, everyone's in the kitchen making pizzas for dinner."

Mac's deep chuckle warmed me. "Eleven people? Do we have enough beds?"

"Sure. The girls can double-up and Jennie and Harley can either take the bunkbed or the living room couches."

"If you have a problem or need anything, call me. We've got snowmobiles out for emergencies and the plows and sanders are working non-stop. But we've got several multi-vehicle accidents, people stranded, others who should've stayed in their homes but didn't. I'm not going to make it home tonight, but I'll see you as soon as I can."

"We'll be fine, don't worry. I love you."

"Love you, too. Kiss the kids and save me some pizza."

The party atmosphere continued through the evening. Our pizzas—individual specialties we each created—were an interesting mix of ingredients and flavors. The power stayed on and the children played together with no mishaps or major upsets.

When the kids were at last tucked into beds, we women turned on a Netflix binge-series and broke out a deck of cards and a bottle of wine for some grownup time. It was something I'd never taken part in before, the sort of girl's night gathering you see on TV.

I watched Jennie, Del, and Harley for cues, figuring they'd spent lots of evenings that way, but all I saw were three young women being themselves and having fun. Even Maria Ana laughed and chatted and, as I relaxed a little, I began to join in. It was one more box to check off my list of experiences, another step in becoming *real.* I no longer cared that things happened late in life for me as long as I got to try them.

ᘐ

The following morning began slowly. The storm passed, leaving downed branches and debris in its wake, but no major damage that I could see. My produce deliveries would wait until the roads were cleared and safe, but there was other work to do.

At six o'clock, I started the coffee maker and slid my way to the barn to do the milking, gather eggs, and feed and check on all the livestock. I used a sled to move the filtered milk and the eggs to the main barn cold room where I bottled some of the milk for our use and inspected and sorted the eggs.

Back at the house, I showered, grabbed a cup of coffee, and checked the news on my laptop. The children slept in but, before long, the adults began wandering into the kitchen, one by one, in search of caffeine and sustenance.

Harley was first, sinking into a chair opposite mine and breathing in the aroma of coffee. "You're so lucky, Shay. Your life is perfect, like something out of a TV show."

I laughed. "You think that now, but you weren't here when I had to go out in the freezing cold to do the milking and feed the animals."

"It's a lot of work, I guess, but you have so much… this gorgeous home, your kids and Mac, your own business right next door."

Even though she dismissed all the hard days and unpleasant parts, I knew *lucky* was a fair evaluation. "What about you and Storm? You seem like you've conquered the single-mom lifestyle. That's pretty amazing."

"We're okay. There's nothing special about us. Normal life, normal days, normal me."

I set a plate of scrambled eggs and sausages in front of her and started the toaster. "Normal is nice. And Storm is a sweet girl. Tell me about your family. They live in Ohio?"

"Yes, in a boring little town northwest of Columbus. There's only my parents, no siblings. My dad works at the Honda plant and mom teaches third grade."

"And you became a hair stylist."

She nodded. "I got my cosmetology license after high school and I've taken a little advanced training to try to keep up with new techniques and styles."

"That's exciting. Sometimes I think I'd like to take classes in horticulture or business if I can ever find the time."

"You should. You have Del to watch your kids. I tried to go back a few times after Storm was born, but it's a struggle for a single parent with no support."

"It must have been hard."

She shrugged. "It was. But I'm pretty independent and, to be honest, Storm's father was more trouble than he was worth… if he even bothered to be around."

"Does he spend time with her?"

Harley spread jam on her toast and took a bite. "Oh, yum. These jams are so delicious. Do you ever dream of a having a huge business like Bonne Maman or Smucker's?"

Her abrupt change in subject and tone took me by surprise. I'd overstepped but, since she obviously didn't want to talk about her past and it wasn't my business, I backed off.

"Bonne Maman or Smucker's," I repeated. "Uh, no… not at all. I never imagined anything like The Farm Gourmet when I started. In the beginning, it was nothing but home-canned pickles that a few of my neighbors wanted to buy. Then I made some jams and… It just kind of grew on its own from there."

"That's fantastic. How long has it been?"

"I guess it's ten years since those first jars. But I was mostly focused on growing fresh produce and running the farm until Terri got involved. She's the one who saw potential and convinced me to expand."

For a moment, Harley fell silent. When she spoke again, it was with another, somewhat bold twist to our conversation. "Are any of your children related to you or are they all adopted?"

I tried not to squirm. People often inquired about us, directly or indirectly, since neither blonde Elodie nor the bronze complected Marin children resembled Mac or me. I found some comments rude and intrusive, the same way I felt when people asked very personal questions about my past. Sometimes I'd reply with a veiled that's-none-of-your-business kind of answer but Harley was now part of our inner circle. I softened my response.

"We're not biologically related. Elodie is adopted and the Marin children's parents died, so they're staying with us until social services can locate their relatives." I got up and took a bowl of berries from the fridge, hoping to put an end to her personal questions. But, when I sat down, she picked it up again.

"You treat them pretty well for not being your own kids."

Anger flared and I tried to count ten but it was pointless. "*Pretty well?* I hope I treat them exactly the way I'd treat *my own*—the way they deserve."

"Sorry," she said, not looking it. "That came out wrong. It's just that most people who take in somebody else's kids tend to treat them… uh, different from their own. Either they're too involved and impressed with themselves, or they neglect or abuse them."

That time, I did count before I spoke. And I got up again to fiddle with the coffee maker which didn't need it. "You sound like you're speaking from experience. Storm's not adopted, is she? Or you?"

Her laugh was sharp. "I'm just talking about all the stories you hear and how you're not like those at all. You seem like a regular family. But I guess you probably grew up in a normal, happy family, didn't you?"

"No."

She widened her eyes as if being an only child was something unusual. "No siblings at all?"

I shook my head.

"What about your parents? Do they live close by?"

"No. My mother died when I was small." Her questions were leading to places I'd rather not go. I opened the fridge and pretended to study the contents although nothing really registered.

"What about your father?"

"Uh, he wasn't around when I was growing up." I knew most people would interpret that remark as a common single-mother, absent-father situation, but I didn't care how she saw it as long as it put an end to the questions. But Harley's persistence was beyond most people's.

"You didn't have either parent? Then who raised you?" She clapped a hand over her mouth. "Sorry, sorry. You're so easy around your kids, so good with them and they obviously love you… I assumed you came from a home like that, too."

When I didn't respond, she relented. "I didn't mean to be rude, Shay. I just imagined a different picture of how you grew up. Sorry."

I decided to put an end to it. "None of us knows the real story of someone else's life. And how we parent doesn't necessarily reflect our past. It's best not to assume anything."

She nodded and reset the conversation as if it had never happened. "Jennie's been telling me about your seasonal vegetable pickles. When will we start making those?"

I took a long breath to steady myself and closed the fridge door. "The spring mix is made with early ripeners—onions, sugar peas, radishes, and carrots—and we'll start as soon as they reach baby-size. The ones in the greenhouse are almost ready and the transplants will follow right after." I took a deep breath and returned to the table. "Once we begin those, you can expect busy days and sometimes, longer hours, straight through the end of the harvests."

A few minutes later, Jennie came in search of breakfast, and Del and Maria Ana followed. Conversation turned to the weather and the day ahead.

Harley's evasiveness about her past and her annoying questions about mine left me with a churning stomach. After getting to know her a little better, I'd been enjoying her company. I also admired her determination and independence. She had no idea how well I understood her struggle to manage on her own and the scars that came from a lack of support but she was too nosey and outspoken for me to confide in her. She had an edginess that—along with her questions—made me wonder about her real story. Was she hiding the truth about her parents or her reasons for quitting her job and moving so far from home? I didn't want to mistrust her and I was hardly in a position to judge someone who didn't want to talk about their past. I was going to have to put that conversation behind me.

ꙮ

By noon, with ice melting and the roads cleared, everyone began leaving for their own homes. It had been a crazy storm but I was happy we'd spent it together.

In the comparative quiet of the house, I straightened the kitchen and started the dishwasher, then went upstairs to change bed linens, with the kids trailing along.

When I got to our suite, I saw Mac's sculptures had been removed from their shelf and were strewn across the carpet. Bibi and Tolo couldn't possibly have reached them but I eyed the Not-Twins, who knew they weren't to touch the carvings without permission.

"Has someone been playing with my statues?"

"Not us." Elodie and Gabi, wide-eyed, didn't hesitate to deny it.

"Someone took them off the shelf." I tried not to sound accusatory but respecting one another's property was an important rule in our house and lying was never acceptable.

"It wasn't us, Mommy. Maybe Storm or Poppy wanted to look at them. Or one of the grownups." I knew I could rely on Elodie to admit her mistakes and there was no reason to suspect her or Gabi. The pieces were intact and no harm had been done.

"Maybe," I agreed. "Can you help me put them back where they belong?"

Relieved, all four children scrambled to gather the figures, handling them gently and discussing how daddy had made them for me. They were beautifully detailed pieces, like a special set of dolls that anyone might be tempted to touch and examine—as I often did myself—so I could hardly blame whoever had done so. I decided Elodie's suggestion made sense and let the matter drop.

CHAPTER TWENTY-TWO

MAC

Batavia

A region-wide emergency situation like the ice storm we experienced meant everyone was on the clock to do whatever was needed. For me, that included responding to sudden death situations, helping transport the ill or injured for medical care—sometimes in side-by-side ATVs or snowmobiles—and shoveling and chopping ice to free people trapped in their homes and vehicles. For twenty-four hours, we went where we were called and did what was required to keep western New York residents safe.

It was nearly noon the following day before those of us who'd worked through the night were released from duty. All I wanted was to go home for a steaming hot shower and as much sleep as I could claim.

Maple Sunrise

Aside from Elodie's and Gabi's presence on a weekday, and the extra bedding stacked in the laundry room, the house seemed fairly normal when I dragged my aching body through the door.

Shay was alone in the kitchen, browning a skillet of beef cubes. Her intense focus on the task or some distracting thoughts in her ever-active mind must have blocked out the sound of the door and my footsteps. But the sight of her made my breath catch and I paused, leaning on the door-jamb to watch.

Shay moved like music: strong, intentional, and lithe as a ballerina. It was something I remembered from the first time I saw her unloading Old Blue at the highway truck stop. When she was engrossed in her work, she showed no self-consciousness and seemed completely comfortable in her body.

As she began transferring the meat to a stew pot, she raised her arms slightly, pivoting to her right, then back, to drop and stir. There were bowls of prepared vegetables on the chopping table and as she turned for them, she spotted me and paused, mid-reach, a smile lighting her eyes and washing across her face.

"Are you spying on me, Investigator?"

I straightened, hands raised, and went to wrap her in a hug. "Not *spying*… let's say *benign surveillance.* I just enjoy watching you work. You move like a graceful dancer."

"More like a disjointed marionette." She gave a snort, flailing her arms.

I shook my head in despair. "No one will ever accuse you of conceit, Blodyn." And kissed her to end the protest.

The skillet spat with inopportune timing and Shay spun back to the stove.

"Priorities," I whined.

She laughed, picked up a bowl of carrots, and stretched to plant a peck on my jaw. "Later. If I don't get this stew going, you won't have any dinner tonight."

"I'll go say hi to the kids then, and get changed. Have you been out to look for damage?"

"Only the animals. They're all fine. The gardens look okay at a glance, but I haven't had time to do a complete check."

But when we went out to inspect them, the gardens weren't all okay. Near the south beds on the Farm Gourmet side of the barns, we discovered ice and wind had split an old eastern cottonwood. One side of the main fork had fallen onto four newly-planted beds, tearing away the frost blankets, crushing bamboo frames, and uprooting and scattering hundreds of vulnerable seedlings.

Shay moaned and ran to appraise the damage. The seedlings—sodden, shredded bits of them—were a total loss. Despite the futility of it, she dropped to her knees and tried to salvage something from the mess.

"Leave it, Shay. There's nothing viable. I'll clean it up later, after I grab some sleep."

She startled, remembering I was coming down from a twenty-hour stint. "I'm sorry. You shouldn't even be out here. It's…" She rose to her feet and scanned the destruction. "You're right."

Without another word, she slid her muddied hand into mine and turned toward the house, her expression almost as battered as the cottonwood but every bit as strong. I understood the inherent costs and scheduling setbacks playing in her mind, but there was no undoing it.

"It'll be fine, Blodyn. We'll replace them and keep going."

ജ

I slept until mid-afternoon. I could have gone longer but disrupting my night sleep and getting too far off schedule would only compromise my ability to function the next day. And there was work to be done.

After a quick meal, I got the chainsaw and an axe and went to tackle the downed cottonwood. Although the temperature had risen only slightly, it was enough to melt the ice and—combined with a brisk wind—left everything over-saturated and sodden. My gloves, barn jacket, and not-quite waterproof trousers were drenched by the time I lopped smaller branches for firewood and kindling and began work on the two-foot-thick trunk. I kept those big rounds fairly deep because, once dried, cottonwood is a fine material for whittling and carving.

Shay came out an hour later, bringing a dry jacket, gloves, and a knitted toque.

I took them gratefully. "You read my mind."

"Put on the hat, it'll keep you from losing body heat. How are your feet?"

"They're the only part of me that's dry." I blotted my face and wiped my nose with tissues. "The work's not hard and the wood is usable. Shouldn't take too much longer."

She unzipped one of her pockets and extracted a bottle of water. "Best to stay hydrated…" she paused at my expression and laughed. "…from the inside. If you make this a habit, you'll never have to worry about getting wrinkles."

"I rely on my job to provide enough of those."

Replacing her own gloves, Shay tossed my wet clothes on top of the firewood sled. "I'll take this wood with me and stack it. Do you want that pile of small branches for kindling?"

"Yeah, but don't worry about them. As soon as I get the trunk sectioned and moved into my shop, I'll bundle them. Then I'm going to quit."

She pulled the sled to the woodshed I'd built near the back door and I returned to sawing.

As the day waned, the wind picked up, and I couldn't help thinking about Drigo, checking his vineyard in bitter weather. He'd been doing it for so many years—keeping fragile vines from freezing, harvesting grapes for ice wine, heeling-in soil and compost for root protection—that he probably didn't mind it the way most of us would. But what about his killer? Why would someone choose one of the coldest nights of the year to steal vines and commit murder? It was possible whoever it was had traveled some distance and their window of opportunity was narrow. Or they might have figured no one would be outdoors given the hour and the temperature. More probably, I thought, circling back, it was someone who was just as acclimated to winter vineyard work as Drigo was. Someone like Keith Sands or Patrick Hogan.

I hefted another wood section onto an old toboggan, dragged it around the barn, and started unloading. Sands had been gone for nearly two months, a pretty good indication he wasn't off on a drunk and planning to return. Someone told us he'd grown up in West Virginia, so maybe it was time to cast our net that way. If we knew where he'd lived, narrow it down to a town or county, at least, we could request assistance from local law enforcement. We needed to talk with Sands ASAP. Because, if he hadn't killed Drigo, we were back to square one.

I turned my attention away from work, focused on spreading out the wood in my workshop to dry. The light was waning and my back was feeling the effects of two full days of physical labor. It was time for family and a big bowl of Shay's beef stew.

CHAPTER TWENTY-THREE

SHAY

Maple Sunrise

Spring appeared as fast as the ice vanished. Overnight, the robust water table and brilliant sunshine awakened pale green sprouts that stretched and reached toward the light. Small buds, tiny tufts of color, flickered and spread until bright-hued splotches threaded themselves across the fabric of the fields and I could almost hear them calling to my veggie seedlings, like children urging one another to come out and play. Nesting birds, ladybugs, earthworms, and lacewings—even Mac's honeybees—heard the call and emerged to begin their work, cleaning, recycling, pollinating, and aerating the gardens. The earth was alive again.

I loved the rare mornings when one of the children woke early and accompanied me on my garden walk. They gave me an excuse to linger while I pointed out busy insects or explained the purpose of some half-hidden, regenerative activity. If it weren't for the arrival of our garden crews, I might have been tempted to stay there all day, lost in a bug's-eye view of the world. But a farm has no time for slackers.

When Mac, Elodie, and Gabi finished barn chores each morning, Mac would report on the last two pregnant does: Bitsy and Pebbles were still holding and everyone was healthy and fine. I also ran checks throughout the days, but it appeared there'd be no goat-midwifery required for a while.

Everyone wore expressions of optimism and positivity—a gift of the season, like Easter eggs hidden in winter. The garden crew fell into a steady rhythm of prepping and planting beds as fast as we were able. It wouldn't be long before lush green leaves and sprouting veggies would cover the long stretches of dark, loamy soil. I tried—and failed—to temper my excitement. Early indicators pointed to excellent harvests.

When the gardeners broke for lunch, I stowed my tools and went to the house. If the twins weren't already napping, I'd catch up with them while we ate. Otherwise, I'd grab an apple or sandwich and keep going. But whether I took time to eat or not, I needed to shower and change before going to the kitchen.

ꕥ

When I crossed the yard to Farm Gourmet, Maria Ana was walking up from the barn. She still carried a cane in case of a mis-step but scarcely used it anymore and her stride looked stronger than it had before her surgery.

"Two CSA customers come for their baskets. Brett is on lunch break so I took care of them." She waved at a small pickup pulling out of the parking area. "Some people want to choose own produce."

"I think it gives them the feeling they're *doing* something. Beth Hanson told me she stops here every week after work because it's like going to the grocery store but without the crowds and hassle. She said, even though she's glad not to spend an hour wandering up and down aisles, she misses seeing and smelling all the fresh fruits and veggies. It's like some sort of aromatherapy, I guess." I chuckled. "Maybe we could charge admission for people to walk through the room. It'd be like an art museum but with food instead of paintings."

I opened the kitchen door and held it for her. But when she stepped through, she hesitated, looking around. Behind her, I found myself doing the same.

Big kettles were simmering on the stoves and a pile of parings for compost sat at one end of the prep table, but there were no cooks in sight.

"Jennie? Harley?" I maintained a calm tone as I called out. "Where is everyone?"

Almost instantly, the two cooks rushed in from the back.

"Sorry, Shay." Jennie looked contrite. "I was making up Easter gift baskets and um…" she glanced at her friend. "Harley stepped away to ask me a question."

Before I could respond, she hurried to the stove to give each pot a good stir. "These won't be ready for another thirty minutes. They're fine."

It was a departure from Jennie's usual conscientiousness and her embarrassment was obvious. I gave her a nod, then glanced at Harley who didn't seem at all concerned.

"Harley, the capital rule in our kitchen is that it's never left unattended when we're cooking. I'm sorry if no one mentioned that to you but it's a major health and safety issue, no matter what else is going on."

"I didn't know. No one told me." Her expression didn't change nor did she apologize, but a glance at Maria Ana's face told me Harley had been advised.

"If you're ever alone again and need to leave, be sure to call one of us to take your place."

She gave a curt nod and turned to the sink.

I glanced again at Maria Ana who moved her head in a tiny negative. Although leaving the kitchen unattended was a very big deal, a single mistake was not. And given Harley's good nature and work ethic, I decided the matter was settled. I put on my smock and washed my hands, checking the afternoon's schedule.

The simmering kettles held final batches of *Moonlight Harvest Chow-Chow*, a tangy relish made from cabbage, tomatoes, and whatever suitable vegetables remained in the root cellar or freezer. I set up the sterilizer and started bringing cases of jars from the storeroom.

When I passed Jennie at the basket assembly counter, she turned to face me. "I'm really sorry about the kitchen, Shay. I didn't realize Maria Ana wasn't there."

"Don't worry about it, Jen. I know you'd never deliberately let that happen. Harley said she didn't know, so we'll overlook it this time." I paused to admire her baskets. "Those are beautiful. I always wish we could add a bouquet of fresh flowers to our spring baskets, but it's just not practical."

"What about a tiny plant? I could make room for a three-inch pot in one corner by switching the Herb Guys' tea boxes for their packets. We might even find a small flowering plant to make them really appealing."

I hesitated, weighing the cost of another item against the estimated sales. "I don't know… maybe, if you can find something for under a dollar? It can't look cheap or cheesy, though and it has to be local and available right now."

"Maybe a potted herb? A little peppermint or lemon balm would complement the teas and I bet The Herb Guys have tons of them."

I smiled at her excitement. "Call Ryan and see what he suggests. If he agrees to the packets and can supply enough plants for our Easter orders, we'll give it a try."

"You want me to call him? I'm not…"

"Jennie, you know how we operate this business and it's your idea. Let's try it. If you run into a problem or have any questions, I'll be in the kitchen." With everyone taking on new and interesting responsibilities, I wanted to showcase Jen's talents, too.

I hefted another case and left, happy to for her and equally pleased with myself for delegating another small task. I was building a real team. We could do this.

ꙮ

The distractions and pressing kitchen duties, along with the awkward moment with Harley, kept my pace high all afternoon. It wasn't until the kitchen shut down that I finally turned to my office work.

My desk was a jumble of mail and product samples and my computer was still open from when I'd pulled the change-order requests that morning.

"What I really need is a secretary."

Muttering at my disorganization, I sat down to deal with the physical mail—much of which consisted of catalogs and promotional material that I set aside for later or tossed in the recycle bin. When I opened my email, I sent new orders to the printer, then prioritized the rest. Clicking on an invoice for Terri's flyers, I began to type a cover note. That's when I noticed several tabs were open—many more than I'd normally use in a day.

I reached to close the files I didn't need, but puzzled over the document names. One, simply labeled *Notes,* was so old I didn't even remember what it held. Another, marked *Personal,* had information I'd collected about the search for my mother in Port Terrence, information from people I'd met in Illinois, and my more recent conversation with Nadia Giordano. It was a chronological record of everything I'd learned or surmised about my birth family. I knew I hadn't accessed that one in the two weeks since Nadia's call.

Opening the document, I double-checked for something I might have added or changed but it was exactly the way I remembered it. I couldn't think of any reason someone else would open it or why that private research would interest anyone.

Deciding I must have mistakenly opened it in my rush to get through the morning orders, I did a quick save-and-close on it and the other opened files. *Haste makes waste*, a distant voice scolded—probably some long ago schoolteacher annoyed by my perpetual impatience.

I smiled at the thought. "If I ever hire a secretary, I'll be certain to request a tolerant, understanding one."

CHAPTER TWENTY-FOUR

MAC

Vignes d'Argent

The workers at Vignes d'Argent were taking full advantage of the sunny day. Crews dotted the vineyards like bees in a field of clover and the bustle carried over to Coteau Hall where staff appeared to be setting up for a large event.

People who bemoan our Buffalo winters either haven't experienced or don't appreciate the contrast and sheer pleasure of witnessing seasonal changes. Spring, that year, absolutely exploded over western New York. It was like that old kids' movie that starts out in black-and-white and then surprises you with a switch to brilliant, full-blown color.

Philippe Beaumont was busy, rushing between his office and the main floor, directing staff with shouts and hand signals, and working his phone. Whatever he was doing, its importance seemed to take priority over everything and everyone in his path. It was unlikely he hadn't seen us, as he'd been facing the doors when we entered. Yet he pointedly ignored us, never acknowledging our presence.

I grinned and exchanged a look with Braun who was working to swallow his laughter at the chaos.

"Big day at Vignes d'Argent, apparently. Do you suppose he'll interrupt his very important business to give us a few minutes?"

"We can convince him." I chuckled, wading into the crowd.

It took a few minutes to catch the man's eye, and another ten for him to break away but, once we reached the mezzanine and the door to his office was firmly closed, he gave us his full attention.

"I apologize for the delay. We're hosting the 50th annual *Vin America Fête,* this year. It's one of the most prestigious ceremonies in the industry. Are you familiar with it?"

Braun shook his head and Beaumont continued.

"It's an annual, week-long celebration featuring presentations by a number of highly regarded experts in the wine industry. We'll hold several exclusive tastings including some debut wines, tours of our vineyards and winery, an en primeur charity auction and, of course, our grand finale—an awards banquet and gala. It's a great honor to be selected to showcase Vignes d'Argent for this occasion."

"It sounds like quite an undertaking." Braun made an effort to appear interested despite his impatience.

"It most certainly is. We'll be closed to the public that entire week and a week prior to prepare. It's going to be sensational."

"I can see you're very busy and I wish you well with it. But the sooner we can run through a few things with you, the sooner we'll be out of your way." He launched into a recitation of our search for Drigo's killer within the area's wine community. "We were told Keith Sands has ties to West Virginia and we're wondering about the possibility he might have returned there. Do you know if he has family or friends he might turn to with some… problem?"

"I know very little about Keith's personal life. He mentioned West Virginia, someplace in Wirt County…"

"Anything more specific? A town or village, maybe?"

Beaumont shook his head. "From the way he talked, there weren't many places that reached that level of populace. I got the impression that a church, some sort of one-room store, and a few cabins scattered around the mountain was about all they had in the way of community."

"The county name helps. We'll check with the sheriff."

"I do think you're looking in the wrong trees, Investigator. Keith is likely taking a break. He'll show up now that there's work available."

"While we wait for him to *show up*, then, we need another direction. We're looking at anyone in the wine industry, local or regional, who might..."

"I know all of our veteran vintners and larger operators—many are close friends of mine. They're honest, hardworking, law-abiding people."

"Not everyone is who they appear to be, and it's unlikely you know every one of them that well."

"There has been a significant number of new wineries in recent years, so it's true that I'm not personally acquainted with all the players... particularly some of the more recent, smaller operations. If you're in need of introductions though, I can probably connect you via a *friend-of-a-friend* in most instances."

"That might be helpful, later on. For now, we'd like to narrow the field. We're looking at vintners with the ability to launch a product to compete with the Cruz EnElCee wine. We understand it would require a large vineyard and substantial financial resources."

Beaumont frowned. "I have to disagree. Rodrigo Cruz already completed the grape development. And an en primeur vintage isn't going to be produced in large quantities, particularly in its initial cuvée."

I watched Braun flinch as he took in the implications of Philippe's assessment. I cut in. "We have the names of some major vintners in the state and a few owners who might have shown strong interest in Drigo Cruz's wine. We'd like to get your impressions of those."

Beaumont's expression held neutral, but he slid a rapid glance toward the window and his right foot began a steady tap-tap-tap against the floor. "This is a very sensitive matter. I'll have to give it some thought..."

A knock sounded and Charlotte opened the door. "I'm sorry to interrupt, Philippe. The caterer for the opening reception needs to speak with you about the garden set-up. He's insisting..."

Beaumont's tone turned icy. "Tell him I'll be there in a few minutes. If he can't wait, we can hire another service."

"I'll tell him."

He reset his expression as Harmon withdrew. "Perhaps we could compromise. If the person you're looking for is part of our circle, I can almost guarantee they'll be at our fête. I'll still get a copy of our membership directory to you and I can suggest who it won't be, but there is a more direct approach. If you'd like to attend the gala it would provide you an opportunity to talk with the members yourselves. Will that help?"

I wondered if he wanted to avoid assigning blame or if he had no idea where to begin. I looked at Braun who nodded.

"We'll have to clear it with our superiors and ensure there's no conflict of interest involved."

"You'd accept then?" Without waiting for a reply, he went to his desk, scribbled a note, and returned with a pair of invitations. "I'm quite confident you won't find your suspect in our group but feel free to bring your plus-ones and you'll at least get to enjoy a stellar evening. You may or may not pick up information but, either way, you have nothing to lose. Agreed?"

ꕥ

We were hoping to intercept Charlotte on our way out. I'd been intrigued by the antipathy we'd witnessed between her and Philippe and curious if it had anything to do with our presence. But we'd barely reached the main floor when my phone pinged with a screen ID for one of our troopers. I stepped outdoors to take it.

"Llewellyn."

"Mac, it's Pete Chen. I'm at the Cruz vineyard. A couple of workers stumbled across something suspicious and called it in. I think you'll want to get over here, ASAP."

"What have you got?"

"There's a pond near the east side of the property, toward the back…"

"Yeah, I know it."

"Okay, so it's pretty deep for its size—probably an old glacier pit. Anyhow, a field crew was working the vineyard behind here and a couple of guys went on break, stopped for a smoke. They spotted something in the water that didn't look right. Turns out to be a submerged vehicle. It's hard to tell, but I'd say it could be a black pickup truck."

I swallowed a curse. "Any occupants?"

"Can't tell. The water's relatively clear but the vehicle's flipped over. Upside-down."

I spun toward the building and signaled Braun. "We're near Silver Rapids right now, Pete. ETA shouldn't be over five minutes."

CHAPTER TWENTY-FIVE

SHAY

Maple Sunrise

I closed my office, double-checking that my computer, desk, filing cabinet, and office doors were all securely locked. But instead of going directly to the house, I detoured upstairs to Maria Ana's apartment.

"Come in, Shay. I'm making tea." She took in my expression and before I could speak, she added, "You look like you could use a cup."

"I'm probably over-reacting again."

"Tea will fix that." She went to her kitchen and retrieved a vintage Quinchymali teapot—part of a folk-art pottery set my father had sent from her home country.

"What happened?"

"I'm not sure. You were in my office today. Did you notice anything… different?"

Maria Ana used my desk daily to order supplies, write journal reports, and take care of other managerial tasks, so I knew she was familiar with how I kept things. She might not spot an extra tab on the computer screen, but she'd probably notice if things were physically moved.

"Different? Like go missing?" She poured lemon balm tea into mugs decorated with scenes of a Colombian village.

"I'm not sure if anything is missing," I admitted. "But there were documents opened on my computer that I'm certain I haven't used recently."

"I used computer to order towels this morning. Only same form as always. Could I click by mistake?"

"No. Those forms are linked to the company's website. They're completely separate. To get to my files you'd have to open the word processing application, locate the folder, and then the file. It'd take more than one accidental click."

"So, somebody else."

"Do you know if anyone else was in my office today?"

She sipped tea while she thought. "Jennie called Herb Guys. She said you okayed it. Brett took in mail and did cleaning. I don't remember any other but I was busy, and with customers."

It seemed like days since I met Maria Ana coming from the barn and we'd walked into the abandoned kitchen. It had been a long day with enough problems to explain an over-reaction.

"Was anyone in the office longer than seemed necessary?"

Maria Ana frowned. "No one I saw."

"I suppose someone could have gone in when you were in the CSA room at the barn."

"Are the files important?"

"If someone fiddled with work files—changing data or orders or something—I guess it could cause problems. But I didn't find anything like that. It was just a bunch that were opened." I flapped my hands, feeling a little foolish. "I guess the one that bothered me most was my personal file. I can't think why anyone would be interested in it because it's… personal. There's nothing in it but notes I made about my family history, no big secrets, or hidden treasures. But it isn't information I want to share, either. It's private."

"Nobody should be looking at computer. That's not respectful. Everything in office is private. I'll watch."

Feeling a little like a whiny toddler, I backtracked. "I'm sure I'm over-reacting, wasting energy on what was probably a simple mistake. A bunch of simple mistakes. Thanks for listening, though. And for the tea."

Again, I started for home, but I only made it to the Farm Gourmet parking area.

Harley and Brett were standing by their cars having an animated discussion about some club where a popular band was performing. Brett, like Harley, had recently been absorbed into Jennie's social circle and I enjoyed watching their friendships grow closer.

Since they didn't seem to be in a hurry, I decided to ask if either of them knew who'd been in my office.

"If you aren't in a rush, can I talk to you each, privately? It shouldn't take more than a few minutes." They both looked startled, so I added, "If you can't, it's okay We can talk tomorrow."

"It's fine." Brett relaxed right away. "I'm not in any hurry. What do you need?"

I looked to Harley who also nodded.

"Thanks. Let's go back inside."

Since I knew Brett had been in my office to drop off the mail, I took him first. But trying to explain the situation without making it sound like an accusation was difficult. "I know everyone uses my office to check orders or handle calls when I'm not here. It's necessary work and I usually leave the door open for that reason. But a few things have happened recently that I need to check on." I fiddled with my pens, unsure how to proceed.

"I only come in here to drop off the mail and to run the vacuum and clean." Brett looked alarmed, his gray eyes wide. "Did I do something wrong?"

"No, nothing like that. It's really about how my files… about the way information is handled. And it's most likely just a mistake."

I searched for a tactful way to ask him without saying what I'd found. "I realize we get changes to orders and questions all the time and staff have to know how to handle those. It's part of the job when we're such a small operation. Have you ever needed to use my files or the computer when you're in here?"

It didn't seem possible his eyes could widen any further. "I've never touched them. Maria Ana told me I wasn't to move or handle anything in here, even when I'm dusting. She told me to dust the surfaces that are clear and to leave your stuff alone, or ask her if there was any kind of problem. And I'm not supposed to answer calls either. She said I have enough to do and the cooks are trained to handle orders and customer questions if you're not here."

"Okay. And no one's ever asked you to look up a file or print something?"

He gave an emphatic head-shake. "Never."

"Have you noticed anyone hanging around my office? Someone who isn't normally here?"

"Not really. Maria Ana usually comes in at closing to write up reports and the work schedule."

"Of course. Anyone else?"

"Jennie or Harley, once in a while, if Maria Ana's busy and a call comes in or they need an order form." His confusion convinced me Brett hadn't been looking at my private records.

"Those are things I'd expect to happen, legitimate reasons to use the office. As I said, this was probably nothing but a mistake. Thanks for your help."

When Harley sat across from me, she seemed annoyed but she might have been expecting a continuation of my earlier reprimand. Her reaction to the same questions I'd asked Brett couldn't have been more different. She was dismissive and barely civil.

"Anybody and everybody goes in and out of here, all the time. Things probably get shifted and moved around. What do you expect when you leave the place wide open?"

It felt like a personal attack and, for a moment, I didn't respond. Then I firmed my posture and my tone. "What I expect is for everyone to treat my office and all company property in a respectful and professional way."

A flash of surprise registered before she reset her tone. "I didn't mean any of us would do something disrespectful. But your office is open and there are a lot of people around—the garden crew, route drivers, people making deliveries, even your kids…"

"The children aren't usually here if I'm not and they shouldn't be unattended anywhere. The others—route drivers, gardeners, delivery people—should never be in the building without good reason and only when either Maria Ana or I are here. If they are, I expect to be told so I can address it." A note of anger crept into my voice and I paused for a five-count.

"I didn't mean anyone came in the building, but they're around. Like, hanging around outside or deliveries coming into the store room. Stuff like that."

"Has anyone unauthorized been inside, lately?"

"I don't know." She raised one shoulder and gave a quick tilt of her head in what might've been a *so what* gesture. Her lips were compressed, her jaw set.

"Look, Harley, I'm not accusing you of anything. But you're in the kitchen so you'd probably notice anyone who shouldn't be here."

"I'm busy helping Jen and Maria Ana all day. I can't be guarding your office, too."

I forced a smile. "There's not much to guard. And I'm not asking you to. I don't mean to upset you, either."

She continued to look at me, silent. I tried another tack.

"If you feel I was too harsh about what happened this afternoon, I apologize. Leaving the kitchen that way is a serious violation that could result in fines and censure or even revocation of my license, so I have to make certain everyone complies. I realize it was a mistake and, as far as I'm concerned, as long as it doesn't happen again, it's over."

She shrugged again, saying nothing.

"We all really like you, Harley. Your work has been excellent and you're fitting in as if you'd been with us forever. I hope you like working with us and I want you to know your ideas and suggestions are always welcome. That's another reason I keep my door open."

Her smile lacked warmth and never touched her eyes. "You out to consider taking some of those courses you were talking about. You really don't know much about managing people."

My fist clenched but I forced a smile. I could see she had nothing useful to say. "You might have a point. Thanks for the chat."

It was four-thirty and I'd failed my intention to be home for Elodie's and Gabi's return from school. If I was going to drop any of the balls I was juggling, that was the wrong one. Nothing was more important than the children.

CHAPTER TWENTY-SIX

MAC

Cruz Vineyard

Emil and Ami Cruz stood behind a rail fence that separated the public winery grounds from the working vineyard. It was a toss-up whether the body of water they faced should be called a pond for its four-acre size, or a lake in lieu of its thirty-foot depth at one end. Semantics aside, it was large enough that it had apparently concealed a good-sized pickup for three months—assuming it was Keith Sands' vehicle and had plunged into the water the night he disappeared.

Braun and I gave the couple a nod, but continued to the far shoreline where a small group of first responders milled around, speculating, while they waited for our arrival.

The gravel track we'd followed began at the Cruz's storage barn and ran uphill, cutting between the water and the newer vineyards. About midway along the north side of the pond, the land rose to form an overlook and it was there we spotted lengths of yellow tape and a pair of sawhorses. Trooper Chen pointed up the slope.

"You can see the truck from up there," he told us. "It's where he must've gone in—the deepest part of the pond."

"How deep?"

"Cruz says at least twenty-five, thirty feet. The other side starts out shallow and slopes to maybe twelve feet near the middle, but after that it drops into a trench. No one knows if it was dug that way or formed naturally but the locals say it's listed like that on the old survey maps, so it's likely glacial."

When we reached the overlook, we checked for ruts or tracks from the vehicle but, if there'd been any when the truck went in, snow melt, wind and rain had removed all trace. At the edge of the drop-off, we scanned the water around a bright orange buoy. A definitive, rectangular shape lay several feet below the surface.

"Cruz says they ran vine checks during the winter but nothing would've been visible with the pond iced over."

Braun looked back the way we'd come. "Where are the guys who discovered it?"

"Sam Blanchard's waiting in my vehicle. He was the first to spot it and pointed it out to his foreman. The foreman, Carbone, is waiting in Huerta's cruiser."

"We'll talk to them first. Llewellyn, you want to call the Underwater Recovery Team and Forensics, get them out here?" Braun took a second to run through protocol. "Maybe we'll get lucky and the truck'll be empty."

ꕤ

It took a while for URT to arrive with their inflatable boat and dive equipment. While we waited, I called Sheriff Cramer to let him know we might've located Keith Sands. When forensics arrived, I helped them set up and Braun interviewed Blanchard and Carbone.

It was no surprise that the vineyard workers had little information to share. Blanchard claimed he saw the truck's shadow in the water when he stopped for a smoke on his way from the field. Not knowing what it was but realizing it wasn't a natural formation, he summoned Carbone, who immediately guessed what they were seeing and called it in.

The divers took some time setting up, checking equipment, and scanning the lake bed with sonar. Once they were satisfied, the divers went in to verify and attach buoyancy lift bags to bring the truck to the surface. By the time they'd towed it onto a flatbed, those of us waiting had fallen silent, anticipating grim news.

The truck wore a thick coat of mud, its windows impenetrable, but the license plate was intact. One of the divers wiped off sludge and read the number aloud. It matched the vehicle registered to Keith Sands.

A second diver moved to the truck's left-side, rubbed a window, and signaled me to join him as he opened the door. A body lay across the seat. Its condition had been partially preserved by being frozen but it was far too fragile to handle or remove.

"There's no way to ID him here and they're going to want us to work fast and keep him on ice so we don't compromise evidence. You can call the M.E." He gave me a nod and we pulled a nylon tarp over the cab to prevent the now-encroaching bystanders and media from looking inside.

We spent another half-hour waiting. Tyler and I walked the upper embankment with a forensic tech, going over distances and angles to gauge the spot where the truck had plunged, and trying to estimate its speed. If he'd gone over at a high rate, we might be looking at suicide; slower could still be that but, more likely, accident or homicide. I wasn't placing any bets.

ꟙ

A small crowd had gathered by the time Dr. Brian Powell pulled his Mercedes onto the curving road, following the body wagon. He stopped near the tow truck and climbed out with the air of man well accustomed to balancing impatient cops with his charges who would never be in a hurry again.

"What have you got for me, boys and girls?"

"One occupant." The guy who'd covered the truck slid the tarp back. "Probably been under the ice for a while."

"ID?"

"We didn't touch him. Truck's registered to an MP out of Maple Valley. Guy named Keith Sands."

Keeping the body intact was always tricky with an underwater recovery and special mesh body-bags and handling were required. Brian leaned into the truck to ascertain the condition but even he avoided any unnecessary handling. When he straightened, he scanned the group. "Whose case is it?"

"That'd be me and Llewellyn," Ty answered.

"All right. We'll try for autopsy tomorrow, probably afternoon. You can check with Willa for the time." He stripped off his gloves and signaled an assistant to bring a gurney. "Llewellyn, you owe me a squash match. I hear that new gym on the highway's got some nice courts. We should give it a try."

I laughed. "I'll check it out, reserve one if I can."

As soon as he left, everyone else began packing up as well. Braun and I stopped at the house to update the Cruzes and ask, again, if they remembered seeing the truck or anyone near the pond around the date Sands had disappeared. Their answers remained unchanged.

Night fell over the Cruz pond and, aside from trampled ground and an overlooked scrap of crime scene tape, the vineyard returned to its silent, timeless existence. I paused to ponder Keith Sands' truths—a man lacking ambition who might have died for someone else's—but no clear personality arose. Victim or killer? Or both? We had work to do.

On the way to HQ to complete our reports and wrap up, I called in an update to the Sheriff.

"Preliminary assessment is the truck went in at a low rate of speed. But that's only guesswork, based on where it landed. It could've been pushed over or he might've been idling and his foot slipped off the brake. Could be a lot of things. Forensics will go over the vehicle, look at accident reconstruction. Maybe we'll get some answers, maybe not." I checked my notes. "The body was still partially frozen, so he'd been down there a while. We'll have more after Doc Powell does the autopsy. That's about it."

"Sounds good, Llewellyn. As soon as ID is confirmed, we can take notification. You want to be there?"

I glanced at Braun.

"Unless the autopsy turns up something unexpected, it's probably not necessary," Braun decided. "But, let us know if his wife has anything new?"

"You've got it. Thanks for your help."

We disconnected and rode the next few miles in silence. We'd found our missing person but picked up the possibility of another homicide. The complications multiplied.

CHAPTER TWENTY-SEVEN

SHAY

Maple Sunrise

Instead of going to the gardens the next morning, I waited for Jennie to arrive. She was the only Farm Gourmet employee I hadn't questioned.

Jennie was outspoken, an open book who either lacked filters or didn't see the point of them. I was confident that, if she wanted to know something about my personal life she'd ask me straight out. She wasn't sneaky. I clung to the possibility that she—or someone--had opened my private file by mistake but that didn't explain how Terri's gift wound up in the trash, or any of the previous *mistakes* I'd discovered.

I was glad to see she'd driven to work alone that day. As soon as she grabbed her smock and coffee, I called her into my office.

"I have to ask you something, Jen. It's a little sensitive."

"About someone breaking into your office?"

"You know about that?"

"Only that it happened. Harley told me you questioned her and Brett. She's a little pissed off. I told her you weren't accusing her of anything, that there'd be private records in here." She lifted her coffee mug but didn't drink. "Was anything stolen?"

I shook my head. "Nothing important. Someone opened a file of notes I'd made—stuff that shouldn't be of interest to anybody but nothing terribly confidential. It could have been an accident, I guess, if they didn't know where to look for a file and went poking around." I huffed, torn between wanting to excuse the incident and not believing it was innocent. "My concern is because this wasn't a one-time thing. Someone's been opening files and snooping in this office a few times and I've found personal things moved around. I can't imagine what anyone would need that isn't in an obvious place."

Jennie bit her lip. "I know I didn't touch or open anything I shouldn't and I can't imagine why anyone else would, either."

"Harley suggested someone came in from outside. It makes no sense but I'm going to keep my office locked when I'm not here, at least until I figure out what's going on. If you need to use the office, Maria Ana will open it for you."

"That's not a problem. I usually tell Maria Ana if I'm going to be in here, anyway."

After Jennie went to work in the kitchen, I rechecked that the file cabinet was secure and I locked the office door. As I handed the keys to Maria Ana and explained what little I knew, I noticed Harley watching us, but when I looked in her direction, she turned away.

I was sorry our discussion upset her but she'd have to come to terms with it. Maybe I was overly cautious in locking the door, but employee records with personal information—including hers—were in there. It was my responsibility to keep those private. I wouldn't back down.

&

An uneasiness hung over the kitchen that afternoon. The food processing was on schedule and everyone performed their usual tasks but the light banter and friendly atmosphere was missing. Harley kept her eyes on her work, making it difficult to strike up a conversation and she ignored Jennie's attempts at conversation.

At quitting time, I intercepted Harley at the door. "You seem quiet today. I hope it's not because of what happened in my office."

She shook her head. "That has nothing to do with me. I'm fine."

"I don't want you to think I was singling you out. I've asked everyone about it, even Maria Ana. No one saw anything, so the only other possibility is the one you suggested, that someone came into the kitchen unnoticed. I'm not blaming you or anyone but I can't let it happen again. You understand, don't you?"

She forced her lips into a smile. "Sure. But like I said, you could benefit from some management classes."

"Hmm." I could tell the chip on her shoulder hadn't moved. "Can we put this behind us, then?"

"No problem. See you tomorrow." And she was gone.

ꕤ

I was at the door when the school bus dropped off the girls. Their excitement at seeing me and their non-stop chatter reminded me of the many times I'd missed those moments. My business might be growing but I seemed to be failing at everything else, lately. I scolded myself that if I needed to learn how to manage a business, perhaps I should also look into parenting classes.

I gave extra attention to school papers and all four children's reports about what they'd done that day. And, when they finished their snacks, I took them outdoors to play.

The warm, lengthening days drew us to the fields and the water. We spent hours floating stick-boats down the creek and gathering pebbles along the lake, our excitement never lessening at the sight of another fawn, a rabbit, or birds constructing nests in the hedgerows.

That evening, I told Mac about the problem in my office. "I'm afraid I didn't handle it very well, although Harley was the only one to take offense."

"Do you think it was her?"

"I'm positive neither Maria Ana nor Jennie would snoop like that, and I thought Brett seemed genuinely surprised. So, unless someone was in the building who shouldn't have been, that only leaves Harley. I know she was upset with me for reprimanding her earlier. Maybe she wanted to find out if I'd written her up or was planning to fire her."

Mac nodded, giving consideration to what I said. "How did her background check out?"

"Um… I didn't find anything negative."

His left eyebrow arched. "Meaning you didn't look very deep?"

"I called her last job. The salon owner said she was a great worker and her customers loved her."

"That was in Ohio?"

"Yes."

"Would you like me to run some checks online? I can show you some accessible sites that are easy to start with. If anything questionable turns up, you'd want to go further but, for most people, that will give you the basics."

"Okay, I guess. Only now, I feel like the snoopy one."

"It's due diligence, Shay. Not everyone is honest about their background."

Mac showed me the most reliable free sites for general facts about a person, then some that charged a nominal fee for basic legal reports. After those, he told me how to search social media platforms and what sorts of things could be red flags. There was a surprising amount of information available but we didn't find anything concerning about either Harley or Brett.

"If you notice conflicting information or a big gap in someone's timeline, it can be a sign of trouble. You'd want to follow up on that—or hire someone to look into it."

"I did call their last employers, though."

"Employers are legally limited in what they can say. And they might have their own reasons for withholding information. Imagine if the person is a close friend or family member, or if there was a situation where the employer had falsified records or didn't comply with employment laws. They might have concerns about retaliation if they revealed a problem. There are all kinds of possibilities."

I huffed. "Harley told me I ought to take classes on how to manage people. Maybe she's right."

Mac grunted "Sounds like Harley could use a class in respect and good manners."

"She was pretty upset when she said it. I guess she had a right to be."

"That's no excuse."

"No, but I really like her, Mac. Everybody does. That's partly why I didn't do a lot of checking. I just had a feeling she was the right person for the job. And we had such a nice time during the ice storm. I learned a little about her life and it sounded like she doesn't have much support. It's just her and Storm, her daughter. She's new in the area and trying to make a good life. I want things to work out for her."

"You can't adopt everybody, Blodyn." He smiled, knowing I how impulsive I could be. "It's important to listen to your gut but it's also wise to get facts to support those feelings... or contradict them."

ꙮ

Later, I was nearly asleep when Mac stirred and propped himself up on one elbow.

"I nearly forgot, Love. Braun and I have invitations to a bash at Vignes d'Argent. It's some kind of week-long get-together for people in the wine industry but we'd only attend the final party… dinner and dancing. Tyler and I are going to talk to people there, to try to pick up something on the Cruz case. We'll attend as guests though, if you'd like to go? Ty's asking Rona."

"You're going to be undercover?"

He laughed. "Not exactly, just quietly incognito. We want to meet the movers and shakers who might know what's going on behind the scenes without alerting anyone they're being questioned about a crime. There was a lot of interest in Drigo's development of his new EnElCee wine and we think it might be what led to his death."

"That's horrible. Are you going to arrest somebody?"

"It's not likely unless someone confesses. We'll be looking for new leads, more information."

I wasn't sure about a fancy dinner-dance but if Rona was going, it might be okay. "Is this party a dressy thing?"

"I think so. I'll show you the invite in the morning. Maybe you and Rona will want to go shopping for new outfits."

"Okay." I grinned. "Should we buy dresses with places to hide a spy camera and a microphone?"

"No wires needed. Your dress can be as low-cut as you can find." He laughed and waggled his eyebrows.

I gave him a light punch that morphed into some playful wrestling and it was very late before we finally went to sleep.

CHAPTER TWENTY-EIGHT

MAC

Iroquois County

Because thawing a frozen body too quickly can create rapid decomposition and destroy evidence, the M.E. postponed Keith Sands' autopsy, raising the temperature incrementally until late Saturday morning.

I got to the morgue at 1030, knowing Braun, who avoided autopsies whenever possible, would wait until the last minute.

Doc Powell was at his desk scribbling notes. "We're just getting started, Mac. Sorry I had to put it off to the weekend, but we didn't want to compromise the organs and tissue." He dropped his pen and slid a stack of photos toward me. "In case you were wondering, Mr. Sands didn't die by drowning. He was deceased before he went into the pond."

I sat across from him and studied the first picture, a close-up of Keith Sands' neck area, from his upper lip to just below his shoulders. "His throat was cut?"

"Indeed. And not particularly cleanly. The instrument used was thin and jagged. It appears to have been drawn across his neck repeatedly in a sawing motion."

"When we viewed the body at the pond, it was angled across the seat, with his head away from us, covered in silt and mud. We couldn't see much beyond the fact he was dead." I laid out a row of three photos for comparison. "They used a pocket-saw, like with Drigo."

Brian smiled, pleased I'd caught it although it hadn't been a huge leap. "Very much like Drigo at a glance. We'll be able to confirm more after we examine him and take some measurements."

"It won't be the same saw. Forensics recovered the one used on Drigo. But, according to Emil Cruz, there are plenty of hand-saws readily available on the premises."

Braun tapped at the door and entered as I was spreading the rest of the photos across the desk. The doc filled him in while I scanned the array. I wasn't certain what to look for since the cause of death wasn't in question but you never know what small item might be important.

"His clothing." I pulled out my notebook and flipped to the interviews at Vignes d'Argent. "Lily Todd, a server at Beaumont's winery and potentially the last person to see Sands, gave us a description of what he was wearing that night." I read aloud. "Tan, weatherproof jacket with zippered pockets—probably a Carhart—and work boots with red-and-gray knitted cuffs."

"So it's not inconceivable he was killed on the same day he went missing."

"And the last person he dealt with that day—aside from his brief conversation with Lily—was Philippe Beaumont."

Braun grunted. "The very person who told us Keith was going to the Cruz vineyard when he finished at Beaumont's."

"I'll have Willa send you the photos with my preliminary findings. And since you no doubt have a full day ahead of you, as do I, we'd better move along." Powell got to his feet. "Ready?"

Braun and I each took a protective equipment pack and put on surgical smocks, gloves, face masks, shoe- and hair-covers.

I never got used to the chilly, death-and-chemical odor of autopsy rooms. But unlike Braun, who really dreaded them, once I was engrossed in the process I could block out the ambience. Some medical examiners willingly shared their knowledge and observations while they worked and I'd stored up a lot of information from the many autopsies I'd attended over the years. The payoff often came when those mini-lectures helped me decipher a crime scene.

Powell's second revelation was that Sands had taken a significant blow to the back of his head. Due to injuries inflicted by his attacker, the impact from the truck's descent, and his lengthy submersion, it wasn't possible to determine how the head injury had occurred. But, going by Drigo's attack and the fact that Keith had no obvious defense injuries—although that was mostly guesswork—I went with a supposition that his killer had struck him from behind before cutting his throat and sending him into the pond. We'd never know for certain unless we found the killer and he described his methods.

There were no other definitive findings but Powell would follow up with tox reports and forensic details.

Braun and I needed to update Lieutenant Cross and plan our strategy going forward. Even though we suspected Beaumont of killing Keith Sands and Drigo Cruz, we had zero proof of either.

"We'll have to circle back and re-interview everyone we talked with on both cases," Braun decided. "Somebody had to have seen something."

"Let's eat lunch while we figure out what we missed. Shay made lasagna for dinner last night and she always makes extra. There'll be plenty of leftovers."

"Oh man, I love Shay's lasagna. Garlic bread, too?" Braun's appetite is legendary.

I laughed. "Of course. And maybe a salad and her *Bonfire Pickles* if she's feeling generous."

But when we got to the house, Shay wasn't home.

Maple Sunrise

"Shay and Rona went dress shopping," Del told us. "She said they'll probably run late but I can have three evenings off next week—with the car—in exchange for watching the kids today."

Ty grinned and eyed the kitchen. "Sounds like a generous mood to me."

I opened the fridge to grab the pan of lasagna and burst out laughing. "You have to see this."

I held up a jar of Hot Surprise Bonfire Pickles with a sticky-note attached, and read aloud. "*Mac, you do not need THREE pickles at one sitting. If Tyler is with you that goes for him, too. XXX.*"

Tyler grinned and grabbed the jar. "We're going to have to change our M.O."

I drowned a loaf of Italian bread in garlic butter and popped it on the grill while I reheated lasagna.

Tyler made side salads and pulled a couple of beers from the fridge, then entertained the kids with his antics. And, Del, like nearly every other woman on the planet, was smitten.

While we ate, we ran down the list of interviews we'd covered. We managed to eliminate at least half of those individuals. There was no point in revisiting anyone we were certain hadn't been near Drigo's lab or hadn't seen Keith around the time he'd gone missing but it still left us with a dozen or so who needed a closer look.

"I think we should stick to a motive connected to Drigo's new grapes and wine," Braun insisted. "Which brings us back to Philippe, Charlotte, Patrick Hogan, Emil, and Ami." He held up a hand. "I know you've eliminated Emil and Ami on a personal level but I can't take them off the list without solid proof they weren't involved. You know how often we wind up arresting family members, even when it doesn't look that way in the beginning."

"No argument here. You're right to pursue it." I was more than okay with my partner's decision. His determination to do the job right, despite my opinion, was the mark of a damn good investigator. "But if Sands was killed the same night he checked Beaumont's vines, they have a solid alibi from Drigo's funeral director and the restaurant where they ate."

"Except we don't know for certain when Sands was killed. Could've been much later that night or some other night."

"Correct." I made a conciliatory gesture with my hands. Braun was lead and he was following protocol. We'd work the case his way. "Do you want to get started on all five?"

"I'd say so. If nothing pans out, we'll still talk to the wine moguls at the gala. In between, we can hit Hope Sands, Nico, Lily, and Jack—not that I expect we'll get much from them."

"Good plan." I got up and started clearing the table. "Let's check in with the L.T. and see if he has anything to add."

"It'd be nice if forensics pulled something from the scene. Or the M.E. found some kind of clear-cut evidence."

I grinned. "Or the killer had an existential crisis and confessed."

Braun shouted toward the playroom, "Who believes unicorns are real?"

Calls of "Me" and "I do" rang through the house.

"There's our jury," he said.

We left laughing, with our stomachs full.

CHAPTER TWENTY-NINE

SHAY
Buffalo

Ronalee Kennedy may have been the best pastry chef in the state, but she also had the lean, sophisticated, statuesque look of a runway model and there was nothing she enjoyed more than shopping for clothes. I, on the other hand, being shorter and unsophisticated, had a wardrobe made up almost entirely of denim and T-shirts which I purchased online whenever a previous, identical version fell apart at the seams—more or less.

It was no surprise that Rona took charge of our expedition to the gazillion stores that comprised Buffalo's Walden Galleria and the Fashion Outlet in Niagara Falls, as well as all the boutiques and shops in between. She insisted that we were going to find perfect, stunning, elegant gowns for *Vin America Fête 50* and she approached the task with the strategic planning of a military general preparing to invade a medium-sized country.

By the time we stopped for dinner, I could say with complete honesty that I had never tried on so many dresses in my entire life as I did that day.

After endless searching and discussions about fabrics, styles, designs, colors, and fashion details that I'd never heard of, Rona had chosen a pale cream strapless gown that made her brown skin and dark eyes glow. But I was still indecisive about my choices.

To give me time to mull the options, we stopped to eat at Made-for-You, a trendy, premium casual restaurant offering individually prepared, customized meals in a relaxed atmosphere. Rona and I were sipped tea and nibbled mezze appetizers while waiting for our entrees—all the while continuing our debate about the dresses I'd tried on.

"The gala sounds pretty upscale and there'll probably be a lot of rich, old people," Rona mused. "But we're young enough to have a touch of sexy, too."

Remembering Mac's comment the night before, I giggled. "Nothing so low-cut I have to worry about falling out of it."

She grinned. "Discreet décolletage."

I was surprised when I glanced up and saw Emil Cruz and an older man walking toward the exit. They'd apparently been seated at a table near the back so I hadn't seen them when we arrived. I lifted my hand to get Emil's attention, to say hello, but as they turned toward the door, I saw both men were scowling and focused on what looked like a tense conversation. They were too far away to hear any words but from their aggressive stance—bodies canted stiffly toward one another—I thought they were arguing.

I returned my hand to my lap and looked away. I was curious, knowing the turmoil Emil had faced recently but I had no idea who the other man was and didn't want to interrupt.

When I returned my attention to Rona, she was still comparing dresses.

"I think we should go back for the emerald green, backless sheath," she announced. "The fit was perfect, the monochrome floral embroidery gives it a haute couture touch, and it shows just enough skin…"

"Too much skin," I protested. "There's no back, hardly any front, and the slit is way too high."

The waiter, who arrived with our food in time to hear my complaint, couldn't cover his grin and Rona laughed out loud. "The back is less than an inch below your waist, Shay. The corset bodice shows off your curves—discreetly—and the side-slit is just right. You hardly notice the slit when you're standing still."

"I felt half-naked in it."

"You looked sensational. And it's on sale. Let's go back. I'll take a picture of you and we can send it to Mac, ask him what he thinks."

"What about the one in the shop before that, the pink one with the full skirt?"

"The teeny-bopper dress? Shay, please." She released a loud sigh and raised her hands toward the ceiling. "We're going to a fête, not a high school prom."

"I never went to a prom," I muttered.

"You didn't miss anything. Getting your feet stomped on in a sweaty, crowded gym with tinsel-draped basketball hoops and a bunch of adolescent boys hoping to get lucky for the first time in their lives is not what our mothers promised us."

I'd never had a mother to promise me anything either, but I let that slide. "It's different for you. You did all those things."

"Trust me." She flapped a hand in dismissal. "You're much better off waiting for elegant galas with grown-up men. And that emerald sheath is perfect for you."

"I'm not…"

"Yes, you are. Now I'm saying we go back, you try on the dress again and send the picture to Mac. If he gives it a thumbs-down, we'll keep looking."

I was tired of arguing and tired of shopping. When we finished our meal, we went back.

On the way, Mac texted to say he and Ty had enjoyed lunch—and the pickles—and I mentioned seeing Emil. He seemed interested but I couldn't tell if it had to do with his case or not.

At the dress shop I followed Rona's orders, putting on the dress she'd picked for me and pinning up my braid. I even slipped on a pair of too high, too tight heels and posed in front of the mirrored wall.

She snapped my picture and sent it off to Mac.

Within seconds, my phone pinged with a text. Mac had sent three hearts emojis and a thumbs-up:

You look gorgeous, Love! It's perfect. Buy it.

He followed that with a winking emoji face and:

How soon will you be home?

Rona walked over and tried to peek at the screen but I covered it with my hand. "Is that Mac? What did he say?"

I shrugged. "He thinks it's… okay, I guess."

"My gosh, Shay. You're blushing."

"I am not. It's just warm in here." I turned away, ducking into the fitting room and rubbing my burning cheeks.

The dress was too glamorous for a farmer, too form-fitting for my body, too bare to wear in front of a whole bunch of people who probably knew how to look confident and which fork to use before they even started kindergarten.

But Mac obviously liked it and Rona insisted it was perfect. And apparently my preference for teeny-bopper prom dresses wasn't even worth consideration. I peeled off the dress and put on my jeans.

I'd buy it and I supposed I'd have to wear it but I knew it was going to be the most awkward, embarrassing night of my life.

CHAPTER THIRTY

MAC
Cruz Vineyard

Lieutenant Cross wanted to review and compare reports on the Cruz and Sands cases before he'd agree they were linked to a single killer. The fact there was nothing solid to indicate a suspect for either case didn't inspire confidence and, although the unconventional choice of weapon held, copycat criminals were as common as ticks on a deer.

"I'd feel better if you at least had a potential suspect," he complained. "But unless we've got a serial killer with some kind of wine trigger, your theory they're tied to Cruz's anticipated jackpot has merit. Chase it down but keep an open mind. Maybe this wine festival thing will pan out."

On the way to the Cruz home, Shay texted that she'd seen Emil arguing with an older man at a restaurant. I read the message to Braun.

"She didn't recognize the other guy but I asked for a description and it could fit Philippe Beaumont. She says Caucasian male, and older—fifties or sixties, she thinks." I checked again. "Tall, graying hair, trim beard. I'm picturing a box-beard, but I've already got that bias. Even if it's correct, it could fit a million men. But Shay says he and Emil were there together and they looked angry, might've been arguing. They were too far away for her to hear anything."

"She didn't speak to them?" Braun took the North River Bridge, crossing to the east side.

"No. She was going to say hello to Emil, but when she saw he was preoccupied with whatever was going on between him and the older guy, she stayed quiet. They were leaving the restaurant by then, so she let it go."

"Might be worth mentioning to Emil. We can see how he reacts."

"You're right. I'm having a hard time imagining Emil involved in his grandfather's murder. We know it happens—a momentary lapse in judgment, a disagreement escalating—but I can't see it with him. Emil's deliberate, methodical. He thinks things through before he acts." I huffed and shook my head. "On the other hand, twenty minutes ago I would've said I couldn't see Emil arguing in public. It's not his style."

"I get it." He took a right onto a narrow town road. "The thing with Drigo might've been a long-simmering issue, some friction that reached flashpoint and he lost control. Maybe the guy with him knows about it. Or, maybe that guy is our man."

"Let's get an ID on him and maybe we'll find out." I still couldn't see Emil as a killer but that was another advantage to having Braun as lead on the case. With no history, he could be more objective than I.

ဢ

Emil was in the yard when we pulled into his driveway. His approach seemed almost reluctant but I put it to normal post-crime anxiety, a tendency to be always bracing for more bad news. Like all cops, we saw it a lot when we showed up at someone's door.

I greeted him with a smile. "Nothing much to report, Emil. We're following up again."

He nodded and led us into the kitchen where Ami was already setting out coffee mugs.

"I know you guys want caffeine. We drink a lot of coffee, too." She poured, then set a box of donuts on the table, with a small flourish. "You're in luck. I had to run to the hardware store this morning and Tim Horton's is right next door. Do you need me to stay or just Emil?"

"Stay, if you would. We'd like to review a couple of points in your statement. See if you've recalled some detail or if anything new has turned up." Braun took a seat and set his phone beside the mug.

I sat back and observed while he walked them through Drigo's last days and the morning Emil found his body. Nothing significant in their stories changed and nothing unexpected arose. Both made an effort to consider each point and the mild restlessness they exhibited could be attributed to impatience with our repetition and lack of progress. Finally, Braun brought up Shay's report.

"How well do you know Philippe Beaumont?" Braun's posture and expression were unchanged but the air shifted and I saw it register with the couple.

"I know him." Emil set his mug on the table, sat a little straighter. "We used to run into each other at vintner meetings once in a while. Not often, because I didn't attend regularly before Abuelo… when he was alive."

"You and Beaumont ever get together socially? Grab a coffee or a meal together?"

The pause was palpable. "Uh… what's this got to do with my grandfather's murder?"

"Maybe nothing. We have to pursue a lot of loose ends before we find the right one." Ty took a slow drink of coffee, letting the silence stretch.

"If you asked me that question a week ago, my answer would've been a flat no, never." Emil inched his chair back, crossed and uncrossed his legs.

"But?" When there was no response, Braun prodded. "We had a report that you were seen with Philippe Beaumont."

Emil turned toward his wife who looked surprised. He took her hand and whispered an apology. "I haven't even told Ami about that yet. It was so out-of-the-blue and, to tell you the truth, I haven't been thinking all that clearly." He cleared his throat. "But, yeah. I met with Beaumont today, although how you found out that fast…"

"Why don't you tell us about it, Emil?"

He looked to Ami again and she squeezed his hand.

"I… the thing is, Beaumont first approached me about buying us out. I told him I wasn't interested but he wouldn't let it go. There were a couple of phone calls, back and forth, and then, today…" He hesitated, seemed to make a decision. "What Beaumont wants is full ownership of Abuelo's chardling blanc stock and the formula for his EnElCee Brut. I made it clear that will never happen, so he counter-offered either buying us out—the vineyards, equipment, and everything—or buying into our business as some kind of leveraged partnership."

I watched Ami's dismay turn to shock and then something close to horror, while Emil dropped his chin to his chest.

"I couldn't do that. He offered a lot of money… more than a lot. But I just… I couldn't. It would be an insult to Abuelo Drigo's memory and his legacy. EnElCee was his gift to our family… not just us but every family member, current, future, even all our ancestors. It's the culmination of centuries of family wine-making." He shuddered as he raised his eyes to Ami's. "Beaumont offered a fortune, Ami. But he'd control everything. I can't do it."

"Of course you can't, *mi amor*. You'd never dishonor our family." She turned her glare on Braun as if he was the one who'd tried to buy them out. "Is that all, then? Are you finished?"

"I apologize for upsetting you, Ami. Both of you." Braun's tone was contrite, patient. "We're on your side, here. But if we want to find the person who killed Drigo, we have to ask uncomfortable questions."

He fiddled with his phone to give them a moment, then switched to Keith Sands' case. "I need to ask you again, about the night Sands went missing… two days after Drigo's death."

"You have our statements," Ami snapped.

Emil shook his head in annoyance, but responded. "We were here until around four o'clock that afternoon. Then we left—Ami, Ruy, and I—for a meeting at the funeral home to discuss Abuelo's arrangements. We were there for over an hour, closer to two, I'd say because we discussed the details, music, photos, and a video for the viewing. We had to choose a casket and flowers… Anyway, it took much longer than we'd expected, so when we left there, we decided to find someplace to have dinner."

"Where did you go?"

"The Stagecoach Inn. It's quiet on a weeknight and we could eat without… a lot of questions and interruptions."

"You got home late?"

"Around ten-thirty. Penn comped us drinks after and let us finish while he closed up."

"Thanks for confirming that," Braun said. Once they seemed calmer, he switched back to Beaumont.

"When was the first time Philippe mentioned an interest in Drigo's grapes?"

"To me? That was about a week ago, I think it was last Monday he called. But I suspect he and Abuelo might've discussed it before. That was the feeling I got." Emil didn't hesitate to explain. "He asked if I was planning to continue developing the EnElCee line and I told him I was. Then he went on about the costs and difficulties of introducing and marketing an entirely new product and how unpredictable the public and the OIV can be."

"What's the OIV?"

"The International Organization of Vine and Wine. They're the ultimate authority for the industry. They're based in France but with members from more than fifty countries."

Braun grunted and typed a note on his phone. "Sort of a United Nations of vintners?"

"That's not a bad analogy." Emil drank coffee, returned to his narrative. "Philippe said we were courting failure. He suggested we'd be in over our heads, financially speaking, and he offered to invest in the line. I'll admit I never got too involved in the business end of things. I'm the production guy. So, I couldn't completely disagree with what he said. But a buyout?" He shook his head in disbelief.

"Was he looking for a partnership?"

"Not in a traditional sense. He said he'd put up some money in exchange for a fifteen or twenty percent share and consultation rights. At one point, he even said he might settle for royalties—a set amount per bottle or per barrel. But he wasn't all that firm on his numbers or on the type or amount of input he'd want."

"You weren't interested?"

"Not at first. He called me again to offer a complete buy-out and that time, he hinted at a huge price that was… well, it was a lot of money. Enough to pay off all our debts and ensure a solid future."

"So, you got together after that."

"I thought I should at least hear what he had to say."

"That was your meeting today?"

"Yeah. We met at a Buffalo restaurant for lunch—the one you heard about—but it was a mistake. There's no way I can exchange Abuelo's hard work and talents for money, no matter how much. I couldn't morally accept Beaumont's offer. My abuelo would be disappointed, devastated if I betrayed him that way."

I saw Ami's fingers press his hand again, signaling her support.

"How did Philippe react to your refusal?"

"Not very well. He tried to convince me we're too small, too uh… too financially unstable, to take on such a big project. He said we'll be bankrupt by this time next year if we try. I told him we'd chance it, so he went back to his initial offer, even increasing it when I kept refusing. It got a little heated." Emil pressed his lips together, one corner curling in disbelief. "I shouldn't have bothered in the first place. Abuelo Drigo would say *if it looks too good to be true, it is.*" He spread his hands. "And he'd be right. I know I made the best decision. What good is money if you can't sleep at night or face yourself in the morning?"

Braun followed up with all the right questions concerning Beaumont's reactions and statements, and whether anyone else had approached with offers or interest.

Emil cooperated through all of it. His remorse at having entertained the offer for even a moment convinced me he'd never been capable of harming his grandfather.

Braun left the Cruz house more confident than he'd gone in. He slid behind the wheel, slamming the car door with a satisfied thump.

"We need to have a chat with Beaumont."

ꙮ

Two minutes into the ride, Braun's phone pinged with a call from the lab. He tapped the dashboard speaker.

"Have I got something interesting for you…" Ji Ho Yoon was a Forensic PhD with a marketer's flair for teasers. "Those tire prints you cast back in February, on the road above the Cruz vineyard?"

Braun's mind had moved on, but he alerted to the excitement in Yoon's tone. "Yeah. Don't tell me you found the vehicle?"

"I did not." The lab director chuckled. "You did."

"Huh?"

"The vehicle you pulled out of the pond the other day, the Ford 150 pickup? Strangely enough, it has Michelin tires on both front wheels and on the left rear. And the fourth tire—the right rear—is a BF Goodrich A/T." He paused for us to express our appreciation but we were both momentarily dumbstruck. "If you read my report on the prints you cast…"

Braun swore. "That pickup was covered with so much mud and gunk when it came out of the water, we didn't give it more than a cursory glance, especially since your guys were going to handle it and we had a fragile DB..."

"You would've gotten there eventually. But, lucky for you, we caught it the minute we ran it for comparison."

"So the guy we were chasing that day was Keith Sands… who was allegedly killed the day after that." Braun looked at me and shook his head, stunned. "Nice work, Ji. We owe you."

Yoon released a hearty laugh. "You can cover your debt at Probable Cause, any time. I'll tell Ike Brannigan to stock up on soju."

CHAPTER THIRTY-ONE

SHAY

Maple Sunrise

Rona's shopping extravaganza left me exhausted. I couldn't understand how she and Terri and hundreds of other women found so much pleasure in wandering around looking at stuff to buy.

I'd thought that once I decided on a dress, we could go home. Instead, it turned out we still needed to look at shoes, jewelry, makeup… and underwear, for heaven's sake. I was one hundred percent positive no one except my husband would know what kind of underwear I had on beneath that dress, in spite of how bare it was. And he already knew what kind I wore.

We didn't stop until the shops began locking their doors and I'd been coerced into buying a pair of strappy, nude-color heels, sheer stockings, a gold necklace and earring set, a bag of assorted face glop, a lacy pushup bra, and panties the size of a band aid, plus the emerald green dress. I expected Mac to have a stroke when he saw how much I'd spent but he only laughed and said I was worth every penny.

At least I'd gotten everything on Rona's list and wouldn't have to do any more shopping. And I drew the line at getting my hair done.

"I don't need some wild, trendy, gooped-up hairstyle," I protested. "I'll brush it into plaits and coil it on top."

To my relief, that got Rona's approval as an appropriate, elegant look that, according to her, would show off my new earrings and necklace and emphasize my over-discussed décolletage.

ℰ

Returning to work on Monday was a relief. Seedlings were growing rapidly and transplanting moved into high gear. I shuttled dozens of flats from the greenhouse to the gardens, where small plants seemed to sigh with pleasure as they reached toward the warm sunshine and fresh breeze. The morning flew past.

Right on schedule, the pace at Farm Gourmet also ramped up. Sugar peas, radishes, pearl onions, and carrots had reached peak baby-size, leading us into one of the high points of the year: processing batches of *Lake Neoka Spring Mixed-Veggie Pickles.*

I found the kitchen bathed in an aroma of a tarragon, mint, and garlic brine, along with the sweet, earthy scent of freshly-harvested vegetables. I closed my eyes and inhaled deeply. It was the fragrance of spring, of new growth and nature's gift for enduring the winter.

Maria Ana smiled at my momentary self-indulgence. "You enjoy now. There won't be time, later."

I laughed, feeling so free I was positive nothing could spoil the day. "We know that happens every year, don't we?"

"These batches will be ready soon." She held up a ladle. "You can fill the first jar of the new season."

I grabbed my smock and was starting toward the range when I had another idea. "I think Harley should get to fill the first jar this year. It'll be her first jar ever, so it's only fair it should be a special one."

Harley looked from me to Maria Ana to Jennie with a confused smile. "Me? I'm not even an official cook, yet."

"You have to start somewhere, don't you? Jennie will show you the steps and, when everything's ready, you can fill the first one." I began lining up jars and lids, preparing them for processing.

When I first created the seasonal veggie pickle line, Maria Ana and I had experimented with several decorative jars before settling on a basic squat, clear-glass style that showcased the bright colors and shapes inside. To me, a set of all four seasons of veggie pickles was as beautiful as a piece of art.

Fifteen minutes later, the first kettle of brine mix was ready and we all gathered around for Harley's debut.

She took the first jar, packed it carefully, the way Jennie had shown her, then filled it with hot brine. She hesitated no more than a half-second before setting the lid in place and securing it. When she set it in the processor and turned for another, we all cheered and applauded the way baseball fans celebrate the first pitch of a new season.

Despite a visible attempt to act indifferent, Harley couldn't repress a small smile. "Is it okay if I keep doing this?"

I knew it would take her longer to pack jars than the rest of us, but if she was going to become a permanent part of our team, we'd have to begin giving her more responsibilities. She seemed so pleased I hoped it would make up a little for our previous difficulty.

"Go ahead," I said. "The repetition can get tiring, though. Let us know when you've had enough and we'll switch jobs."

I signaled Jennie to start a second line and she moved to set up at the other end of the table while Maria Ana and I took over prepping veggies for the next batch.

Sparkling jars of colorful pickles filled the finishing table as the hours spun away. Harley worked slowly but she was careful to maintain the uniform standards she'd been given. In time, I was certain I wouldn't be able to tell the jars she'd filled from anyone else's. In spite of our brief disagreement and the addition of another salary, I wanted her to stay.

Around mid-afternoon, Jennie went to the storeroom for more cases of pickle jars, returning minutes later, empty-handed.

"I can't find any more mixed veggie jars."

"They ought to be in the last row." I scooped up a handful of freshly-trimmed baby radishes. "There are extras stacked in the backup loft but we shouldn't need to pull those yet."

"Maybe they got moved when we took inventory. I'll look again." Jennie turned back.

"Try up top." Maria Ana set her knife aside and went to help. "If no more here, Brett can bring some from the loft."

They'd barely left the room when my phone sounded with a call from Nadia Giordano. I'd all but given up on hearing from her but maybe her daughter remembered something, after all. I rose as I answered.

"I have to take this call," I told Harley. "Are you okay for a minute? Jennie and Maria Ana will be right back."

She gave me a wave. "Go ahead. I'm good."

Ducking into my office, I closed the door.

"I have some news," Nadia said, her voice ripe with emotion. "Not what we expected…"

"About Betty?"

"No. About Shinny. I think she called me."

I was bowled over, speechless. Dropping into my chair, I could only manage to parrot her words. "Shinny called you? What do you mean? When?"

"Last night. A woman called and said she was your sister, that she's been looking for you…"

"What's her name? Did she give you her phone number? Or say where she lives? Can I call her?" I hadn't meant to blurt out so many questions but one followed the next as if I'd been waiting to ask. It took a moment for Nadia's answers to even register.

"She wouldn't tell me anything. No, no. I don't know…"

I took a breath. "Tell me everything she said."

"First, she asked if a Flaherty family used to live next door. I told her yes. Then she wanted to know if I remembered the children. At that point, she hadn't said who she was, so I asked her. She said she'd been adopted but she thought she was one of those children."

"Was it really her?"

"Well… I don't know. You can't be too careful these days. People are always getting phone calls that turn out to be criminals trying to steal their money. So, I pretended I didn't remember you very well, I only said that I thought there were a couple of children. The woman—she never did tell me her name—she said she found out she'd had a sister and she was trying to find her. And she asked if one of the Flaherty children was named Shay?"

"It was her." I gripped my phone so hard my fingers cramped and I had to switch hands.

"I don't know if it was or wasn't," Nadia said. "It bothered me that she wouldn't say who she was. I told her I didn't remember a child named Shay. That was the truth. We called you Shannon or Shanny when you lived here.

"That didn't slow her down, though. She said something about getting the name wrong or not being sure. But she started asking questions about where you went, whether you were adopted or did some relative come for you. Finally, I told her I could ask around the neighborhood, see if someone else remembered your family, and I would call her."

"You got her number, then?"

"No. She made up some ridiculous story about going out of town and her cell phone not working. All baloney, in my opinion."

I felt like a balloon somebody had popped. "But if it wasn't Shinny, it had to be someone who knows her. How else would she know about me and where we used to live?"

"Maybe or maybe not. The police are always warning people not to give out personal information on the phone. Callers can tell you anything. They can even get a thing that will change their voice."

"Maybe she'll call you again. If she does…"

A loud crash and a scream sounded from the kitchen. I leaped up and ran to the door.

Harley was between the range and the work center, staring at the shattered remains of jars of pickles and an overturned kettle, as steaming pickle brine spread across the floor.

"I have to go, Nadia… an accident." I ran into the kitchen as Jennie burst in from the back with Maria Ana following.

"Are you hurt, Harley? What happened?"

"I'm okay. I was trying to move the kettle to the work counter. I didn't realize how heavy it was."

"Move over to this side so you don't cut yourself." I signaled her away from the broken glass and ruined pickles. "Jennie, can you call Brett to help? He's working in the cold room."

Maria Ana set an armload of kitchen towels on the table and reached for a push-broom.

"Leave it, Maria Ana. You'll cut yourself or re-injure your hip."

The next several minutes were chaotic as I tried to contain the spreading brine and remove the larger shards of glass, while Brett resorted to a bucket and shovel.

Once the immediate crisis was handled, I turned to Harley who'd retreated to the far end of the room.

"You're lucky you weren't burned," I told her. "Why were you lifting that heavy kettle?"

"I thought it'd be faster to have the brine on the counter where I had the jars lined up, instead of filling only a few at a time."

"But the brine needs to stay hot. That's why we have it set up that way."

She twisted the hem of her smock. "I didn't realize. I'm really sorry."

I'd already counted ten, several times, and I knew what Mac would say about *crying over spilled milk*… which apparently also applied to spilled pickle brine.

"What's done is done. But we might as well close down for the day. Brett and I will clean this up and the rest of you can go home."

Minutes later, she was gone.

CHAPTER THIRTY-TWO

MAC

Vignes d'Argent

Our first stop on Monday morning was at the winery on Silverdust Lake. Braun wanted to confront Philippe Beaumont directly but the truth was, we still had no leverage. Expressing an interest in purchasing or investing in a business wasn't a crime.

Braun mulled our approach while we drove. "We could start off with the news that Sands stole the chardling blanc vines. I'm curious whether Beaumont already knows that."

I considered it a high probability. "I can't see Sands acting on his own. He didn't own any land or have money for a startup vineyard. It's likely he'd either lined up a buyer—Beaumont or another vintner—or someone hired him to steal the vines. And for that, it'd have to be someone he knew well, someone he'd already worked with, legitimately or otherwise."

The parking lot in front of Coteau Hall was jammed with delivery vans and trucks, the occupants shuttling carts and hand trucks into and out of the building. To avoid the crush, Braun parked in a side lot, away from the crush and we walked up.

"Looks like gala preparations are in full swing."

The lobby was a madhouse with a dozen voices calling out questions and instructions, people moving furniture and utility carts, climbing ladders, and carrying assorted material in every direction.

I spotted Charlotte, holding court with a half-dozen people in food service uniforms. Her expression was intense and her focus so narrow she didn't even notice our arrival.

Braun scanned the room and headed for the stairs. "Let's find Philippe."

The vintner's office door was ajar. Two men in coveralls stood in front of the desk where Beaumont was scribbling on a notepad. He looked up, exasperated, when we tapped on the doorframe and stepped in.

"Not today, gentlemen." The words were firm but he rose, sweeping an arm at the overlook to the main floor. "Whatever it is, it'll have to wait. There's far too much going on right now."

Braun stayed neutral but matched the man's tenacity. "You might want to give us a minute. There's been a break in the case."

His tone and demeanor caught the workers' attention. They gave us a three-second study and edged toward the door.

"We'll get started downstairs and check back later, Mr. Beaumont." The older one signaled his men.

Philippe started to protest, then waved them off and sank into his chair. "Very well. Close the door and let's get this over with."

"We actually have a couple of new angles to discuss." Braun positioned a guest chair in front of the desk and sat. "The first thing is that we know who stole Cruz's chardling blanc vines."

I remained on my feet, casually moving toward the exterior window but keeping my eyes on Beaumont. His expression at Braun's announcement was pure surprise. He froze, eyes wide and mouth gaping. Then, as if abruptly awakened, he clamped his lips, flexed his neck and shoulders, and shifted in his chair.

"Who is it?"

"Your man, Keith Sands." It was a flat statement but Braun's gaze never wavered from his prey.

Again, there was a protracted pause, followed by a slow head-shake. "That makes absolutely no sense."

"We have proof that Sands, or at least Sands' truck, was involved in that incident. And before you suggest it, we followed up on the possibility someone else used his vehicle. According to his wife, that wasn't something he would have allowed."

Philippe shook his head again. "Someone stole it?"

Braun shrugged. "There's nothing that says so." He waited for response but nothing came. "There's something else we'd like to discuss, though… Tell us about your meet-up with Emil Cruz on Saturday at the Made-For-You restaurant."

That time, the man appeared more annoyed than surprised. "Emil told you about that?"

"Someone else reported seeing you there but we did follow up with him. You want to tell us your side of it?"

"My side? It was a discussion, not a war. If you've already spoken to Emil, you must know what it was about."

"Give us your version and maybe we can move on."

Philippe summarized his offer and Emil's rejection, varying only in subjective terms and his avowal that Cruz was courting failure.

"That must've made you pretty angry," Braun observed.

"Disappointed, I would say. Not angry."

"You had a heated argument."

Beaumont drummed a hand on his desk. "I feel quite strongly about his decision to risk an exceptionally fine product—not to mention the years of research and development—on a project that's destined to fail. Once the chardling blanc grapes become common currency, there will be dozens of wines developed to compete with the EnElCee label. Assuming it even survives that long. There are no second chances in this business."

"So, stopping him from developing his grandfather's wine was pretty important to you."

"Investigator, you're putting words in my mouth. I can't force Emil Cruz to sell his business. I couldn't even convince him to accept an investment, money and guidance, that could ensure his success."

"I guess somebody thought differently about forcing out his grandfather. Given that, do you want to amend your statement about where you were on the dates Drigo Cruz and Keith Sands were killed?"

"You can't be serious." The vintner paled, shook his head. "If you have any further questions, I think you'll need to speak to my attorney."

I had an urge to applaud Braun's performance even if he'd leaned a little dramatic toward the end. He gave Beaumont a nod, got to his feet, and we left the office.

Our conversation with Charlotte was brief, uninformative, and interrupted several times as she insisted on staying available to her staff and service people. She claimed she knew so little about Keith Sands that whether or not he had criminal inclinations had never crossed her mind. But neither did she have an opinion about who might have killed him or why.

"I know Philippe thought Keith was some kind of genius but, to me, he seemed like many of the field workers we employ."

"How's that?"

"Just… getting by with as little effort as possible."

"Lazy?"

"Lazy, complacent, willing to settle for a paycheck to cover his rent and his beer, I suppose." She spread her hands in a what-can-you-do gesture. "There are people who are incapable of envisioning anything beyond their most immediate needs. I don't pretend to understand them but, like most things in life, they serve a purpose."

"Just to review, where were you on February first? Let's say between six and nine that morning?"

"At home. Given the weather and our reduced hours at the winery, I rarely came to work before nine or ten o'clock."

"How about two days later? That'd be the third of February and let's go with a time-span from five that evening up to mid-morning on the fourth."

"Are you deliberately obnoxious or just dense? I'm certain I wasn't out prowling around in the night. I do require sleep, you know."

Braun hard-eyed her for an extended moment. "Start with five o'clock. You don't turn in that early, do you?"

Charlotte spread her hands, gazed at the ceiling, exasperated.

"February third. Five P.M." Braun fired his words like bullets at a sitting duck.

With a brief glance around the room, Harmon pulled out her phone and scrolled. "We had a full evening on February third, beginning at five o'clock. No, actually beginning around three for preparations." She tapped her screen. "There was a full tasting—forty-three guests—that started exactly at five, followed by a second presentation with eighteen attendees, at seven-thirty. That would have taken us until nine-thirty or ten to complete."

"You left here at ten?"

She hesitated, glanced again at her screen. "Presumably. And then, I would have driven straight home."

"Did you go out again, anytime during the night?"

"Hardly."

"Is there anyone who can support your statement?"

"I live alone, Investigator. And I'm not in the habit of wandering around after dark without good reason."

ꙮ

We were on our way out when I noticed Lily Todd perched on a stone wall that separated the lawn from a recreation area. There were two other girls with her, all nibbling on sandwiches that looked like an assortment of caterer samples.

I elbowed Braun. "Let's check in with Lily, see if she has anything new."

The young women all smiled as we approached but Lily said something in an undertone and the other two took their tray and moved on.

Lily directed her attention to Braun—something that might have paid off in his pre-Rona days. "Hi, guys. We heard what happened to Keith Sands. Everybody's been talking about it. Was it an accident?"

Braun ignored the question. "We're following up to see if anyone else remembered seeing him on February third or if you've thought of something. That was the night you and Jack worked two events."

"Right. You already asked me about Keith and Philippe." Lily's smile held. "I don't think there's anything else."

Tyler continued to avoid any discussion of Keith's fate. "I do have a couple more questions about the schedule that evening."

She sat straighter and her smile broadened. "Ask me. I've been working on improving my observation skills."

He grinned, acknowledging their last conversation. "Okay. Let's see. You told me you talked to Keith in the lobby. Then you went into the tasting room to serve the guests. Have I got that part right?"

"Yes. We always start serving the flight boards while Charlotte explains the curated selection and the five esses—see, swirl, smell, sip, and savor—that guests should use to evaluate each wine."

"And that time you began at…" Braun glanced at his phone as if checking his notes. "Five, o'clock, you said."

"Yes. Charlotte insists on punctuality."

"So, she tells them what to do and they start drinking?"

Lily giggled. "It's called tasting, not drinking, and they aren't supposed to just jump in. First, the sommelier—that's Charlotte—introduces the wine, one at a time, and explains a little about the origin and the grapes used, the vintage, what to look for when you evaluate it or maybe an odd fact if there's something interesting about a particular one. She's strict about the schedule but she presents them at a slow pace so if somebody actually does drink them, they're less likely to get drunk." She giggled again. "You're not supposed to drink the whole flight but some people do."

"I'd drink them. Seems a shame to waste perfectly good wine." Tyler was rewarded with another laugh. "So, what time did you finish?"

Lily gave that some thought. "Usually, a tasting takes between sixty and ninety minutes, depending on how many guests there are and how much they want to discuss the wines. That was a large group that I think ran over, coming up on two hours, partly because there were so many questions but also because when Mandy stepped in..."

"Mandy?" Braun's expression and tone didn't change but I saw him register the new name, as did I. "She took over for you or for somebody else?"

"For Charlotte. Mandy is Charlotte's assistant. She got her level two sommelier certificate last year."

"What happened to Charlotte? Did she leave the wine tasting?"

"She had an important call she had to take. It might've been an international one? Usually when they come in during evening hours like that it's because they're in a foreign country or a different time zone. Anyway, she knew she was going to have to take it in the middle of everything so she had Mandy there to co-host and step in for her."

"Is Mandy here, today?"

Lily looked disappointed, but nodded. "She's helping Charlotte select the wines for the gala."

Braun gave her a smile. "Thanks, Lily. You're the best. Can I ask one more question?"

She nodded again.

"Did Charlotte return, after her call?"

"I'm not sure. I didn't see her. We finished the tasting, helped the guests get their coats and bags, and bused the tables."

"You left after that?"

"Uh-uh. We had another tasting. Two back-to-back ones that night, remember? We had to go from clean-up right into set-up. And Mandy did the second presentation on her own so it ran longer. I didn't get out of here until after ten o'clock."

"Are you saying Charlotte never came back from her phone call, even after… what, three or four hours?"

"Maybe she got tied up in the meeting or something?"

We started toward the building to find Charlotte and Mandy, but Braun stopped and went back.

"Lily, does Philippe ever do the presentations?"

"Not very often. Sometimes he comes in to welcome the guests and to… introduce himself, I guess. He doesn't like dealing with the tour groups very much. The tastings probably exceed his charm time-limits." She giggled, covering her mouth. "Don't tell him I said that."

"My lips are sealed." Braun obliged with a laugh. "But he wasn't there for either of the tastings or the international phone call?"

"Nope. I know he left early that evening because I saw him go out right after Keith left."

ℬ

Amanda Perry, a thin, skittish version of her boss, combed fingers through her tangled curls and clutched an armload of papers. "This isn't really a good time…"

"Two minutes," Tyler insisted, steering her to a comparatively quiet corner of the room. "It's important."

To my surprise, since she seemed otherwise incapable of asserting herself, she tapped her cell to start a timer.

"Two minutes," she repeated before flashing an apologetic smile. "I'm working on time management skills."

"I'll be quick." Braun jumped straight in. "Question one: on February third you took over a tasting event that Ms. Harmon was conducting. Do you recall what time that was?"

"A little past six. I remember that because Charlotte told me to be ready at six but she was in the middle of answering a complicated question that took a few minutes longer."

"Okay. Did Charlotte return before the end of the evening?"

"No."

"Was that unexpected or had you planned it that way?"

"That was the plan. Charlotte said she might not make it back before the end and I should be prepared to take over the rest of the evening."

"Do you know why she left the tasting?"

"She had a phone conference." Mandy chewed the top of her pen. "Or a Zoom meeting. Something like that. She's here if you want to ask her…"

"We already spoke with her and I know she's pretty busy today. I only need to verify the timeline before I write up my report. So, you didn't see her again that night?"

"No."

"How about Philippe Beaumont? Did you see him?"

"I'm not positive but I don't think he was here that evening."

"Last question: did you see or talk to Keith Sands?"

She hesitated before answering. "I know I didn't talk to him because I barely knew who he was until everyone started talking about what happened to him. I do remember seeing him here right before the program began but, to be fair, that's only because Lily Todd mentioned she spoke with him before the tasting and that reminded me. When I went to ask her to direct a group to their tables, he was saying goodbye."

"That was at six?"

She shook her head. "It was just before we began. The program started at five so probably a few minutes to."

"Was anyone with him?"

"Not that I noticed. I wouldn't even remember that much if it weren't for what happened to him."

Her phone trilled a repetitive note. She tapped and nodded. "Two minutes. Is it okay if I go back to work now?"

"That's fine. Thanks for your help, Mandy."

ꕥ

On the way out, Braun spoke kept his voice low. "Do we have enough to pull Harmon's and Beaumont's phone calls?"

"Probably not for a content warrant. We could subpoena phone logs to prove or disprove Charlotte's conference call and see if that gets our foot in the door…"

"Let's try it. Meanwhile, we should talk to Hogan, again."

CHAPTER THIRTY-THREE

SHAY

Maple Sunrise

Farmers don't have weekends. That's one of the reasons Mac's crazy schedule never affected our marriage the way it did for some law enforcement couples, because my schedule is equally crazy. Milking, caring for livestock, and managing crops can't be ignored when the calendar turns a page. But our work is so integrated into our life we've learned to accept the disruptions, each of us picking up unfinished chores when the other is called away.

That week, in addition to our usual work, Mac and I helped deliver six more baby goats, completing the herd's freshening for the year. Some of those would be sold or traded to other farms through a complicated plan intended to strengthen and improve the herds.

Until the kids were weaned and ready for new homes, our farm became a never-ending circus. Homework, meals, daily chores, and even games were frequently dropped and forgotten while we all ran to watch our four-legged kids leap and climb over everything in sight—including one another. We all spent far too much time in the barn and pasture behaving like manic caprines, ourselves.

Somewhere in the midst of the turmoil, I found a quiet moment to tell Mac about Nadia Giordano's strange phone call.

"Nadia said the woman asked a lot of questions about me and my family but she wouldn't even give her name. Nadia thought she might be a scammer so she pretended not to know very much. She told the woman she could ask some neighbors if they remembered anything and suggested she call her again in a few days."

"That was smart. Did the woman call again?"

"I don't think so. Nadia said she'd let me know if she did."

"How about Warren? Did anyone let him know about this woman? He might be able to find out who she is."

"I didn't think of that. And Nadia didn't mention him so, probably not."

He nodded. "I'll give him a call. He's in a better position to follow up if it's not a random scam."

"Do you think it might really be Shinny?"

"Let's wait and see what Warren can tell us." He gave me a steady gaze but no smile. "Anything's possible but it does sound sketchy. Don't get your hopes up just yet."

ꙮ

I spent a few hours on Saturday morning updating my journals and reworking the schedule. Harley's accident cost us nearly eighty units of veggie-pickles in addition to the ten gallons of brine and herbs, the broken jars, and the loss of two or three hours' work. It was going to be difficult to recover but, for a product that popular, I'd have to find a way even if it meant shorting a lower demand product later on. I couldn't understand Harley's actions that day but neither could I undo it. I had to accept the loss and move on.

Right after chores and breakfast, Mac and the kids went to furnish the newly-completed tree house. Rather than a rough cubby perched on a branch that I'd once imagined, Mac had built a perfect, scaled-down, one-room house with a real door, windows on each side, and a properly shingled roof. A sturdy railed deck encircled the house with a basket-and-pulley system to lift items from the ground.

Besides the strong maple it surrounded, Mac had installed thick stilt-legs for added support and, in place of a ladder, he'd built a child-safe staircase with railings and flat wooden steps.

By the time I joined them, the children were all clambering up and down, trying out everything while Mac unrolled a colorful, weatherproof rug. Small beanbag chairs and a box of toys sat in the grass below.

"Climb up and see it, Mommy." Elodie shouted as if I were miles away instead of only seven or eight feet below.

Gabi panned a pair of binoculars across the landscape. "You can see the whole world, almost."

I wasn't sure if there was room for all of us, so I looked to Mac—who was grinning like an overgrown six-year-old.

"Come on," he urged. "We need your stamp of approval before we bring out our sleeping bags."

"You're not planning to spend the night up there, are you?"

"Of course we are. So are you."

It sounded like a crazy idea but I wasn't going to spoil their fun. When I reached the deck and looked inside, I was as enchanted as the kids. "It's like a real house."

Mac beamed. "It is a real house. If we hooked up electric and water, we could live here."

I laughed and entered, surprised at how bright and cozy it felt. I helped Mac with the chairs and we spent the rest of the morning watching the kids raise and lower their toys in the pulley-basket. We even ate lunch there—a pulley-delivered sandwich and juice picnic in the trees.

"This is a wonderful playhouse, Mac. You come up with the best ideas."

"Every kid deserves a tree house. Even when they're grown." He nudged my side, his own kid-happiness evident.

ജ

After lunch, I pulled everyone away from the tree house long enough to transplant the Oregon Trail roses I'd brought from my mother's ancestral farm in Illinois. There were only five of them, but I split the largest with Mac so each member of our family could have their own rosebush.

We helped the children set their stocks in the places I'd marked along the perimeter of our wrap-around porch. Mac added little wooden signs where they wrote their names and the date. And, last of all, he and I planted our roses on either side of the front steps angled to grow tall and join at the top, someday. They were starting out as only small, bare bushes but, if Crystal's prediction was correct, we'd eventually have a thick hedge of yellow roses wrapping our home in history.

I guessed, for the children, it was only a fun family activity with no huge meaning attached. But for me and for Mac, it represented the planting of heritage as well as our future.

"Your roots are set, Blodyn," Mac whispered as we stood and admired our work. "No matter where the children go, they'll always be rooted here… with us."

Vignes d'Argent

That evening, Coteau Hall sparkled and gleamed with thousands of fairy lights across its façade and strung through the trees and shrubs surrounding it. Bollard lights lined both sides of the entrance walkway that was covered with a flamboyant red carpet. And the rooms beyond the glass walls were a glittering fantasy straight out of Hollywood.

I'd never seen so much opulence in real life. The mingling guests in formal gowns and tuxedos looked like celebrities. As we were greeted by deferential, uniformed valets and doormen, I began to feel like an actress, myself—and perhaps not overdressed after all.

Mac, in his tux and a bowtie that matched my gown, could have passed for a movie star. I loved seeing the looks he got when we entered—the sort of expression someone might give a pasta-bowl sized ice cream sundae. He smiled warmly, accepting handshakes and introductions and sliding into brief conversations as easily as if he'd known those people all his life. His guiding hand at the small of my back kept me steady enough to at least smile and not say anything stupid.

I didn't relax until we found Tyler and Rona in the crowd and Rona, barely managing not to squeal, mirrored my excitement.

"I could get used to this." She kept her voice low but couldn't suppress a giggle as roving waiters offered us glasses of wine and hors d'oeuvres.

"You look gorgeous, like somebody famous," I whispered.

"So do you… and you'd better keep tabs on your man. He is sizzling hot tonight."

As the evening evolved, keeping tabs was out of the question had I even been inclined that way. Mac's conversations became more and more focused as he elicited guests' stories about their vineyards and their work. Sometimes I'd wind up in a separate conversation with a vintner's wife or plus-one but, when I could, I simply drifted away to find Rona and enjoy the music and entertainment.

There were mini-wine tastings in one room that Rona and I decided to try, despite the fact neither of us was certain how it was done.

Charlotte Harmon, the sommelier, seemed to know who we were, right away. She treated us the same as the other guests—who all appeared to be familiar with the tasting rituals—but she directed us in subtle ways like demonstrating how to swirl a glass and explaining what to look for in color and clarity, so we could pretend to know what we were doing.

As we were leaving, Charlotte stood near the doorway, offering a word or two to each guest. When Rona and I paused to thank her, she touched my hand lightly. "I hope your partners are having a successful evening?"

The question was unexpected. I didn't know if she was involved in the investigation as an informant or something, but Mac had told me only the basics of the case. I settled on a neutral response.

"We're all having a wonderful time."

Not long after, we were seated for dinner, a multi-course meal with a different wine for each course. After a number of speeches and conversations about wines and grapes, the president of the organization announced the winners of several annual awards to cheers, applause, and more speeches. It seemed like hours passed before Philippe Beaumont took the podium and informed us the reception area had been cleared and a band set up for dancing.

"I have just one more announcement," he said. "At the end of this banquet, Coteau Hall and all public areas of Vignes d'Argent will be closing until July. Ms. Harmon and I will be away, sourcing adjunct vineyards for a new venture." He paused for a spate of comments and questions.

"While I intend to focus on certain areas in Asia and the Middle East, Ms. Harmon will be in South America. If all goes well, we should have some very exciting news by mid-summer. Please enjoy the rest of your evening and thank you all for attending."

The room erupted in discussion as we left the table and moved toward the reception room. I realized the announcement had taken everyone, including Mac and Tyler, by surprise.

"They're closing down and leaving the country within hours." Ty sounded worried. "If we don't get something tonight, we could lose this whole case."

CHAPTER THIRTY-FOUR

MAC

Vignes d'Argent

Philippe's announcement at the end of the banquet appeared to shock everyone in the room—no one with more urgency than Braun and me. If either he or Charlotte were involved in the murders of Cruz and Sands, their exit from the country could be for more than research. I wasn't familiar with the current list of non-extradition countries, but I knew there were a couple in South America and several in Asia and the Middle-East. If they landed in one of those, we might never get them back. And we had no grounds to prevent them from leaving.

Braun and I kicked into high gear. We'd already spent a good part of the evening chatting up vintners about their business interests and about the future of chardling blanc grapes and EnElCee wines. Some of it was mind-numbing because we were trying to appear part of the wine community and the guests, assuming we shared their interest, were immersed in the culture. The good news was, most people accepted us as potential investors and no one seemed bothered by our questions. The two exceptions—Bull Duncannon and Patrick Hogan—had agreed to keep our identities private.

I'd spent a fair amount of time with Hogan and, as far as I could determine, he wasn't our man. In fact, the more he talked about the grapes he'd claimed Drigo had stolen from him, the less he became convinced of his own theories. In the end, I passed on something Philippe had told us about the prevalence of copy-cat vines and suggested he might want to go back and try to get his own on the market. Slightly mollified, he agreed… and I mentally crossed him off the list.

After dancing a few numbers with Shay, she and Rona went to the restroom, leaving me not far from a guy who'd been bragging about his ability to blind-test wines. He'd been contesting his title on and off all evening and, as far as I could tell, his backers had won some serious money. I asked him if it was a learned or innate talent.

"It takes a lot of education and hard work to become a master sommelier," the man told me. "But I think you have to be born with a sensitive palate, the same way a talented musician has to begin with a good ear."

"You're a master sommelier?"

"I am."

For a moment, I tried to think of a way we might use his skill but we were looking for stolen vines, not the finished product. Still, he might have heard something.

"What's your opinion of that new EnElCee wine everyone's talking about?"

He winked and edged closer, lowering his voice. "If you can afford to grab some en primeur, do it. It's going to be huge."

It was impossible to tell if he had inside information or was simply expanding on his *expert* persona. "Have you tried it, then?"

"I have. And I couldn't be more serious about its potential." He glanced around to see if anyone was listening before continuing. "Rodrigo Cruz was a genius. Whoever killed him should get the death penalty."

I feigned surprise. "I heard some theory it might've been a rival, somebody he knew."

"You can put money on that. Nobody's asked my opinion but, if they did, I'd tell them to look close to home."

I spotted Shay and Rona across the room, searching the crowd, so I half-turned toward the man, hoping to signal them to hang back for a minute.

"This place, right here." I indicated Vignes d'Argent by pointing to the floor beneath us. "It's probably the closest vineyard to Cruz's. You don't think someone here could be involved…"

He blinked, jerking his head back and pulling his chin. Then lifted the glass in his hand. "I need to get a refill, if you'll excuse me. Nice talking to you."

Before I could recover my error, he was gone like a rat up a drainpipe. I wanted to kick myself. The guy had an insider's view of the community that I should have exploited. Instead, I'd blown it with impatience and a rookie mistake.

Pushing back against premature frustration, I scanned the crowd, trying to prioritize. Had we missed someone, a key person with more wealth or avarice than we realized? Or had we been chasing smoke while the killer never blipped our radar?

I was debating whether an attempt at a second interview with the master sommelier was advisable or even possible, when I spotted another familiar face shuttling trays from the tasting room.

"Lily."

The young woman turned at the sound of her name and I raised my hand, hurrying over to her. "We're in a bind, Lily. Can you spare a minute?"

"I guess…" She peered behind her where Charlotte was talking to a group of people.

"I don't want to get you in hot water with your boss. It'll only take a minute."

Lily smiled. "Let me get rid of these trays. I can take a quick break before the next setup. Meet me by the back door?"

Five minutes later, a jacket thrown over her shoulders, she exited the building to a shadowed path where I waited. The windowless entryway prevented anyone inside from seeing us and a pair of dumpsters blocked the service road.

"I didn't know you guys were going to be here, tonight." Lily was clearly surprised and pleased to see me—likely for the prospect of seeing Tyler, again. He had that effect on women.

"We're here as guests," I told her. "But we're also working. I'd appreciate it if you didn't mention us to anyone."

She made a zipped-lips motion and grinned. "You're like, undercover? That's so cool."

"You told Ty you remembered seeing Keith Sands with another worker, someone he was friendly with. Do you remember that?"

"Gus? Yeah. He's the vineyard supervisor, probably the person Keith worked with most."

"That's the one. I didn't get his last name."

She hesitated. "Friedland, it's Gus Friedland. If you want to talk to him, he's actually here, tonight. He came in because one of the workers had an accident this afternoon. I think they're in the equipment shed with a mechanic."

"Where's that?"

She pointed to a barn at the end of the service drive. "He'll be in the last door on your right."

"Thanks, Lily. You think he'd mind if I talk to him here?"

"Nah. Gus is okay."

"You're the best. Thank you."

"Tell your partner *Hi* from me, in case I don't see him." She ducked back into the hall and I crossed to the barns.

ꕥ

The equipment shed was like an automotive garage on steroids. Tractors, cultivators, sprayers, forklifts, and some kind of giant bins on wheels filled the barn, along with other vehicles I couldn't name. Three men were examining the rear axle on a forklift. They turned at the sound of my footsteps on the oil-stained, concrete floor.

A heavyset, bald guy intercepted me before I got too close. "You need help with something?"

"I'm looking for Gus."

"Well, you found me. What can I do for you, mister…"

"Llewellyn, Mac Llewellyn. I wonder if I could speak with you privately, if you have a minute?" I extended a hand but he held up his own oil-smeared ones.

"What's this about?"

I lowered my voice. "You were friends with Keith Sands?"

"I'll be right back," he told the others, pointing me back to the door. "You're gonna ruin that monkey-suit in here. Let's talk outside."

Since the gala was nearly over and I didn't think Gus would be mingling with the guests, I flashed my ID and got right to the point.

"We're investigating the possibility that Drigo Cruz was killed by someone within the wine community, someone he knew, and that the same person targeted Keith Sands. I understand you knew him pretty well, so I'm hoping you can help us figure out who had a problem with Keith."

"I take it you think the person is here tonight?"

"It's a strong possibility."

"And you're in a time crunch because they're going to scatter all over the map when tonight's bash is over." Gus's tone was direct. He wasn't taunting; he took what I said, processed it quickly, and presented his conclusions. The guy was sharp.

"You've summed it up pretty well."

"I don't think this is the best place for this conversation, Investigator Llewellyn. If you give me a few minutes, I'll tell the boys you're having car trouble and I'm going to give you hand. Meet me at Pilcher's Saloon, half-a-mile from the state road and wait in the lot. Unless you've got a change of clothes—say, jeans and a sweatshirt—you'd stand out in the bar." He grinned and started back toward the barn. "Five minutes."

"I'll be there."

CHAPTER THIRTY-FIVE

SHAY

Vignes d'Argent

I wandered through the event space but didn't see Mac. He'd probably cornered someone he hadn't already questioned, although it seemed to me there couldn't be many he and Tyler had missed.

Rona was still dancing but I was tired of making small talk with strangers, too full of rich food and wine, and my stiletto heels beginning to pinch. I spotted an empty chair in a conversation area overlooking the dark lake and headed for it. But before I'd taken three steps, I felt a hand on my arm.

"I hope you've enjoyed the gala, Mrs. Llewellyn, even though your husband is working." Charlotte Harmon smiled but her eyes looked as weary as I felt.

"It was a fantastic evening. And you must be looking forward to your trip."

"I am. As much as I love Vignes d'Argent, I'm counting the hours." She held up a pair of wine bottles. "I have to return these to the wine cellar. Did you get to take one of the tours this afternoon?"

"No. We didn't arrive until the reception. The tours had already ended."

"Then you didn't get to see the Grande Lounge à Vin. You don't want to leave without experiencing that. It's the highlight of the entire complex." She tucked her bottles under one arm and linked the other through mine. "Come with me and I'll give you a private tour."

I looked around one more time for Mac, who was nowhere to be seen, and Rona, who was talking to someone on the far side of the dance floor, facing away from us. Even though every tiny bone in my feet was protesting, I smiled.

"I'd like that."

ꕤ

The passageway we entered was exactly the way Mac had described when he'd told me about his first visit to Vignes d'Argent and the wine cellar: a long, curving hallway built from stone and leading downward beneath the building and into an underground cavern. As we descended, the air on my bare arms and shoulders grew colder and the gala's music and chatter faded until silence coiled around us like a thick wrapper.

Charlotte unlocked two sets of doors and we passed into the tasting room—the Grande Lounge à Vin—where a long, gleaming table and deep, leather chairs stretched beneath the most incredibly beautiful chandelier I had ever seen.

I must have gasped or made some sound because Charlotte chuckled. "Lovely, isn't it? It affects everyone the same way. As often as I've seen it, it still gives me goosebumps."

"It almost took my breath away." I couldn't stop gazing at the tiny purple lights, hanging in grape-like clusters from graceful, twining, silver vines. It was truly a work of art.

"We host small group tastings down here," Charlotte explained. "Usually they're reserved for wine executives, foreign dignitaries, or celebrities—movie stars, famous entertainers, people who don't mind the premium price. Personally, I'd have installed it on the main level because I find the temperature down here too chilly. But this is Philippe's baby and he wanted the cellar ambiance. You're not too cold, are you?"

"I'm fine." It was cooler than I liked, but I wasn't shivering and we wouldn't stay long.

"This is the tasting area, obviously." Charlotte set the bottles on a narrow bar and led me further in, where glass doors revealed another room with floor-to-ceiling wine racks.

"That's the racking room. Beyond that are the tunnels where we age our wines. Those areas are set at specific temperatures, some even lower than in here. Tonight, after we leave, it'll probably be months before anyone else sets foot in here." She turned in a circle, viewing her underground domain. "We should drink to that. Let's sit at the table, and I'll pour one I think you'll enjoy."

Without waiting for my agreement, she signaled me back the way we'd come, while she went into the racking room. A moment later, she returned with a bottle and a pair of glasses.

"This is a Merlot we started producing a few years ago that Philippe believes has potential. I'd love to get your opinion."

I sat at the table, below the beautiful chandelier, and accepted a glass of brilliant, deep-red wine.

Taking the chair across from me, Charlotte conducted the see-swirl-smell-sip-savor ritual, then raised her glass. "*Santé*," she toasted. "Or, if you prefer, I could say *prost* in German, *cin cin* in Italian, or *kanpai* in Japanese."

"Mac would say *lechyd da*. That's Welsh."

"And I'll bet you're Irish, right? So, *sláinte*."

Laughing, I responded in English. "Cheers."

She leaned back in her chair and sipped. "It feels good to sit. I've been on my feet for close to fourteen hours straight. And that's after standing most of the day, yesterday. You can't imagine how much work goes into one of these events."

"I can tell it was a lot. Just the meal, itself…"

"We used a caterer for that. But still, I had to do the planning and organizing, and keep track that everything was done the way it's meant to be." She laughed and stifled a yawn. "But it's nearly over, now. Everything went perfectly and everyone seems to be having a good time. And by noon tomorrow, I will be high in the sky on my way to Buenos Aires."

"That's exciting."

"It will be. The first thing I plan to do when I get there is to spend at least a week catching up on my sleep." She took another sip, eyeing my glass. "What do you think?"

"It's…" I scrambled through the muddle of terms I'd heard all evening but couldn't remember which was which. "I like it."

Charlotte laughed. "That's the most important thing. I like it, too." She continued to describe the wine with some of the phrases she'd used at the tasting.

I took another sip and tried to match the terms to the experience without much success. "How can you distinguish between an ordinary wine and one like this or like the EnElCee everyone's been talking about?" At the mention of Drigo's wine, Charlotte frowned and I realized I might've slipped, mentioning a competitor's product. "Sorry. I mean…"

"It's a fair question. And honestly, for most people, it's not that important. They measure the way you did, by whether they like it or not. Imagine if I offered you pieces of the finest chocolate in the world and a two-dollar candy bar. You'd probably notice some difference in taste and texture, but not to the degree the price tags would indicate."

Even though I wasn't trained or educated, I was fairly sure my palate was more discerning than that but I wasn't there to argue. "That's probably right."

"You'd judge them based on what you like, not on their price or any awards." She grinned. "The holder of that prize—in case you were wondering—is a chocolate crafter in Bangkok. But chocolate snobs are no different than wine snobs. Our holy grail may differ but whether its existence is real or a marketing dream we've accepted remains to be seen."

"So the EnElCee Wine isn't as special as people are saying?"

"Let's say that's still to be determined. But it is getting a lot of airplay from people in the know." She paused, sipped. "Do you have some special interest in EnElCee?"

I shook my head, not wanting to mention Mac's investigation. "Not really. I just heard a lot of talk about it today and… well, Drigo Cruz was a neighbor."

Charlotte's eyes narrowed. "The EnElCee vintner? I was sorry to hear about what happened. Did you know him well?"

"A little. I met him through his son and daughter-in-law."

"Then maybe our wine craziness wasn't a complete shock to you. It's just what happens when you get a group of connoisseurs together… Oh." She pulled her phone from her pocket and put it to her ear.

"Hello, can you hold on?" Lowering her voice, she leaned toward me. "Sorry. Reception in here is terrible. I'll just step outside the door for a second, if you'll excuse me?"

"Of course."

ꕤ

I stretched my legs under the table, wanting to take off my heels, but worried I might not be able to get them back on my feet. I wished I'd worn a shawl or something, too.

After several minutes passed and Charlotte hadn't returned, I checked the clock hanging in one of the alcoves. It was 11:40. The gala officially ended at midnight and Mac would be looking for me. I took out my phone to call him, but—as Charlotte had indicated—there was no reception. I'd have to go into the hallway like she had.

When I stood, my feet hurt more than before I'd sat down. I hobbled to the first set of glass doors but Charlotte wasn't in sight. Hoping I wouldn't have to walk too far to get a signal, I pulled the door handle.

Nothing happened.

I pulled again and realized the door must have jammed. I set my phone down and used both hands to tug with all my strength. The door still wouldn't budge.

"Charlotte?" I called out. "I can't open the door, Charlotte. Charlotte!"

I leaned close to the door and called louder, several times, but there was no response. I retried my phone… still dead. And still no Charlotte. The door was stuck and it looked like I couldn't call Mac until she returned.

With a twinge of impatience, I released the door handle. I would have to wait but I didn't have to do it standing on my aching feet. I might as well sit down.

I was starting to turn, to go back to the table, when all the lights went out.

CHAPTER THIRTY-SIX

MAC
Vignes d'Argent

When I returned to the winery after meeting with Gus Friedland, the gala crowd was starting to thin as guests departed for their homes or hotels. I spotted Braun and Rona near the fountain, saying goodbye to some guests, but Shay wasn't with them and didn't appear to be in the event room. Thinking she was probably with other guests in one of the tasting rooms or getting her coat, I bee-lined toward Braun.

"Change of plans," I told him. "You and I are going to make an arrest tonight."

Ty spun toward me, surprised. "Who?"

"TBD. I'll explain in a minute. Shay can drive Rona home or to our place."

He looked at her. "Are you good with that?"

"Sure. Should we leave right now?" Rona had been with Ty long enough to take such moments in stride, the way Shay did with mine.

"As soon as you're ready. Don't wait up. It could be a late night for us." He gave her a kiss and she went to find Shay.

I tried Shay's phone. She didn't respond but I figured she'd have set it to vibrate and left it in her bag. I sent a text to explain our change of plans, knowing she'd get back to me when she saw my message.

I signaled Braun away from the exit to speak privately.

"I talked to Philippe's vineyard foreman, a guy named Gus Friedland who was friends with Keith Sands. He told me he saw Sands here the morning we chased him from the Cruz place, the same day he disappeared."

"Before or after we saw him?"

"Apparently not long after. Gus thinks the vines he stole are here, too. He's waiting for us, up at the greenhouse. We're going to need warrants and some backup."

"It's coming together that easily?"

"Almost. We're down to Beaumont and Harmon now. We just have to determine whether it's both of them or only one… and if one, which? But we're going to get those answers, tonight."

ꕤ

Gus had the greenhouse lights dimmed to avoid attention, even though the barns blocked the view from the event hall. We stepped inside and he led us between rows of grapevines, stopping at a group of smaller ones with bluish-green leaves. I asked him to repeat his statement for Braun.

"As I told Mac, I was out on the slope, checking for storm damage the morning he says you saw Keith in the Cruz vineyard. When I came over the hill, coming this way, I spotted Keith's pickup parked just back of where you see my truck now. I didn't really think much of it, but I walked down to say hello and see what he was up to. Tell you the truth, it was damn cold out there that day and I was glad for any excuse to come in here for a minute and warm up.

"Anyhow, I got to the door just as he was leaving. I asked him how he was doing, complained about the weather, that sort of thing, and I said I was surprised he'd been called in since there wasn't much to be done. He told me he'd been asked to drop off something. I can't remember his exact words but I know he didn't say anything about vines. My impression was that he'd picked up some supplies, something Philippe needed or… I don't know. I didn't really give it much thought." He shrugged his broad shoulders. "This greenhouse isn't my responsibility so I don't pay a lot of attention to what goes on in here."

Braun looked up the hill, then back the way we'd come, probably gauging the distance or fixing the men's positions in his mind. "Do you recall what time that was?"

"Sorry, no. It was morning. Not crack-of-dawn but still a while before noon. Maybe nine or ten?"

"Close enough. So, Sands said he'd been asked to drop off something. Did he mention who asked him to?"

"No. But it would've had to be Philippe or Charlotte because I'm his supervisor in the vineyard and the three of us are the only ones he reported to. And I know it wasn't me."

"Then what?"

"Then he locked the door and left and I went back to work." Gus glanced at me and I gave him a nod to continue. "The thing is, Keith wasn't himself that morning. He seemed jumpy and kind of evasive. I mean, I was about finished so I said something about grabbing coffee. Keith hemmed and hawed, claimed he needed to get home so Hope could get to a parent-teacher meeting for one of the kids, and that he needed to clear the snow off his porch roof because it was leaking, that he might need to swing by Home Depot for new snow guards in case we got another storm… It was too many excuses and details just to avoid a cup of coffee.

"At the time, it crossed my mind he might be having a rough morning, that he was hung over, you know? Because sometimes that happened. But that wasn't exactly right, either. When Sands is hung over, he clams up, doesn't talk to anyone. That day, he was talking too much."

"You didn't see him again, after that?"

"No. I heard later, after he disappeared, that he'd come back for something that afternoon, but I'd gone home by then. Turns out, that was the last time I'd ever see him. You have to wonder, if I pushed for the coffee or…" He studied his boots, considering.

It was the kind of speculation we heard on more cases than I could count. "No point in second-guessing, Gus. Sands had already put things in motion. A cup of coffee wouldn't have stopped it."

Braun pulled him back to his statement. "How did you make the connection between him and the stolen vines?"

"I didn't. Or, not exactly. What happened was the HVAC in here got a little wonky with the extreme cold. It's an old system and needs to be replaced but Beaumont was trying to get through the winter before he invested in a new one. He had me tinker around with it a couple of times when it glitched and that's what happened a few nights after that storm. It's worn out, doesn't have the capacity to run 24/7 at full power, so it glitched and they asked me to see if I could get it working again. That meant almost a full day in here, some of it waiting around to see if the thermostat and fans would kick in when they were supposed to, stay on schedule, and what-have-you. While I was killing time, I wandered around looking at what's growing in here because that's something I do know about, grapes and grapevines.

"I was standing right about there, where you are now, when I happened to look at those vines on the end and I noticed how different they are. Take a look at them." He gestured toward the blue-green plants.

"Now look at these and those and those over here…" Gus indicated groups of vines with leaves that were shaped differently and in varying shades of green. "I know all the others like I know my kids' faces. They're all varieties we grow in these vineyards. They're familiar. But those odd color ones on the end? I'd never seen them before. So I was kind of studying this bunch and thinking some of the features on these are similar to some of the vines I do know. And that made me think these might be a new plant grafted from some combination of other ones."

Gus scrunched up his face and looked from Braun to me. "I'm not a scientist. I don't know a lot about how you do things like that but I do know that's how they come up with new grapes. So I'm standing here, thinking all this, and I remember Keith being in here, acting strange, and… bingo."

"*Bingo*, is right. Did anyone confirm your theory?"

"I didn't tell anyone. First off, I was busy in here and with my regular work and second, like I said, I'm no scientist. Besides, if that's what they are, Sands said somebody in here asked him to drop them off and they must be taking care of them, so it wasn't my business. It didn't occur to me they were Drigo's vines. After a while, I kind of forgot about it."

I studied the blue-green vines more closely. "Is there any way to tell if these actually are Drigo's vines? Some kind of plant identifier or something?"

Gus scratched at his chin, thinking. "Emil would know. Or his son, Ruy. And Drigo would've kept records of everything he did, I think."

Braun ended the recording and jumped into action. "Mac, can you get a warrant started and call Emil Cruz? See if he'll come over and ID these vines. I'm going to request backup to collect the records for all this stuff. We'll want the warrant to include journals, invoices, anything they used to keep track of where they get their vines or how they grow them. And we need a botanist or one of those oenophiles to tell us what's involved."

"Yoon has a guy who specializes in this kind of thing," I said.

"Call him, will you? And we'd better get Beaumont and Harmon before we do anything else or they'll be long gone, out of the country and out of our reach."

CHAPTER THIRTY-SEVEN

SHAY

Vignes d'Argent

Darkness in an underground wine cellar is nothing like an unlit room or a field at night where there's always some degree of nightglow. The subterranean cavern was pitch black nothingness.

For one moment my heart stopped and I couldn't breathe. I stood absolutely still and ordered myself to stay calm. Power outages happen. They're temporary—sometimes as brief as a minute or two. I wasn't in any danger. Even if it lasted a bit longer, Charlotte knew where I was and she'd come back or send someone with a flashlight.

I closed my eyes because it was somehow easier to not see if I wasn't trying. I turned to my right, facing the direction of the table and extending my arms in front of me. I took one step forward, sweeping my arms to feel for a wall, the table, a chair. Another step. Sweep. Another step. Sweep. Another. And again. After more than a dozen steps, my hand brushed the tufted leather of a chair and I groped my way around it, holding one armrest and sidling slowly until I felt the leather seat-edge on the back of my legs. I eased onto it, reached out for the solidity of the table, and planted my feet. At last, I felt anchored to something again. Now I only had to wait for help to arrive.

Several minutes passed. I wasn't sure how long I'd been gone from the gala, but it had to be ending soon. Mac or Rona would have noticed I was missing. Were they looking for me and would they think to check the wine cellar? If the power was out in the whole building, what were the guests doing? Was there a generator or would everyone leave? If the party was nearly over, they'd probably go home. But Mac wouldn't go without me. He'd be looking for me, asking if anyone had seen me, and Charlotte would tell him where I was.

I couldn't understand why she hadn't come back for me. Was it possible I was locked in because of the power outage, that the doors couldn't operate without it? And, if so, might other doors be locked? Maybe Charlotte was stuck in the passageway, too. Someone would certainly look for her, and when they found her, she'd tell them to come for me.

Then I remembered Philippe announcing the winery closure and panic rose in my throat. What if everyone assumed we'd left early, that Charlotte had left on her trip and I had somehow gone home? What if they closed up the building without searching? We could be locked in for days. Or months. They might not find us until July.

The room seemed even colder and the darkness, threatening. It pushed at me from all sides. My throat tightened. I tried not to think about what might inhabit the cold tunnels beyond the racking room, what dangers lurked there, or the possibility I could starve or freeze before anyone came.

But that was ridiculous. Mac wouldn't allow that to happen. And Charlotte's absence would be noticed. When it became clear we were missing, people would search the whole building, the places we were last seen. It wouldn't be long. Getting upset and screaming wouldn't help. I'd focus on controlling my breathing, staying calm.

I couldn't guess how long I sat there, only that my measured breathing, combined with the silence and darkness, began to numb my body. I was cold and tired. I curled my legs into the chair, pillowed my head on one arm, and began to drift.

ꕤ

I didn't think I'd slept long. I wasn't even sure I'd been fully asleep when my body startled awake—a sort of jumping upright before awareness kicked in. Immediate panic struck when I couldn't see, but the frigid air prodded my cognitive mind.

"I haven't lost my sight. I'm only locked in a wine cellar with the power gone out." Speaking the words aloud sounded so dramatic I nearly laughed. But there was nothing funny about my situation or the pain in my body.

Turning to straighten stiff, cramped limbs and feeling for the floor with my toes, I tried to stand up. My legs were wobbly and uncooperative. I struggled to remove my shoes, setting my bare soles against the cold floor until the needles-and-pins feeling dissipated.

Automatically, I reached for my phone, remembering it was in my bag, somewhere on the table. I leaned forward, sliding my hands carefully over the surface to find it, then fumbling to open the flap. My phone lit up with a tap but there was still no service. I couldn't text or call for help.

The time display read half-past midnight, more than an hour since Charlotte left and a half-hour since the gala ended. Why hadn't anyone come for me?

I was about to put the phone back in my bag when another app caught my attention. I tapped the icon and the flashlight came to life. I could see! For a few moments I shined the light around the room, trying to think of some way I could use it to get help.

First things, first. I got to my feet and carried the phone to the exit doors. They still refused to open and the passage beyond was still dark. My flash, reflecting off the glass, barely penetrated what might as well have been a blank wall. I checked again for service, but it still failed to connect. Maybe it was only spotty. It might work in another part of the room.

Using the light to guide me, I returned to the chair and tried to put my shoes on, but my feet were so swollen and sore, I gave up. The floor was cold but at least I could walk.

I held the flash in front of me, moving along the table, past a tall sculpture and two wine barrels in alcoves. The room was longer than I realized. A bistro table and a pair of chairs sat in an odd nook where a tunnel angled into the rack room on one side, then there were four more alcoves containing barrels of wine. When I reached the opposite end of the room I retried the phone with no better luck.

I turned back. When I reached the side tunnel, I aimed the light that way and saw a second set of doors that opened into another tunnel. There, an aisle stretched away into darkness, flanked on both sides by rows of giant barrels. The floor was bare stone and the dank, damp cold seemed to seep through my feet and into my bones. I was shivering, and with only my thin gown covering what little it covered, I wondered if hypothermia was possible.

I hesitated, peering into the tunnel, considering the array of hidden dangers in a place like that. But if waiting for rescue wasn't working, what choice did I have? The tunnel had to lead somewhere, maybe to an exit that wasn't locked, or to an area where a phone signal could penetrate.

Shining the light as I turned in a circle, I oriented myself as best I could. Then I took a steadying breath and opened the tunnel door.

CHAPTER THIRTY-EIGHT

MAC

Vignes d'Argent

One of the pluses of having our own crime laboratory system is that it's never closed. The labs are staffed around the clock, seven days a week, with specialists in every imaginable branch of science and probably some unimagined ones. Crime scene techs are often ready to roll when we call.

I parked my vehicle at the far end of the winery lot, well away from the buildings and guest parking areas, so I could work unobserved to complete the necessary phone calls and computer forms. For once, I lucked out at nearly every step.

Bud Kowalski, a brilliant young soil and plant specialist who'd helped us crack a difficult case the previous year, was on the job and eager to help. Additionally, despite the hour, Emil Cruz was more than willing to examine the grapevines Gus believed were chardling blancs. While we waited for them to arrive, I handled the warrant requests and requisitioned troopers to assist in our search. They began arriving soon after. It was a lot of work that took time and involved multiple individuals, including the district attorney and a cooperative judge but, even in the middle of the night, the wheels kept turning.

Emil brought a chardling blanc grapevine for comparison purposes and, to my untrained eye, it looked like a match. There were obvious similarities in color and leaf shape between his vine and the ones Gus had tagged, and he pointed out some unique feature in the tendril formation. When Kowalski arrived, he expanded on those observations, indicating small hair-like fibers on the backs of the leaves, the comparative size and shape of the lobes, and other less noticeable, more cryptic, characteristics.

"We'll extract DNA from them," Bud told us. "But there's no doubt in my mind the morphology will be identical."

I considered the often lengthy delays we faced with human DNA tests and my impatience soared. "What's ETA on the results?"

Bud's response was a surprise. "Couple of hours to extract it. If you want it fast, give me a day and I can probably get what you need."

"That fast? Terrific." I raised my eyebrows at Braun, thinking he might be looking at his first closed case as official lead.

"Okay, then." He gave a sharp nod, rubbing his palms together. "Where are we on the warrants?"

I checked my requests. "We've got a green-light on the Beaumont and Harmon searches—both their offices and homes. Also, phone records. I'll send those to their cell providers, ask for a rush. And the one for Sands' records is…" I tapped my phone again. "Approved and received. We're good to go."

Braun told Emil and Gus they were free to leave, thanked Bud, and told the troopers we were ready to move. We left the greenhouse and jogged downhill toward Coteau Hall.

It was 0112 when our team converged on the building. The gala had been over for an hour but there were still a few guests milling near the entrance. As Braun and I crossed the drive, Rona tore from the group, her fists pressed to her cheeks and terror in her eyes. We all spoke at once.

My heart slammed my ribs. "Where's Shay?"

"Why aren't you home?" Ty's tone brought everyone to a halt.

"Shay's missing. She's not here." Tears filled Rona's eyes. "We've looked everywhere. We can't find her. No one's seen her."

Rage surged in my gut. "Why didn't you call me?"

"One of the troopers…" Rona broke off and we all turned as an unmarked with strobes full-on rapid, slammed to the curb alongside us.

Before it had fully stopped rolling, Lieutenant Cross was out, coming at us, as grim and menacing as I'd ever seen.

"Trooper Lyski, I want all witnesses to the missing person detained, now. Move them inside. Braun, take four troopers to deal with your search warrants. I want all others—including the teams on their way in—organized and searching every inch of this property. Morales is on the way. He'll take charge of those." He turned his glare in my direction. "Llewellyn, stand down. You're off this case. Everyone else, move it. Now."

The small crowd dispersed, hustled, leaving me and the L.T. facing off on the trampled red carpet.

"Rosie, you can't…"

"Mandatory recuse, Llewellyn. Don't waste my time arguing." Softening his tone and volume slightly, he set a hand on my shoulder. "When did you last see Shay?"

I closed my eyes and inhaled, trying to recall. "God, it was hours ago, after dinner. We'd been dancing. Then she and Rona went to the ladies' room and I spotted a server we interviewed a while back. I wanted a follow-up and we met out back by the dumpsters, so I could get more information. She told me Sands' foreman was here, on the property, and I went from there to find him." I watched troop cars and unmarkeds pulling in, personnel reporting to Trooper Morales and shunting off in teams. I needed to join them, not stand around talking.

"Focus, Llewellyn," Cross prodded. "Sands' foreman?"

"Yeah, Gus Friedland. He was in the equipment shed with some other guys. He didn't want to talk at first, but agreed to meet me outside Pilcher's, down the road. That's where he told me about the vines he thought Sands' stole from Drigo Cruz. We came back here, I grabbed Braun and we met Gus, up at the greenhouse."

"Where was Shay then?"

"She… I don't know. Rona was with Braun when I came back from Pilcher's. We told her to get Shay to drive them home in my vehicle but…"

"Shay wasn't with her?"

"Not then. It was late and I figured she was getting their coats or something. I guess I didn't think about it because Rona agreed they'd go home together. After that we were at the greenhouse with Gus. Then I called Emil Cruz to come by and Kowalski drove up from the lab. I was requisitioning warrants and…"

"Okay. So Rona was the last person to see Shay?"

"As far as I know."

"I need to talk to her. You want to go home?"

"I can't, Rosie. I'm not leaving without her."

He nodded. "Come inside with me, then. But you're off duty."

CHAPTER THIRTY-NINE

SHAY

Vignes d'Argent

If the Grande Lounge à Vin resembled a surreal fantasy, the wine tunnel was a grotesque horror. Crude, coarse walls of raw, rough-hewn stone arched upward, while endless rows of giant wooden barrels loomed three-high on either side. The floor, pitted and uneven, was littered with puddles where water had dripped or seeped in and settled across the path. The pools were mere inches deep but ice cold and it was impossible to avoid walking through them. The stone felt slick under my bare feet and I tried not to think what I might be stepping on.

The ceiling hung inches from the top barrels, oppressive and suffocating, as if it might suddenly compress and bury me. And though my flash app allowed me to see a short distance, it also cast giant, menacing shadows that pulsed and shifted as I moved.

Twice, I started to turn around but going back felt pointless. I already knew there was nothing to help me, there. A few times, I passed entrances to other tunnels, offshoots going right or left but I stayed in the main one, afraid of becoming trapped or lost in a maze. Sometimes the path dipped slightly or angled up a small rise, occasionally it bent in long, shadowy curves. Nothing else changed and I began to wonder if I were walking in circles, passing the same barrels, over and over and over.

"I'm okay," I told myself. "I won't panic. I'll find a way out of here or a place where my phone will work. Nothing bad is going to happen. Mac is looking for me and we'll laugh about this tomorrow."

A stream of water ran from somewhere between rocks, flooding a wide section of the floor, and I could hear it falling away beyond the barrels on my right. As unlikely an exit as it seemed, I shined my flash between the barrels to locate the opening. But whatever gap the water had found was hidden from view and impossible to reach.

I was discouraged. I was a little scared. I was bone-tired and bone-cold and everything, including my actual bones, hurt. I shivered and began to sniffle. I wanted to go home to Mac and our family but I couldn't think about that or I'd drop where I was and cry. Instead, I returned my focus to the tunnel ahead. And kept going.

"I'm okay. I won't panic…"

&

It felt like I'd been walking for hours, although it might have been weeks or only minutes. I hadn't checked the time since I'd entered the tunnel, had seen nothing but barrels and rock and puddles. The path, which had been fairly straight for some distance, rounded into another curve and a small incline. And as I trudged to the top of that rise, something in the air seemed to change. It was too far for my flash to reveal anything but there was something different about the path ahead. It seemed… not as dark?

It was dark but not black as pitch dark. It was more an almost black gray. A very, very dark gray that wasn't quite black.

Baffled, I came to a stop and squinted down the tunnel, trying to decide if what I thought I was seeing was a mirage or my imagination. I closed and opened my eyes. Whatever I was seeing—or thought I saw—was still there. It was like an absence of something rather than an actual thing. It seemed elusive, intangible. I was afraid to name it in case it wasn't real, but why shouldn't it be? The tunnel had to end somewhere. There'd have to be another exit, a second way out. Wouldn't there?

Hope bubbled inside me and I started to run. My sore, swollen, frozen, blistered feet pounded and splashed as I wobbled between those rows of barrels, moving as fast as I was able to go—which felt impossibly sluggish. I tripped. I stumbled and fell, soaking my clothes and splattering mud in my face and hair, banging my knee on the hard ground. But I scrambled up and kept going, gasping, but moving, until I was close enough to see it truly was not pitch black ahead. There was some sort of lightness—a glimmer of not-exactly light that was too faint to see but that I could feel. It was something… real.

In that place, the tunnel also widened into larger area where tools and debris and parts of metal racks were piled. And there was the thing I'd wished for: a door with a small square of glass… the source of light.

I didn't stop when I reached the end of the tunnel. The sight of that door propelled me into it, grabbing the handle and bracing myself, pushing and pulling with every ounce of strength that remained.

It didn't budge.

Of course it was locked. I don't think I was even surprised it was locked. What did surprise me was the fury that rose in me that it dared to prevent my escape. That, in spite of all my pain and effort, I'd found only one more impenetrable barricade. Another dead end.

But as I stood there, gasping for air and fuming with rage, I looked through that tiny window, irrationally expecting the glow of daylight. Instead, what I saw was a security light, a sort of streetlight, off in the distance in what I guessed was some remote part of the vineyard. It was still night, still dark outdoors. But if the power was out, how could that light be working? And if it was restored, why hadn't anyone come for me?

I backtracked in my mind to the moment Charlotte left the lounge. She'd pulled out her phone and said *hello*. The phone hadn't rung, although it might have been set to vibrate. But she'd answered and rose to her feet, even as she said *hello hold on a minute*—as if it was all one word—not waiting for a caller to speak. She couldn't have known who it was, wouldn't have realized there was no reception before she'd even answered. And when she went out, she closed the door and locked it… with her keys.

I remembered hearing the sound of the lock without recognizing it for what it was, but it came back to me exactly as it happened: there'd been a light clatter of keys bumping the glass and then a solid *thunk* when the lock engaged.

Charlotte had deliberately locked me in. She'd probably also turned off the lights. She'd left me there, knowing the winery was about to close and I might not be found until July. But why? She didn't even know me. We'd never met before that evening. What could she possibly gain by hurting me?

I couldn't answer those questions and I honestly didn't care about her reasons. All I knew was that she could have killed me and I wasn't going to let that happen. I was not going to let some stupid, crazy psycho take everything away from me and destroy my life and my family. She. Would. Not. Get. Away. With. It.

Everything was a blur after that. Fury blinded me more than the dark tunnel had. Everything began to speed up and slow down at the same time. I know I grabbed up tools—a hammer, an axe, some heavy thing with an electric cord, even pieces of metal racks—and I swung and hurled and pounded them against the locked door. The window shattered but didn't break open. Dents, scrapes, and gouges marred the door but the lock held.

I screamed. I shrieked and yelled and howled as loud as I could, shouting until my throat was raw and my breath ran out and another sound—a blaring, ear-piercing, high-pitched wail like a hundred sirens—smothered my voice and deafened me.

As I fell to the floor and covered my ears, I understood I must have set off a security alarm. Maybe more than one. An alert would go out to the police or an alarm service and someone would have to respond. Someone would have to come to see what was wrong. And I'd be found. I would finally be rescued from that horrific dungeon.

CHAPTER FORTY

MAC

Vignes d'Argent

Sitting around while everyone else searched for Shay was out of the question but, following orders, I accompanied Lieutenant Cross to the courtesy office where a trooper was setting up a tactical base.

The L.T. signaled me to a chair but I couldn't settle. I paced out a cramped triangular path—door to chair to wall and back—recognizing the room from the day Braun and I first questioned Lily and Jack, almost two months before.

I'd already called Shay a dozen times. She didn't answer, didn't respond to texts. But I couldn't stop trying. Attempts to ping her location put her in range of the Maple Valley tower but that coverage stretched for miles in multiple directions. And finding her phone wouldn't necessarily mean finding her.

I wracked my brain, digging for a logical explanation for her absence. There was no reason to think she'd been abducted but she would never have purposefully left the gala without letting me know. And she hadn't taken my vehicle, so how did she leave? And why? As far as I could recall, she hadn't known anyone at the banquet except for Ty and Rona. There'd been no one with a common connection or interest who might have asked her to go somewhere, for some reason. I'd been busy interviewing attendees though, and she'd been circulating, talking with other guests. I struggled to trace her steps throughout the evening, recalling conversations, shared reactions and comments, the people who'd spoken to her, those she danced with. I was grasping at impractical ideas that made no sense, knowing I hadn't paid enough attention. I'd been too distracted with the job. Again.

I sent her another text. Then I tried Delyth. And Maria Ana. And Jennie. And Terri. No one had heard from her. No one had any suggestions about where she might be.

Lieutenant Cross and the trooper were working their comm units, talking to searchers and sticking pins in a map. The initial team had cleared the event area and mezzanine level of Coteau Hall and moved on to the sheds and buildings used for processing, grape-pressing, and wine-making. As more personnel arrived, teams sectioned and converged on the vineyards, the equipment barns, parking lot, and guest houses. I watched as yellow pins—indicating active searchers—were replaced by green—cleared—ones. But there was a lot of terrain left to cover. I needed to be out there.

Cross turned away from the map and eyed me. "Sit down, Llewellyn, before you wear out the floor. Let's go over who Shay spent time with during the evening. You're certain she didn't run into someone she knew?"

"I don't think so." I dropped into a computer chair, rolled it back and forth while I recited the names of people at our dinner table, guests with whom she'd danced, everyone we talked with during the reception or after dinner.

"But I was working the crowd, interviewing vintners. We drifted apart during a lot of that. I didn't pay attention…"

"We're talking to Rona, other guests, staff. People saw her, spoke with her, she made an impression. We're getting a pretty clear timeline."

I pictured my animated, elegant wife in her beautiful new gown. She'd been glowing. "Funny enough, Shay did a lot of socializing last night. That's never been her thing—large groups, people she doesn't know well. She used to freeze up, get tongue-tied, but she has a lot more confidence now."

I heard emotion creeping into my voice, pushed it down. "She talked with a lot of people during the evening. When we were dancing, one of the guys from our table asked to cut in. She danced with him and later, some others. Braun and I were moving around, trying to get info. Shay and Rona were mingling."

"And no one saw her when she left?"

I shook my head. "Rona said she thinks it was after 2300. She remembered checking the time around 2215 or so, when they were at one of the dessert tables, talking with other guests. Then the band started up one of those group things—a conga or line dance or something—and they all went out to join it. She thinks she might've seen Shay on the dance floor after that but she's not positive."

He wrote the number *2300* on a sticky-note and slapped it on wall by the map. "Did Rona know the names of any additional dance partners or people she talked to?"

I slid a piece of paper to him. "There are a few Rona and I remembered. Some are only partial names, and the thing is, I don't really know any of them. There are some I'm sure I talked to but none of them are known to me, personally. And I doubt Shay'd ever met them before."

"Maybe an opportunist." He scanned the list and called in another trooper, Dusty Stearns. "Grab Huerta to help you run these names. See if any of them are still on the property. If they are, bring them here. If they've already left, get their contacts from Beaumont."

Stearns took the paper and rushed out. Cross turned back to me.

"Did Beaumont leave the party at any time? Did he show any particular interest in Shay, spend time with her? Did they dance?"

"I didn't see anything. I introduced her when we came in. They exchanged a few words but that was about it. He was working the crowd all evening but I can't swear to anything toward the end. I was working." I ran a hand through my hair, wanting to leave. I needed to get out and search. I got to my feet.

"I can't do this Rosie. It's not…"

The rest of my protest died as an ear-splitting alarm shrilled through the building and the whole place erupted in response.

CHAPTER FORTY-ONE

SHAY

Vignes d'Argent

The alarm was the deafening. It shrieked down the tunnels and rebounded off the rock walls. It came from every direction at once in a long, continuous, pulsing howl at an impossible volume that made the very air vibrate.

I gave the door handle one more frantic tug, before I sank back to the floor and covered my head with my arms. The noise filled my head until there was no room for thought, it sucked the air from my lungs and invaded every cell in my body until I felt swallowed by it. Nothing existed outside the alarm's scream as it continued pulsing on and on and on.

ꟃ

When they came, I didn't see or hear a thing. I only sensed some disturbance or sudden movement. But when I looked up, the door crashed inward and people burst in—a small crowd of bodies, pushing and scrambling over the jumble of tools I'd thrown.

There were troopers, firefighters, and deputies, some with drawn weapons and all with hard, focused eyes and moving mouths as they appeared to be shouting questions or orders—a pointless exertion since the alarm was still going and my ears completely numbed with it.

Then the noise stopped as abruptly as it had begun.

Yet, somehow, the silence held a comparable volume and my ears rejected the change, my hearing refused to respond. Apparently, I'd gone completely deaf.

A pair of medics crouched beside me, checking my vitals and looking for injuries. I shook my head, trying to signal I wasn't injured, but communication was impossible.

They wrapped me in a silver blanket and strapped me to a stretcher and, moments later, I was carried out of the cave, into fresh night air. Air that smelled of pure earth and greenery and freedom.

And there was Mac, legs flying, arms pumping, racing full-out across the vineyard like he was about to cross a marathon finish line. He was gasping for air but already talking when he reached me.

I shook my head and touched my ear and, with no hesitation, he grabbed my hands, leaned in, and kissed me.

My emotions exploded: all my terror, fear, worry, and despair whirling into gratitude, relief, and a soaring, boundless joy that rose from my soul until I thought I would break down in tears. To my own shock, instead, I burst into breath-taking, rib-crushing laughter that set off Mac, and the medics, then everyone around us. I couldn't hear a sound but I could see the grinning mouths, crinkled eyes, and the hands that reached to slap Mac's shoulder and back, and shake his hand.

Maple Valley

Rona met us at the emergency room. She cried when she saw my bandaged feet, my scratched, bruised face and arms, filthy, tangled hair, and the so carefully chosen gown that was reduced to tattered, mud-covered shreds.

I was oblivious to all of that. My dulled brain, muffled hearing, and total exhaustion created a barrier to everything but relief at being alive. That was enough. I floated, detached and somewhere outside myself while doctors and nurses poked and prodded with various devices. They attached IV lines, an oxygen mask, hot packs, blankets, and bandages.

I think I fell asleep long before they finished.

ඞ

When I opened my eyes, the sun was shining through the window of my hospital room and Mac sat slumped in a chair beside my bed. I looked around, confused.

"How long have I been here?"

"It's eight hours since they brought you in." Mac's voice sounded watery and far away. "The doc says you're doing well. How do you feel?"

"Weird. But… okay." I tried a smile as my mind cleared. "It confused me when I woke up and saw you sitting there. It felt like before."

"I had the same thought: *déjà vu all over again.*" He chuckled and ran a hand over my hair, brushing loose strands from my face.

"Are the children all right?"

"Everyone's fine. I called Del. She told the kids you hurt your foot and wanted the doctor to bandage it, didn't give them any details so they wouldn't worry or be frightened."

"You told her I'm okay?"

"I've been giving her updates all morning."

"Can I go home now?"

At that, he laughed. "And there you are, my lovely, impatient wife. You'll have to wait for the doctor, but you shouldn't have to stay too long if you behave yourself and rest."

Later, I found out I'd been treated for moderate hypothermia, that my speech had been slurred and unintelligible and sometimes, irrational. I'd also developed trench foot from walking through dirty water with blisters and open wounds on my feet. But it was all treatable and I would recover. Even my hearing began to gradually improve.

CHAPTER FORTY-TWO

MAC

Maple Valley

Rona and Ty arrived as Shay was finishing lunch, both looking tired but satisfied with the way things turned out. Their timing was good as Shay was approaching that impatient, stir-crazy stage where she might threaten escape.

Once they'd fussed over her and covered a few details of her escapade, Rona began mourning the loss of Shay's gown. Tyler and I chose that as our opportunity to slip away to the cafeteria for coffee.

"To bring you up to date," Ty began when we settled into a booth in a quiet corner. "Charlotte Harmon was picked up overnight at her home. Sorry you couldn't be in on the bust but we've got her solid, thanks to Shay's statement, the evidence Gus provided, and some corroboration from Beaumont. In the end, Harmon couldn't keep her own mouth shut so we have a partial confession." He was justifiably riding high on the arrest.

"Congratulations. You handled it well." My disappointment at not being in at the last was more than overridden by Shay's rescue. "Are you saying Beaumont knew it was her?"

"He claims he didn't know what she was doing. But he was able to place her with Sands at crucial points that align with events—particularly Drigo's death and the day he stole the vines—as well as significant withdrawals from her bank account that align with deposits to his. It was her own statement that clinched it, though."

"What I don't get is why she went after Shay. Did she think it would stop us or had she completely lost her mind?"

"Her attorney shut us down but, from what she said initially, it seems she and Shay were discussing wines and Shay made some reference to the chatter about Drigo's EnElCee. It was a perfectly innocuous comment as far as I could tell but Harmon got it in her head that we were onto her and Shay was working for us. Paranoia, I guess, but it was enough to tip her over the edge. And she was confident she'd be in South America long before we put two-and-two together." He gulped coffee and leaned back, grinning.

"Piecing it together, it seems she'd been planning the theft for a long time. She'd purchased a sizeable property in Argentina that included a vineyard where she planned to grow Drigo's chardling blanc grapes and duplicate his wine. She had copies of his notes and some details about how he made the wine… nearly everything was in place. But the morning of the storm, when she went to steal the vines, Drigo showed up and found her in the greenhouse. She took a pocket saw from the bench and lured him outside where she killed him. By then, Emil was out looking for his grandfather so she was forced to leave without the vines."

"That's when she recruited Sands?"

"Nope. He was in it from the beginning. We think she'd already paid him to get copies of Drigo's journals and steal his paperwork. Supposedly, she offered him a job in Argentina and paid him to help her export the vines and keep his mouth shut. But after Drigo's murder, Sands tried to back out. That's when she decided she'd have to get rid of him, as well."

"For somebody with all those degrees and certifications, she wasn't very bright."

"I don't think she's as smart as she pretends. Or maybe her intelligence is twisted."

"The DA's on board with everything?"

"Absolutely. Harmon's looking at consecutive life sentences if all goes well. And that's without adding in charges for fraud, theft of intellectual property, grand larceny, plus aggravated kidnapping, and attempted murder of Shay." He grunted. "If we can prove she was intending to stay permanently in Argentina, we could throw in flight to avoid prosecution, too. Probably won't need that one, though."

I shook my head at his exhilaration. "You don't do things by halves, Braun. Guess I'm going to have to look for a new partner."

He ducked his head, clearly struggling with mixed emotions. "Don't get in a rush to replace me. They don't hand out those appointments every day."

CHAPTER FORTY-THREE

SHAY

Maple Valley

Getting discharged from the hospital was the best news I could have received. I wanted my own home and bed and I wanted to see the children. Even though I'd been gone less than twenty-four hours, it felt like months had passed.

By the time Mac and Tyler returned from getting coffee, a nurse had arrived with my discharge instructions. And before long, Mac was pushing my wheelchair through the exit doors. I inhaled, filling my lungs and consciously appreciating the pure, fresh air—for the second time in as many days. It was something I knew I'd taken for granted and I promised myself to change.

Maple Sunrise

At home, fussy Mac insisted on carrying me into the house and setting me on the couch, presumably afraid I'd suffer instant bleeding or gangrene if I walked.

I told the children he'd mistaken me for a baby, which they found hilarious. He said we were all his babies and he picked them up, one by one, and bounced them on the other couch.

When the squealing and laughter passed, Mac went to shower, Maria Ana plumped my pillows and Del prepared tea and brought it to the living room.

"The kids wanted to welcome you home with a little party, so we baked cookies."

I laughed. "I was only gone one night."

"Enjoy it while you can."

Gabi and Elodie came running with enough cookies and snacks for an army and the twins carried paper towels in anticipation of the inevitable spills.

"This is the best party," I told them. "With the best people."

"We missed you," Elodie said, studying my wrapped feet. "Are your feet broken?"

"No. They're just a little sore. The bandages are mostly to keep them warm."

Mac, returning to join the party, caught my remark. "Mommy's feet are healing, so we have to let her rest."

"But can we still sleep in the treehouse tonight?"

He eyed my shock, then grinned and gave me a wink "You have school tomorrow. That means we wouldn't be able to stay up late to make s'mores and look at the stars and tell ghost stories. How about a treehouse sleepover on Friday night instead?"

The children, who'd been preparing to fuss and whine, burst into cheers.

Del snorted a laugh. "Nice save, Mister Smooth."

ꟹ

That evening, after the children were asleep, Del in her room, and Maria Ana at home in her apartment, Mac took me out to sit by the firepit and look at the stars. As he'd done six times before, he handed me a wrapped gift that I immediately recognized as one of his whittled figures.

His smile was tender and self-effacing. "I'm not sure I got this one right. I was trying to show how successful you've been in expanding Maple Sunrise and The Farm Gourmet."

"It's perfect." I stroked the smooth, fine-grained wood—a woman, identifiably me by her long braid and overalls. She stood beside two miniature bushel-baskets overflowing with fresh produce, and holding up Mac's favorite Farm Gourmet products: a jar of Hot

Surprise Bonfire Pickles in one hand and Maria Ana's Spicy Roasted Corn Salsa in the other. He'd even managed to replicate tiny painted labels on them. I giggled at his not-so-subtle hint. "Interesting product choices."

"I was hoping you'd pick up on that… in case you weren't planning on making enough."

"Then you'll be happy to hear we're planting extra beds of cucumbers and peppers, and Chau Sai has increased her corn acreage to cover what we'll need for our expanded territory. There should be a lot of salsa and pickles this year. Although you will have more of competition for them."

He made a Tolo-like pout. "Can't you to reserve some for me?"

"Don't worry, there'll be plenty." I laughed and returned my attention to the figure. "I almost want to put this one in my office instead of with your other sculptures. Is that wrong?"

"It's yours to display where it makes you happy."

"What if I get Terri to take some pictures and put it on our webpage… kind of like a company mascot or logo?"

He squeezed my hand. "I'd be honored."

I settled in his arms and we leaned back, gazing up at the star-filled sky. I easily found Ursa Major in the north and Mac pointed out Leo, to the south.

"If we're lucky, we'll get to watch the Lyrid meteor shower on Friday night. The kids will love it."

"They're going to love looking at the stars and sleeping in the treehouse, no matter what," I murmured. "I'm starting to think I might even enjoy it."

"You've never camped out before." My list of new experiences was growing so fast, he didn't even bother to make it a question. "Another first."

That was only if I didn't count the nights I'd been homeless, I thought. But I was certain sleeping in the treehouse with Mac and the children would be nothing like that.

"I never realized being a parent would be so much fun. I love watching the children have all these new adventures… and getting to enjoy them along with them."

"The way I love watching you enjoy them."

"Rona says it's better to do all these things as an adult, that I appreciate them more than I would have as a child. I wonder if she and Ty have ever slept in a treehouse?"

His laugh rumbled in his chest, where my head rested. "Maybe this summer we can invite them use ours for a get-away."

"The children want to invite their friends for tree slumber parties, too. Poppy and Storm, the Kellogg kids…"

"We'd better stock up on chocolate, marshmallows and graham crackers."

We lay still for a while, listening to the crackle of the fire, the fast-running creek, and occasional calls of owls or nightjars. My life was full of everything my childhood had lacked—security, happiness, love, and fulfillment... and a family. None of that would have happened without Mac.

"Thank you."

He shifted as if he'd been almost asleep. "For…"

"Our life and everything in it."

"We're a team, Blodyn Tatwes. I'm grateful to you for all of it, as well. We did that together."

"I'm happy we did." I sighed with satisfaction. "Let's do some more."

ACKNOWLEDGEMENTS

I'd like to mention a few of the many people who helped guide this book to publication.

As with all of the Mac & Shay books, special thanks must go to Patrick O'Donnell and his Cops and Writers group who do their best to keep me from procedural pandemonium… with a special tip of the hat to Jennifer Eskew for *cutting* to the heart of one difficult problem!

To Judith Moore, who thoughtfully read and directed my often-incoherent scribbling throughout this process and for cheering me on even when I didn't deserve it, thank you, thank you, thank you.

Thanks also to Jessica Brody, Peggy Sue Patton, and the many wonderful members of Writers Mastery whose prods, discussions, and support keep me motivated.

Once again, I want to thank Martin Vestgard and Neslihan Yardimli for another great cover. I never tire of lining up the books to "read" the illustrated progression!

Most importantly, I want to express my utmost gratitude and appreciation to the loyal and enthusiastic readers who have followed Mac & Shay throughout their adventures and who frequently write, text, or call to express your feelings and thoughts, and to let me know that you're awaiting the next book.

ABOUT THE AUTHOR

Fran Sheldrick is a native upstate New Yorker with extensive writing and artistic accomplishments. She's held many occupations, from waiting tables and street busking to corporate management and liturgical exposition, but her award-winning television scripts and the book you are holding remain among her favorites. She now resides in the beautiful Shenandoah Valley, just over the mountain from the nation's capital, but rural New York will always hold her heart.

Get the latest news about the Mac & Shay SEEDS Series on Fran's website at www.fransheldrick.com or in the author pages section at amazon.com.

MAC & SHAY SERIES

SEEDS of UNCERTAINTY – Mac & Shay Book #1
SEEDS of DISTRESS – Mac & Shay Book #2
STOLEN SEEDS – Mac & Shay Book #3
SEEDS of EVIL – Mac & Shay Book #4
SEEDS of VENGEANCE – Mac & Shay Book #5
SCATTERED SEEDS – Mac & Shay Book #6
SEEDS of AGGRESSION – Mac & Shay Book #7

www.ingramcontent.com/pod-product-compliance
Lightning Source LLC
LaVergne TN
LVHW010648110826
845149LV00014B/2989

* 9 7 9 8 9 9 3 2 9 3 9 2 9 *